Alfie's Story
Little Boy Growing Up

Alfie's Story
Little Boy Growing Up

by

Henry A. Buchanan

ISBN: 1-58721-987-5

1stBooks – rev.10/05/00

About the Book

Alfie's Story is autobiographical fiction. Or it is a fictional autobiography. Anyway, I am, or was, a little boy. And I was blessed, or cursed, with photographic memory. I remember everything that happened to me until I was old enough to want to forget some of the things that happened to me.

So I developed the talent for remembering things the way I wanted them to be. I also became adept at adding what I thought was missing from a good story. The line between fact and fiction got erased in the interest of...well, interest. The way I remember it now is better than the way it was then.

And I was eager to grow up and tell my story... Alfie's story. Here it is. Starting when I, that is, Alfie, was about four years old, and Papa knew everything and was able to do everything, a condition of life which, in fact, declined with age – mine – but which in fiction is not so bad, or noticeable.

Now, looking back over more than seven decades of remembering I think I, that is, Alfie, may still want to be as tall and as strong as Papa was.

Introduction to Alfie's Story

Alfie was a very little boy but he was growing rapidly. He was the littlest boy in his whole world but he was filling that world as fast as he could. Alfie's world was Colaparchee County and Colaparchee County is right smack dab in the middle of Georgia. Tobesofkee Creek runs through the heart of Colaparchee County. Parker's Branch, which comes from a spring under a big oak tree on the farm where Alfie was born, is so shallow that Alfie could wade barefooted in it and catch minnows and crawdads. Parker's Branch runs into Tobesofkee Creek at the Rattling Bridge, and the Tobesofkee runs all the way to Ocmulgee River.

Alfie's Papa used to seine the Tobesofkee for catfish. Papa never had the patience to sit with a fishing pole in his hands. Sometimes he would catch eels in the seine. Once he caught a water moccasin. You have to be able to tell the difference between an eel and a water moccasin because if a water moccasin bites you it is Katie Bar The Door. That's what Papa told Alfie.

You have to be able to tell an eel from a snake by lantern light too because Papa only seined the Tobesofkee at night. Some people may tell you that was because Papa didn't want to be seen, but that's not the reason. Papa was too busy plowing corn or picking cotton to go fishing in the daytime.

Alfie had big brown eyes like Mama's and a shock of brown hair that grew down, or at least fell down, almost to his big brown eyes. That was all right with Alfie, even though Papa's eyes were blue and he was fair haired, because Alfie had long blond hairs on his arms like Papa, which meant that he would be a successful pig raiser, if he decided he wanted to raise pigs when he grew up.

Margaret had big brown eyes too but Alfie was so little when Margaret died that he was never quite sure whether he remembered Margaret's sparkling brown eyes, or if he had just heard Mama talk so much about Margaret that he thought he remembered. It amounts to about the same thing.

Papa wouldn't talk about Margaret after she died. He would go with Mama to take flowers to Margaret's grave, but when Mama started crying Papa would walk away putting his feet down real hard on the ground and leaning into the wind, but he wouldn't say anything. Alfie could see that Papa's blue eyes were misty and it made a lump come up in Alfie's throat and he would run to keep up with Papa so that he could hold onto Papa's hand.

Junior was bigger than Alfie but not enough bigger to boss him around even though he tried. And Cliff was bigger than Junior. Cliff tried to boss Junior and succeeded in bossing Alfie. But Willie was bigger than Cliff and he could boss both Junior and Cliff. Willie would take up for Alfie when Junior and Cliff tried to boss him too much.

Cliff always looked as if he were about to run some where, and Gran'ma said "If he can find a wheel or a hoop to roll he will run to the jumpin' off place an' then jump off after it."

Junior had freckles on his face which was usually red in the summer time because of the sun and in the winter time because of the wind. Junior wouldn't wear a hat, summer nor winter, and he defied the weather to try to make him wear one.

Willie looked a lot like Papa, with blue eyes and wavy blond hair. The wave was not natural. Willie pushed it in with his fingers while his hair was wet, and if somebody messed it up, somebody was apt to wish he hadn't done it because when Willie set his jaw and his blue eyes blazed like agates somebody was going to pay for what he'd done.

Even Willie was not as big as Papa though. One day Alfie heard Papa giving Willie a dressing down. It must have been a day when Willie noticed that he was getting almost as tall as Papa, because Papa said "You will mind me if you get as big as the barn door." Barn doors were big enough to drive a wagon through, hitched to a mule. Papa's mule was named Kate.

Everybody had to mind Papa. Except Mama. Mama was not as big as the barn door, but she was big enough, and she had ways of making Papa think twice about things he would just think about once if it were not for Mama.

Alfie was not quite sure how Mama did it but he noticed that she did, and especially when Papa would get on a rampage because the boys had been more destructive than usual in their frolicking, like the time they climbed all over the scuppernong arbor and ate all the scuppernongs before they got ripe and shattered the leaves off too. That was the time Mama said "I will take care of the Baby's punishment." And Mama switched Alfie's bare legs with a broom straw. It didn't hurt but he cried anyway so that Papa would know that Mama had punished him enough.

It was Gran'ma who always called Alfie "The Baby." Gran'ma lived at Alfie's house most of the time, but some times she would go to stay at Uncle Babe's because Babe was bringing up Mutt and Aggie by the hair of their heads like heathens because they were motherless. But Gran'ma was always glad to get back to her Baby, and Alfie was willing for Gran'ma to baby him because Gran'ma made the best tea cakes in Colaparchee County, and maybe in the whole world but Alfie had never been all over the world.

Anyway, if you are going to get special treatment you just have to accept being called The Baby, which Alfie did, and was until Jody was born but that is a way down the line and there were lots of people who came in between Alfie and Jody. There was Miss Lily who lived across the cotton patch. Papa said Miss Lily kept the path packed hard running to bring all the gossip to Mama. Papa didn't say whether Miss Lily came to get gossip from Mama too.

Chapter One: Tom Tom Tom

Miss Lily sighed and let out a gush of air from her lungs as she settled into the rocking chair because she had just crossed the cotton patch in the heat of the morning. She picked up a cardboard fan which advertised Hart's Mortuary and started fanning herself. The fan had a picture of Jesus holding a little lamb in his bosom and Jesus and the little lamb went back and forth in front of Miss Lily's red and perspiring face.

"Lordy mercy!" Miss Lily said. "It's hot!" She lowered her voice, held the fan up beside her face to direct her voice toward Mama, and leaned forward to lessen the distance her words would have to travel in order to reach Mama's ears. "Tom says it's hotter 'n the hinges of hell, but I tell him if he don't quit talkin' thataway he's mighty apt to find out if he's right about it."

Miss Lily was perspiring freely from the exertion of crossing the cotton patch under the blazing sun, and the sweat gathered in little beads on her forehead. Then it ran down her cheeks in little rivulets. When the rivulets reached her short, stout neck, they gathered themselves together to form one river, and flowed down between her ample breasts and became lost. After that, one might assume that the sweat spread out in all directions though, because her pink and white gingham dress was soaked and stained.

The gingham dress was stretched tight over Miss Lily's short, plump torso and it was hitched up almost to her knees, exposing her short, plump legs. Miss Lily was quite conscious of this exposure but she was more concerned for comfort than for decorum. Mama glanced once, disapprovingly, and then looked away. Beneath her sweat soaked dress Miss Lily's body bulged at all the places where a female body is apt to bulge if it is well fed, and if that body has given birth to, and suckled, many children.

Miss Lily had given birth to many children and she had suckled every one of them, weaning each one just in time for its successor to take its place. To have relied upon some other source of nourishment would have been to go against Nature, and Nature punishes those who take such risks.

"Tom says if you put a baby on cow's milk an' the ol' cow goes dry before the baby's weaned then you're up a dry creek for sure."

So that matter was settled and Miss Lily never considered the burdensome option of washing and sterilizing bottles and nipples, nor of suffering the inconvenience of getting up in the middle of the night to fix a bottle for a crying baby.

After the babies learned to toddle, and before they learned not to wet their own pants, the equally burdensome task of washing diapers was greatly diminished by letting the toddlers go bare-assed most of the time, especially if they were playing outside the house.

Making adjustments to Nature did not disturb Miss Lily's composure much. Even the heat did not greatly diminish her pleasure in life. Her round, flushed face wore an expression of contentment and well being. She stirred the air in front of her with the cardboard fan from Hart's Mortuary and patted her graying blond hair. It was done up in a tight bun on the back of her neck. She smiled at Alfie.

"Lordy mercy!" Miss Lily exclaimed. "It's hot!" But that was not a complaint against Nature. It did not mean that Miss Lily felt unjustly treated by the Creator Who gave both Summertime and Wintertime and placed her in easy walking distance of Mama's house where she could find a listener. It was only an opener, an exclamation aimed at getting her listener's attention.

Mama was prepared to listen to Miss Lily. She would not give her undivided attention because she had work to do. But she could give enough attention to Miss Lily to show her respect for her.

Mama's mouth was set in that determined expression that women have about them when they are doing women's work. She was doing women's work. She was hemstitching a shirt waist for Alfie. High cheek bones, together with prominent eyes and a firm full mouth gave Mama a patrician countenance. She was ready to hear Miss Lily, so long as it did not interrupt her work.

To listen to what a close neighbor has to tell is both a privilege and an obligation. It is a way of learning what is going on and sharing the burden of bearing what is going on. Miss Lily was a close neighbor. She lived across the cotton patch from Mama. A footpath cut across the rows of cotton, missing the growing stalks of cotton by making many twists and turns as it joined Mama's house to Miss Lily's house. When Papa plowed the cotton he did not plow up the footpath. He lifted the plow point as he came to the edge of the path, then set the plow point in the ground again beyond the path. This gave Papa an opportunity to shake the grass and debris from the plow point. For a short while this littered the footpath, but the passage of many feet soon beat the path clean again.

The footpath was the line of communication between two families living in houses not more than an eighth of a mile apart. Papa would no more cut that line than you would cut the telephone line that connects you with the world outside your house.

Mama listened attentively and respectfully to what Miss Lily had to say. Mama was always attentive and respectful, even if she had heard it before, and sometimes Miss Lily did repeat herself because the sphere from which she gathered her information was limited. The focus of it all was her own family. Her husband Tom and her fourteen children. The Lord had given her fourteen children, with Tom's willing participation, and at times she sounded boastful. "Fourteen of 'em jest like stair steps and ain't nary a one of 'em ever been in jail!"

Was this self praise, or did Miss Lily simply stand in grateful awe before a benevolent Providence? "Well, I hope not!" was Mama's reply to Miss Lily's boast, or her gratitude. For Mama thought that staying out of jail was the lowest common denominator of performance for decent farm people. People in town, where sin was to be found on every corner, might be expected to fall into the hands of the Law now and then, but not people like her family, or Miss Lily's fourteen children.

Mama was restrained about her own four boys when she talked with Miss Lily. She did not live with the spectre of arrest and imprisonment of them, although she was not above threatening them with the chain gang when she caught them at their worst. And at times she did prophesy that they would wind up in the poorhouse if they did not stir themselves out of their natural laziness or give up such wasteful practices as peeling off too much potato with the peel.

At times, when Mama was exasperated with the boys' deviltry, she would hold up before them the departed but never forgotten Margaret as the paragon of all virtues and the example to be followed if they were ever to amount to anything. "I could raise four girls with less trouble than one boy!" Mama would say when they were a sore trial to her.

Mama did not question many of God's actions, but she could never understand why He had given her four boys and only one girl and then had taken the girl away. It was a mystery hidden in the inscrutable ways of an all powerful but not necessarily all beneficent Providence.

Why God had taken away that one girl in the bloom of her young maidenhood was the deepest mystery of all. It was one which Mama could neither fathom nor accept. But it is a historical fact that Mama's statement "I could raise four girls with less trouble than one boy!" came after Margaret's death and was never spoken before, which means that at the time of Miss Lily's visit, and when she was preparing to hear Miss Lily out while continuing to hem the blouse for Alfie, Mama had never made such an uncomplimentary comparison. For Margaret was still alive, vivacious, and on the point of "spoiling Alfie rotten."

Margaret had, in fact, given Alfie the comic section from the Ocmulgee Sentinel, and she had taught him to recognize Moon Mullins, Joe Palooka, Little Orphan Annie and all the rest of the comic characters. He was happily engaged in gazing at the pictures as Miss Lily fanned herself and Mama looked up from the shirt waist she was hemming on the Singer Sewing Machine, looking up frequently enough to meet the requirements of politeness. She held the thread between her teeth as she reloaded the bobbin. Little beads of perspiration stood on her upper lip.

Her hands then guided the thread and the cloth toward the finished product, a shirt waist for Alfie, but her big and expressive eyes enveloped Miss Lily and conveyed the message that she was in complete agreement that Tom was placing his soul in mortal danger when he used such language as "hotter 'n the hinges of hell" to describe the weather. Mama also sought by her looks to let Miss Lily know that even though she attributed the words to Tom and took no responsibility for their origin, she was endangering herself by repeating them. And she certainly thought it was improper for Miss Lily to quote Tom on the subject of hell's hinges in Alfie's presence.

Alfie himself sat quietly on the floor near Mama, listening. And watching to see where Mama would lay the scissors when she had snipped the thread. As he watched, Alfie's eyes seemed bigger even than Mama's but this was a matter of relative proportion. His face was smaller than Mama's. He was a very small boy and Mama was making a very small shirt waist to fit him.

"Does it look like a fit to you, Lily?'' Mama held up the little shirt and shook the loose threads from it. Alfie's big brown eyes were following Mama's movements. He was watching the scissors and when Mama laid them down, he watched to see when her attention was fixed on Miss Lily. Mama eyed the shirt critically and waited for Miss Lilie's reply.

"Depends on which one you aim to fit." Miss Lily laughed. She fingered the material lightly and examined the buttonholes. "Tom says it don't matter if I cut holes in a meal sack it'll fit one of 'em an' there's always a youngun' to fit any size meal sack."

Miss Lily rocked happily, bathed in the cleverness of Tom's perceptiveness. "Tom says we never miss with the baby crop even in a dry year."

Alfie reached for Mama's scissors and drew them quietly to himself, then started to cut some pictures from the comics. Mama saw him just in time. "Alfie!" she scolded. "How many times have I told you not to cut paper with my good scissors! You'll dull them so they won't cut cloth."

Mama picked the scissors out of Alfie's hands and appeared aggravated, but she tried to appear to be paying attention to what

Miss Lily was saying to her. "Cutting pictures from the funny papers with my good scissors! Lord help you!"

"Speaking of the Lord," Miss Lily followed Mama's cue without hesitation. "I guess you heard about Charles Earl joining the church." She had hoped to draw from Mama a comment on the dry weather and Tom's observation thereon, but Alfie's action in pilfering the good scissors had side tracked that discussion. Temporarily.

"No." Mama had started the Singer Sewing Machine, but now she stopped. Her foot was still on the treadle.

"Isn't Charles Earl rather young to be joining the church?" Mama's eyes met Miss Lily's now, demanding an explanation for her lack of parental control in a matter of such serious and far reaching nature as joining the church.

"Oh, Charles Earl's young all right. He's about Junior's age, I reckon, but Tom says by the time there's water enough in the creek to baptize 'im in Charles Earl'll have hair on his lip an' then he'll be fair game fer the devil. Tom says he never seen such a dry spell as this 'un."

Miss Lily had maneuvered the conversation back to the hot dry weather without losing the main thread of the conversation which was Charles Earl's joining the church. This pious act on Charles Earl's part was unquestionably commendable at face value and it might even help to maintain the perfect conduct record in respect to staying out of jail.

"When did Charles Earl join church?" Mama went to church almost every preaching Sunday at the Midway Baptist Church and she was not going to let Tom's observations on the weather deflect her from the main line of the conversation. Charles Earl's act of joining the church was a momentous event and it should not have escaped her notice. Mama was a bit miffed that it had occurred without her knowledge. She had already indicated that it did not meet her full approval because of Charles Earl's youthfulness, a condition which might preclude the good judgment and the seriousness requisite to taking such a step.

Miss Lily fanned furiously. Jesus and the little lamb waved back and forth in front of her face. She sensed Mama's mood and set about to justify Charles Earl's action in joining the church, and to place the event in a time frame which excused Mama's ignorance of it. She also found in this an occasion for more of Tom's risque humor. "It was durin' the protracted meetin'. The night the preacher give the sermon on hellfire and damnation. That musta' been the night you wasn't there."

Mama was on the verge of saying that if that was the subject of the preacher's sermon she had chosen the right time not to be there, but Miss Lily did not pause long enough for Mama to say it. Her mind had quickly gone back over all the nights of the protracted meeting and confirmed what her lips had spoken, so she said "That musta' been the night you wasn't there. Anyway, Charles Earl an' one of the Tidwell boys, the one that don't talk too plain, both of 'em come down an' joined church together that night."

Now Miss Lily paused and allowed the movement of the fan to slow down to a drag, so that Jesus and the lamb could recover from the dizzying motion. "Tom says he ain't sure whether Charles Earl got a real case of religion or if the preacher jest skeered hell outta 'im with that sermon on hellfire an' damnation."

The sermon had been one to make a young man rethink his ways, whether he had found opportunity to stray far enough from the paths of righteousness to land him in jail or not. Mama could imagine the fright that moved Charles Earl as he sought the extended hand of the preacher to save him from the flames of hell. Quoting Tom on that aspect of Charles Earl's conversion, Miss Lily put the fan in front of her mouth. Jesus and the lamb were perfectly still but tilted slightly so that Miss Lily could see over the fan as she cut her eyes at Alfie to see whether he had noticed her reference to the preacher scaring hell out of Charles Earl.

This drew Mama's attention back to Alfie and she saw that he had her good scissors again and was cutting paper with them. He was excising Moon Mullins whole from the Sentinel's comic strip. Mama's mouth dropped open but Miss Lily was still talking so Mama didn't say anything because Mama considered it impolite to interrupt. But this did not preclude remedial action. She snatched the scissors from Alfie's hand and rapped his bottom sharply with her open palm just as Miss Lily, having met Mama's objection to Charles Earl's premature joining of the church and reduced it to its proper size with one of Tom's witticisms, repeated the last line in order to make certain that Mama had got the point, which it is reasonable to assume she might have missed because of Alfie and the good scissors.

"Tom says the preacher mighta jist skeered hell outta Charles Earl with fire an' brimstone."

Mama's attention was upon Alfie now and she could not give Miss Lily's account of Tom's theological speculations its due. "Didn't I tell you not to cut paper with my good scissors?"

She laid the scissors on the Singer Sewing machine after she had looked at them carefully to try to determine whether they had been dulled by the action of cutting paper with them. Then she looked blankly at Miss Lily because she was ashamed of having lost control.

Miss Lily laughed nervously at what had happened. Then, remembering something Tom had said that seemed appropriate for the occasion, her own mood lightened. She slapped her bare leg with the hand that held the fan, an act which seemed a desecration of Jesus and the lamb. Laughing freely now, Miss Lily said "Lordy! Tom says you can't lay nuthin' down but what one of the younguns'll pick it up an' make a play toy outta it."

Alfie was sitting now in the midst of the paper clippings and the cloth snippings, but even the cutout comic characters had lost their attraction. He averted his face from Miss Lily and looked down at his own empty hands and he scattered the comic characters with an angry swish of his hand. He was trying not to cry, but his chin trembled, and he thought of Miss Lily going home and telling Mister Tom and the fourteen children that she had seen Alfie get a spanking. So he could not keep back the tears any longer. They welled up in his eyes and rolled down his cheeks.

The tears stung his eyes and he rubbed at them with his hand and with his shirt sleeve but he could not keep them away. He was feeling very little and helpless because Miss Lily had used language that was denied him by Mama's inflexible moral code. He wanted to lash out at Miss Lily just for being there and seeing him get a spanking from Mama. Miss Lily's laughing eyes were worse even than the stinging of his buttocks where Mama's hand had smacked him. His voice trembled uncontrollably as he turned defiantly toward Miss Lily.

"Tom Tom Tom!" Alfie now brought the name up from his throat where it was like bile. "That's all you can say is Tom Tom Tom!"

Mama's foot was suspended over the treadle of the Singer Sewing Machine. She dropped the scissors into her lap. She slowly lowered the little shirt waist she was holding up again for inspection. The little shirt waist lay on top of the scissors in Mama's lap. Mama was struggling with her own face because of the emotions churning inside her.

Then the storm of rage inside Alfie broke with a last spasm of pain. It shook his body with violent sobbing. Mama opened her arms and her face. Alfie flung himself into Mama's arms and buried his own face in Mama's bosom, hiding his face from Miss Lily, closing his eyes against the presence of both Mama and Miss Lily and the whole world of big, overpowering people.

Mama held Alfie close, hugging his trembling shoulders. She felt she had to reprimand him for what he had said to Miss Lily; she wanted to hug him close to herself and let the warmth of her own being flow into him. She said "Alfie! Aren't you ashamed of yourself? Saying a thing like that to Miss Lily!" But Mama was so torn by her own conflicting inner feelings that it didn't come out as a reprimand. Mama was trying to keep from laughing and she was trying to keep from crying too.

Miss Lily was not at all upset by Alfie's outburst. She laughed a high pitched shrieking cackle and her body shook with merriment. She fanned her red, perspiring face. Jesus and the little lamb flipped back and forth rapidly in her hand."Lordy mercy! That child!" Miss Lily said when she could get her breath.

"Tom says when a youngun' opens his mouth there jist ain't no tellin' what'll come outta it!"

Chapter Two: A Greyhound Bus Driver or Nuthin'

Papa was scraping up the last of the eggs and grits from his breakfast plate and he was thinking about what he would do as soon as he finished eating, but Mama was thinking about what happened the day before with Alfie and the scissors. Papa reached for another of the thin brown biscuits Mama had made and he wiped his plate clean with it.

"You're the best cook in Colaparchee County," Papa said, turning his blue eyes directly on Mama's thoughtful face. "Maybe in the whole State of Georgia."

Mama smiled, pleased, but she ignored the compliment. She was thinking about Alfie and wondering if she could find some way to make it all up to him. After all, he was The Baby, and the scissors didn't seem to be hurt. "What are you going to do this morning?" Mama paused for a moment. Papa had wiped up about as much black pepper as egg yellow with his biscuit and his eyes were watering as a result of it. "Is it something Alfie could help you with?" Even if Alfie just sat and watched Papa it was considered helping.

"I'm going over to Robb's" Papa said, pushing back the cane bottom chair and getting up from the table because he was ready to go. He straightened up to his full six feet of height and looked down at Mama who was still sitting at the table. Her deep brown gaze was fixed on Papa as she waited. "I have got to see Robb about a hay rake. I don't know whether I ought to take the baby with me. He's mighty little for ridin' a hay rake."

Alfie turned big expectant eyes on Papa, and Mama began gathering up the dishes and scraping them, but she was studying Alfie's face. His plate was as clean as Papa's because he had swabbed it out with a biscuit the way he had seen Papa do it. Mama said "He won't have to ride the hay rake. But he'd rather ride in the car than to eat when he's hungry."

Papa was stalling for time by rolling a cigarette. He had his little sack of Bull Durham and was pouring the tobacco into a thin paper which he held cupped in his hand. "Can I Papa? Can I go with you in the Dodge? To Mister Robb's?" He hesitated on

Mister Robb's name but gathered courage as he thought about riding in the Dodge with Papa.

"I thought you needed the boys to help you in the flower garden. To tote the manure for you."

"Junior can help me." Mama was insistent; she knew why Papa was resistant. "He's bigger and stronger. Take Alfie with you."

"Aw, I don't want to stay here an' carry ol' stinkin' manure." Junior had been pouring syrup into a hole in a biscuit. He had punched the hole with his finger, and the finished product was called a "syrup in the hole." Now he pushed a lock of thick dark hair back with his hand and realized too late that his fingers were sticky with syrup. "Let me go with you, Papa."

Papa viewed the prospect of taking Junior with him more dimly than taking Alfie. He might be able to get a pint bottle of moonshine from Robb without Alfie knowing but nothing escaped Junior's sharp eyes. "One of you at a time is enough," Papa said. "I have got business to talk over with Robb and I don't need the two of you scufflin' and squabblin' with one another."

Papa inhaled, blew the smoke out and squinted his eyes in the smoke. He shook the flame from the match and looked around for some place to throw the match stem. But his eyes returned to Junior. "If your Mama can't find enough work to keep you busy 'till I get back you can go to the corn crib and shuck corn."

"Aw Shucks!" Junior said, licking the syrup off his fingers. "I don't never git to do nuthin' I wanta do. Just carry ol' stinkin' cow manure an' shuck corn for the ol' stinkin' pigs."

Papa was going to reinforce his instructions to Junior with harsher words, but Mama said "I'll keep Junior busy. You just get your business with Robb over with and hurry back." She wiped Alfie's face with a damp wash cloth and said "You stay right with your Papa and don't get out of his sight. I don't want you to get hurt playing around on that old broken down machinery he has got over there." Mama was confident that with Alfie clinging close to Papa there would be no opportunity for

Papa and Robb to make any illegal transaction involving a pint of moonshine.

Junior was unhappy. He poured more syrup into his biscuit, stuck out his tongue at Alfie and said "Baby!"

Alfie glared at Junior, stuck out his tongue at him and was about to protest being called "'Baby'' but Papa said "Well, if you're goin' with me make haste. I can't wait around all day while you and Junior make monkey faces at one another." Alfie ran toward the old touring Dodge which was parked under the chinaberry trees but Mama called him back.

"Come and wash your hands first. You can't go to Mister Robb's with all that dirt on you." Mama got the wash cloth again and dipped it into cold water which she poured out of the well bucket into the enamel wash pan. She washed Alfie's face again. Alfie squinched his eyes and tried to avoid the octagon soap Mama had rubbed onto the wash cloth. His nose was now under assault and he jerked his head sideways.

"Aw Mama! I washed my face an' hands before I ate breakfast. Ouch! That's cold!. Besides, we're just goin' to Mister Robb's and he ain't never clean!"

"You hush your mouth!" Mama scolded. She was in perfect agreement with Alfie's judgment on Mister Robb but a child must not be allowed to say things like that about a grown person, even if the things he said were true. She checked behind Alfie's ears. "Good Lord! Just look at the dirt behind your ears. And your neck. And you went to bed last night with all that dirt on you. Hold still. You can't go to Mister Robb's with dirt behind your ears."

Alfie grimaced, remembering the dirt on Mister Robb's neck but unable to imagine how he was to look behind his own ears. Junior grinned at Alfie, thinking that carrying manure for Mama's flower beds might not be as bad as getting scrubbed up for a trip to Mister Robb's. He slipped another biscuit into his pocket just in case there was not enough manure to keep him busy and he had to go to the corn crib to shuck corn for the ol' pigs who could just as well shuck it for themselves because they didn't have anything better to do. But the more he thought about

Mister Robb the less grievance he felt about not getting to go with Papa.

Papa slammed the door of the Dodge on the driver's side. He turned on the ignition and pressed the starter button in the floorboard with his foot. The engine turned over slowly, whining and complaining. It picked up a little speed as Papa pressed the starter insistently, and finally caught. The Dodge roared to life under Papa's brogan clad foot and he brightened. Maybe the hay rake would be all the business he would do with Robb. "If the hay rake ain't broke," he said silently in his mind, "It'll be because he ain't hitched it up lately."

Alfie was relieved too by the engine's roar. It meant that all the face washing was not entirely wasted. He sat up beside Papa and peered over the dashboard, straining his neck to see. Papa shoved the clutch in with his left foot while he kept the engine alive with his right foot. Gears clashed and scrunched, the Dodge lurched forward. The tires crunched the sand beneath them as they rolled along under the overhanging boughs of pecan trees lining the driveway. A lone Blue Jay in the top of a pecan tree screamed his greeting, or was it a protest? "Jay! Jay!'' Alfie's eyes brightened at the sound of the bird and he searched among the branches. He was rewarded by a flash of blue crossing the driveway directly in front of the car.

"That ol' jay bird musta forgot what day of the week it is." Papa's face gave no indication of what was behind this cryptic remark. And when Alfie looked puzzled, his lips parted, waiting to receive the mystery, Papa followed the Blue Jay with his eyes and said "Jay birds carry sticks to the ol' Bad Man on Fridays so he can have his fires burnin' good an' hot by Sunday mornin'." Alfie thought about Charles Earl and what Miss Lily had said about the preacher "skeering hell outta 'im'" with threats of fire and brimstone. The Blue Jay flapped lazily along the edge of the cotton patch bordering the driveway. Then he swung back and swooped to the top of a pecan tree near the junction of the driveway and the county road.

"That 'un musta forgot what day of the week it is," Papa repeated. "Now he don't know what to do with hisself."

Alfie searched Papa's face until the little twinkle showed in Papa's blue eyes, and the little crinkle flowed back along his temple and behind his ear. Then Alfie's face broke into a self conscious smile. "Aw Papa. You're jest teasin' me, ain't you?"

Papa didn't say whether he was teasing or not, but he swung the Dodge to the left when they reached the road that ran in front of Mister Charles' house. Then they bumped along over the ruts caused by recent rains and Papa looked closely at the fields of corn beginning to tassle and the cotton showing pink and white blossoms peeping from the dark foliage, and he made mental comparisons of his neighbors' crops with his own. Then Tobesofkee Creek was just ahead and when the Dodge mounted the wooden bridge spanning the Tobesofkee the floorboards of the bridge made a "slap slap slap" sound beneath the wheels of the Dodge. The water in Tobesofkee made a softer sound, "lap lap lap" against the concrete pillars supporting the bridge. Then the sound changed to "whoosh whoosh whoosh'' where the water flowed around the pillars and flowed away toward the Ocmulgee River, which is where Papa said all the water went to when it flowed out of sight.

Then Papa reached over and plucked playfully at the silky blond hairs on Alfie's forearm. "I bet you're gonna grow up to be the best pig raiser in Colaparchee County," Papa said. "I always heard that hairy arms is a sign of a good pig raiser."

Papa's own sinewy bare arms were sunburned to a dark brown up to his elbows. Above the elbows they were white because Papa rolled his sleeves up when he was working. Curling red hairs covered the forearms. "Is that what you're gonna be when you grow up? A pig raiser?" Papa plucked at the hairs on Alfie's arm. Alfie squealed with a mixture of pain and pride.

"Ouch! that stings!" It was like pulling off adhesive tape.

Papa put his hand back on the steering wheel as the Dodge cleared the other end of the Rattling Bridge."

He looked inquiringly at Alfie. "You gonna be a pig raiser when you grow up?"

"I ain't gonna be no pig raiser." Alfie rubbed his arm to make it quit stinging, and when Papa looked at him in mock surprise, Alfie's face became grave and proud at the same time. "I'm gonna be a Greyhound bus driver when I git big."

They were clear of the bridge over Tobesofkee Creek now and they could see Mister Robb's house and the barns all around it, some of them leaning at a slant which indicated the direction of the prevailing winds. House and out buildings were of unpainted pine weatherboarding. Farming implements and tools - plows, rakes, harrows and wagons - were scattered about the place, rusting. Papa threw his head back so far you might wonder if he was sitting in the back seat, and the early morning sunlight glinted off his thinning reddish blond hair. Most of it was on the top of his head and there was no danger of Papa's hair ever getting into his eyes the way Alfie's hair got into his.

"A Greyhound bus driver, eh?" Papa said, and he was impressed with the magnitude of Alfie's aspiration. "A Greyhound's a mighty big bus. I reckon it's about the biggest thing on the road. You think you can handle somethin' that big?"

Alfie glanced shyly at Papa and then looked down at his own short legs dangling from the seat of the Dodge. He thought that someday he might grow to be as big as Papa, or almost as big, if he kept drinking plenty of buttermilk and didn't ever drink any coffee which would stunt him and turn him black too, and he said in a hoarse whisper "When I git big."

Then they swung into Mister Robb's driveway, narrowly missing the rusty, battered mailbox because the post was leaning out over the driveway. The mailbox bore the single word Robb and the letters had been painted on and had run down at the bottom. Papa shifted into second gear and drove up to the gate swinging half open in front of Mister Robb's house. He pressed hard on the horn button with the heel of his hand. "Ah-ooo-gah! Ah-ooo-gah!" They sat there for a minute, listening to the engine going "Chack-a lack. Chacka-lack." Then Papa turned it off and waited for Robb to come out of the house.

At the sound of the horn two blue tick coon hounds rose from their cool place under the doorsteps and came out barking dutifully but without a whole lot of enthusiasm.

Then Robb appeared in the kitchen doorway, hitching up the galluses of his overalls and squinting into the slanting rays of the sun. He was a big man in his middle years, and already beginning to show a paunch about the middle. He was not wearing a shirt. The bib of his overalls came high on his chest, but the curling black hairs showed above the bib in stark contrast to his white skin. Farther up, his neck was reddish brown from exposure to the sun and the wind.

A three day stubble of dark beard covered a lean, leathery face. When the sun's rays struck the stubble on his chin, it glistened. Then he looked down at the hounds bristling and moving stiff legged, taking their job of guarding the house more seriously now that the master had appeared. The rays of the sun were now absorbed in the shock of unruly black hair crowning Robb's head. He picked up a stick of stove wood from the porch floor and hurled it viciously at the nearer hound and spoke roughly to it.

"Shut up an' git back under the house!" The stick struck the ground near the bristling dog and bounced away. The dog's bristles fell, he yelped as if he had been hit, and ran under the house where he cowered, but continued barking complainingly, sporadically, now at the intruders in the Dodge at the gate, then at his harsh master standing on the porch floor above him. The other hound backed away, scratching at the ground with his hind feet, but keeping a safe distance from Robb and turning to bark half heartedly at the Dodge and its occupants.

Robb moved toward the porch steps, putting one hand up to shade his eyes from the sun's slanting rays. Loose shoe laces flapped about his bare ankles. Now he recognized Papa and he called out in a rough but jocular tone, "Git out an' come in the house. The dogs ain't gonna eat you." He descended the steps and the shoe laces flapped wildly as he walked toward the Dodge.

Papa ignored Robb's invitation because he knew Robb was merely observing social custom without expecting him to come inside the house. He sat in the car and waited. Robb came on and leaned against the car door, squinting in at Papa and Alfie. He had not washed his face and there were what Mama would have called "cracklings" in the corners of his eyes. Papa said "I didn't aim to git you outta bed but I got work to do and I hate to wait around all day to git started on it. I come to talk to you about the hay rake."

Robb ignored Papa's reference to the hay rake. He turned his face to one side and spat tobacco juice into the sand. "Ain't no hurry about gittin' all the work done. Come in the house and eat some breakfast."

One of the hounds had followed Robb to the car and was sniffing the left front tire and preparing to leave a message on it for the next dog who might encounter it standing still. Robb kicked the hound in the ribs and said "I done tol' you to git under the house. Now git!" The hound yelped and fled. "Damn' dog ain't got no manners," Robb observed.

Robb spat again and turned back to Papa. "You better come in the house and have some breakfast."

Papa said "I have done had my breakfast so long ago I have forgot about it." Robb made a face that indicated he didn't believe Papa but he was relieved anyway. Alfie was relieved too because he did not want to go inside Mister Robb's house. He huddled beside Papa and looked up from under a heavy shock of dark hair at Mister Robb who now leaned against the car and looked inside to see who was with Papa.

The exertion of disciplining the dogs had brought out the sweat on Robb. It stood in drops on his bare shoulders and among the black curling hairs on his chest. Bushy tufts of hair under his armpits gave off a rank, stale odor. He looked inside the car at Alfie and said to Papa "That the same boy you had with you the last time you was here?" Then he reached past Papa to tousle Alfie's hair with a rough, calloused hand. "He has got so much hair hangin' down over his face he looks like a Airedale."

"Where' d you git a boy with so much hair on his head?" Robb said as a sly reference to Papa's thinning hair. Then he gripped the top of Alfie's head and said "What's your name boy?" Alfie twisted his head out of Mister Robb's grip and wouldn't say anything so Mister Robb said "Cat's got your tongue, has he. Well, I know your name. It's Puddin' n Tame."

"Tell Mister Robb your name, Son." Papa looked at Alfie with pride mixed with impatience because Alfie would not respond to Mister Robb. "Tell him your name."

The odor from Mister Robb's armpit assailed Alfie's nostrils, his nose twitched, and he pressed his lips closely together. Robb had pushed his face in close to Papa's in order to reach Alfie who had retreated to the far corner of the seat, and Robb's foul smelling breath coming through brown stained teeth with gaps above and below, was beginning to bother Papa and he leaned away from Robb. This enabled Robb to reach farther inside and he now made a new discovery.

"He's got hair on his arms too." He gathered up the fine silky hairs on Alfie's arm between a thumb and stubby forefinger. The golden hairs stood out in stark contrast against the blackened nails on the fingers clutching them. "You gonna be a pig raiser when you grow up? With hairs like them on your arms you oughtta make a good pig raiser."

Tears were forming in Alfie's eyes now and he stared back at Mister Robb and shook his head but he would not open his lips.

"You ain't gonna be no pig raiser?" Mister Robb twisted the hairs in his grip and said "Well, what are you gonna be?"

"Tell Mister Robb what you're gonna be when you grow up Son." Papa was thinking of what Alfie had told him about being a Greyhound bus driver and he wanted Alfie to say it to Robb but Alfie did not want to share his dream with Mister Robb and he even wished now that he had not told Papa because if he had not told Papa, then Papa would not be trying to get him to tell Mister Robb.

"Tell Mister Robb what you told me you are gonna be when you get big, Son." Papa looked into Alfie's face and tried to encourage him to tell Robb his secret.

"So he's tol' you, has he? And now he won't tell me." Spit flew out through the gaps in Robb's teeth and he belched sour breath inside the car. "Well, I'll jest hafta sweat it outta 'im." And Mister Robb twisted the hairs tighter between his thumb and forefinger.

But Alfie jerked violently away from Mister Robb,almost falling into the floor of the Dodge. He screamed with pain. The gorge rose in his throat and his eyes were blinded over with the tears that gushed from them now. As the wave of anger and frustration swept over him, it lifted him from his crouching position and brought him right up into Mister Robb's startled face. Mister Robb had started to form the words again "What are you gonna be?" But Alfie's mouth was open now and he spat the words into Mister Robb's brown stained teeth.

"I ain't gonna be nuthin'!" he screamed. "I'm just gonna be like my Papa!" Then he hurled himself into Papa's lap and buried his face on Papa's chest and his body was racked with a storm of great shaking sobs.

Mister Robb was so startled by Alfie that he drew his head back so quickly that he struck it against the roof of the Dodge and between his laughter and the pain of striking his head he began to choke on his tobacco juice. He turned his head to spit the tobacco juice and gripped the door of the Dodge to steady himself.

"God A'mighty!" Papa said, throwing his arms about Alfie and holding him tightly against his chest. "And I was hopin' this un' would amount to somethin' when he growed up!"

Papa pushed the starter with his foot. The Dodge roared to life. Robb stood back. The hounds rushed out from under the house and barked. Alfie buried his face deeper in Papa's chest as the tarnished vision of the Greyhound bus faded behind the mist of tears that washed his big brown eyes and prepared them for other dreams to come.

"I reckon we better go home." Papa said, his blue eyes both merry and troubled as he swung the Dodge away from Robb's house.

Chapter Three: Sandy

"A dog's the best cure for a boy's troubles." Papa said it to Mama that evening after Sandy came and the final decision had not been made to let Sandy stay.

Mama was not fully convinced. "Every stray dog that takes up here just makes more mess for me to clean up after. Digging up my flower beds to find a cool place. Lying on the porch and scratching fleas."

Sandy was lying on the porch at that very moment but he was not scratching fleas. He was lying with his head stretched out on his front paws and gazing up at Mama as if he thought she was the Queen of Heaven. She looked back at him and Sandy thumped the porch floor with his tail and smiled at her.

Papa had told Mama about Alfie's run in with Mister Robb and it had made her mad, but she couldn't be mad with Papa because it was her idea for Alfie to go with him to Robb's. Besides, there was the incident about the scissors which she didn't mention to Papa because he wouldn't understand about the good scissors just being for cutting cloth and not for cutting paper. Mama thought "First Lily and now Robb." But out loud she said "Well, I just hope..."

"We'll give the dog a chance," Papa said. "If he ain't no account we can get shed of him."

And Sandy's tongue lolled out, saliva dripping off it.

His eyes were on Mama and Papa who were sitting on the porch, resting and reviewing the happenings of the day. His ears were cocked to the sounds of Alfie and Junior who were running and calling to one another in the gathering shadows of the summer evening. Sandy was touching all the bases at once. But he knew that he already had it made with Junior and Alfie, and that the real decision rested with Mama and Papa.

Sandy had come that very morning, the day after Alfie's unhappy experience at Mister Robb's, which was the day after Miss Lily came with all her talk about Tom. Alfie and Junior were playing Fox and Hound, and as usual Junior made Alfie be the Hound. As usual too, Junior, the Fox, could outrun Alfie because Junior had long legs and Alfie's legs were short and stubby. So Alfie was not enjoying the game of Fox and Hound much because no matter how hard he ran after Junior he could never catch him, and so he had stopped to rest near the chopping block in the woodpile. He was just starting to sit down on the chopping block when he heard somebody say "Woof!"

At first Alfie thought it was Junior teasing him into taking up the fruitless chase, and he wouldn't even look up or let on that he heard him say "Woof!" But then he heard "Woof!" again and it was accompanied by loud breathing, and when he looked to see who it was, there stood Sandy. Sandy sat down and looked at Alfie. His tongue dripped saliva and he wiggled his body at Alfie.

Of course he hadn't been named Sandy yet but it didn't take long because when he sat down and looked at Alfie with his mouth open dripping saliva and his ears standing up and then flopping over at the tips, and his eyes dancing in his head as if he expected Alfie to run up and throw his arms around his neck, Alfie thought of Little Orphan Annie's dog Sandy. And when he told Junior that he was going to call him Sandy, Junior said "I had already thought of that myself and it's what I was goin' to call 'im."

Sandy was reddish brown with a white collar, a white brush at the end of his shaggy tail which was in constant motion, and three of his feet were white but the other one was black.

Papa said "I reckon he's mostly collie but mixed breed dogs are smarter 'n the pedigreed ones anyway, so it don't matter what he's mixed with. He's mostly collie." Papa looked at Sandy critically for a while and said "The only question is whether he is any account."

Sandy set out to prove that he was of some account by playing with Alfie and Junior and showing great concern for their safety and welfare. Once, when they were wrestling and hasseling, Junior fell over and pretended that Alfie had hurt him so badly that he couldn't stand up. He just did it to tease Alfie but Sandy ran up to him and began whining and licking Junior's face, and then when Junior still played hurt, he ran off to Mama making sounds of distress and Mama came to see what was wrong.

It didn't take Mama more than two seconds to see through Junior's trick and she scolded him for it. "The Lord will surely punish you on Judgement Day for doing a thing like that to a poor dumb brute and I have a good notion to give you a switching for it right now."

Mama might have done it too but she thought that might cause Sandy even more distress. After that Junior and Alfie would play the trick on Sandy but they would always recover just before Sandy ran off to get Mama. Then Sandy would be so happy he would forget about going for Mama. But Willie was watching from the barn door one day and he said "They ain't foolin' that dog one bit. Sandy's smarter 'n Junior and Alfie put together." Then Willie laughed silently which meant that Willie was pleased with what he had seen.

Papa said that he reckoned Sandy had proved that he was of some account by the way he settled the matter of the Blue tick hound. It was just the way Mama said it would be. "Every stray dog in Colaparchee County will want to take up here when the word gets around."

The word that Mama referred to was that free room and board could be found at her house together with small boys to love stray dogs. And the Blue Tick hound was standing at the yard gate the very next day after Sandy established his claim. Sandy saw that the Blue Tick hound wanted the same thing he had already laid claim to and he ran at him and bowled him over and stood over him stiff legged. The Blue Tick hound lay belly up and pleaded innocence of any malice, so Sandy left him there with a warning growl, but he did not go off very far, and when the Blue Tick hound got up and ran to Alfie, wagging and twisting his whole body and trying to lick Alfie's hands, Sandy came back and hit him harder than he had done before. Then he kept snarling and exposing his long white canine teeth to let the hound know that he meant business. The hound made for the open gate and Sandy chased him until he was heading for Mister Tom's and Miss Lily's house where he was welcome to lick the hands of all fourteen of Miss Lily's children.

Papa said "I could use a good hound dog if he would run rabbits in the day time and possums at night, but if he won't fight I don't reckon he deserves to be fed."

That was the end of the Blue Tick hound's short stay. Mama said it was good riddance and agreed that Sandy might be worth his own feed if he would just keep all the other beggars and strays away from the house and yard.

Sandy was tenacious about his new home and he proved to have tenacity about anything he sank his teeth into, especially a croaker sack. Papa had sent Junior and Alfie to the corncrib to get a croaker sack because he was going to gather some roasting ears for dinner. Roasting ears are the ears of green corn at the right stage for people to eat and before they get hard enough to feed to a mule. And a croaker sack is a burlap bag that you can carry almost anything in by slinging it over your shoulder.

It had not yet occurred to Junior and Alfie that there is a far more exciting use for a croaker sack but Sandy soon discovered it. He sank his teeth into the end of the croaker sack that was dragging on the ground behind Junior and he started jerking and tugging and growling at the croaker sack as if it had been some vicious animal that he had to kill.

"Look at Sandy!" Alfie laughed, and Junior started jerking and tugging and growling back at Sandy. Alfie was jumping up and down and shouting and laughing and so it became a real tug of war with spectator support but most of the support on Alfie's part was for Sandy who wouldn't turn loose but just dug in, shook the croaker sack violently and growled.

Junior started to run in a circle with Sandy hanging onto the sack and soon Sandy's front feet were off the ground and he was dancing around the circle on his hind feet. Junior kept running and swinging the croaker sack then until Sandy's hind feet began to skip along and when Junior ran faster Sandy's hind feet left the ground entirely and he was floating through the air suspended at the end of the croaker sack with Junior swinging him in a circle about him and the faster Junior swung the higher Sandy got off the ground but he wouldn't turn loose. His teeth were clamped on the croaker sack and his eyes were set on

Junior, and on Alfie whenever he would pass him in his circuit. He kept up an ominous growling deep in his chest.

Papa thought that Junior and Alfie had been gone long enough to bring a croaker sack from China and so he went to see what was going on and he walked right into what was going around, which was Sandy. For just as Papa turned the corner of the corn crib in his search for Junior and Alfie and the croaker sack Sandy swung past the same corner of the corn crib in his flight on the croaker sack. Sandy's feathery tail was floating out behind him and his hind legs were extended to give him balance and when Papa walked into the arc of Sandy's flight Sandy's hind feet struck Papa in the chest and almost bowled him over.

Junior dropped his end of the croaker sack and Sandy tumbled to the ground with his end still clenched in his teeth. He rolled over three times and got up looking very surprised but he quickly recovered and ran off with the croaker sack, shaking it and growling to let it know that he had won the game.

"God A'mighty!" Papa said when he had got enough breath back into him to say it. "That damn' dog ain't been here more 'n a week and you younguns have done made a airplane outta 'im already!"

So Sandy had given a good account of himself, proving that for dogged determination and devotion to duty, there just was no match for him in Colaparchee County.

And Alfie's troubles with Miss Lily and Mister Robb were almost forgotten if not completely cured.

Chapter Four: "Watkins Man, Pearl!"

The Watkins Man was the first intruder - with the exception of the Blue Tick Hound, of course - whom Sandy challenged. As the self-appointed Protector of Alfie, it was Sandy's job to bark at anyone who came into the yard. So that Alfie, and presumably, Mama too, might know of the approach of either danger or opportunity, Sandy heralded the Watkins Man with a "Woof!"

"Ah-ooo-gah! Ah-ooo-gah!" The old Ford rattled, chugged, banged and steamed into the sandy spot in the shade of the big oak tree which stood at the corner of the fence on the East side of the front yard. The sound of the horn floated away on the morning air as the sound of the engine died away under the vibrating, shuddering hood.

Now a sound came from the rear of the Ford. It was the sound of anxiety. In a wooden crate tied with baling wire to the rear bumper and spare tire of the Ford, the Anxious Ones gave forth their sounds of anxiety. Three Rhode Island Red hens and a Barred Rock rooster poked their heads through the slats of the crate. Their beaks stood open, gasping for air. Their eyes glittered with fear and they made a sound akin to a strangled squawk.

This was a strange world attached to the rear of the Watkins Man's Ford, this chicken crate tied with baling wire to the rear bumper and the spare tire.

"Ah-ooo-gah!" The horn sounded once more, but weakly this time. Without the engine to keep the power supply up, it soon diminished to the disappearing point, and the Watkins Man prudently decided to conserve the energy stored under the metal covering for propelling the machine. He would make his presence known by voice.

"Watkins Man!" he called out in a loud rasping voice. "Watkins Man!" And he let himself down stiffly, somewhat painfully from the driver's seat, first onto the running board, and then onto the ground. He stood slightly bent over, he pressed his left hand to the lower area of his back to relieve, or perhaps to call attention to, the pain of his lumbago.

He was a short, swarthy man. That is, his face, neck and forearms were sunburned to a deep brown. But where his blue chambray shirt stood open at the neck, there was a V shaped exposure of white skin covered by short, curly black hair that seemed to push up from his barrel chest. Her wore a black felt hat which he now pushed back from his forehead, the better to scan his surroundings. The upper part of his forehead, the part which his hat had covered before he pushed it back, was white too.

The Watkins Man's arrival had not gone unnoticed. His descent from the Ford was not undetected. Two pairs of bright eyes watched from beneath the steps that led up to the porch. The eyes of the small boy were watchful and even anxious. The eyes of the mostly collie dog were challenging.

The Watkins Man took two steps toward the gate and the collie dog said "Woof!" The small boy remained silent and motionless under the steps. The Watkins Man put calloused, hairy hands on the rail that ran around the top of the yard fence and called out again "Watkins Man!" Sandy looked at Alfie inquiringly, whined and said "Woof!" again.

Mama had heard the Watkins Man's announcement of himself the first time he called. She had heard the sound of the horn before he called. She had heard the rattling and the clattering of the old Ford even before he sounded the horn. The Watkins Man's extra heraldic efforts were not needed. Mama had already said under her breath. "That will be the Watkins Man."

It was the tenth of the month, and the Watkins Man always came on the tenth of the month, unless the tenth fell on a Sunday. And it was too early in the morning for Miss Georgia to come calling in her clattering, swaying Ford. Miss Maggie's did not make that much racket because it was newer. So it had to be the Watkins Man. But he would just have to wait. "If he wants to keep blowing his horn and calling out, then he will just have to do it, but I can't stop what I am doing to run to the gate right now."

Mama was lifting the butter out of the churn and when you are lifting butter out of the churn you can't stop and run to the gate because the Watkins Man has come. But when Mama had all the butter in a crockery bowl, and had covered the bowl with a clean dish towel and had wrapped another towel around the dasher on the top of the churn to keep the flies out, she wiped her hands on her apron and said "I am coming." This was said in the kitchen and nobody heard her say it. But then, pushing her heavy dark hair back from her face, she walked to the front porch where she stood for a moment, smiled, and said "Get out and come in."

The Watkins Man had already got out, and his business did not require him to come inside. Rather, it was for Mama to come outside to the Watkins Man's old Ford which was a veritable store on wheels. So even while Mama was saying "Get out and come in," she was walking toward the porch steps and mentally making a list of the things she needed to buy from the Watkins Man. She was fingering the coin in her apron pocket, placed there earlier because she knew he would come today, and thinking about the things she needed. Her eyes, big and dark, were on the Watkins Man who was leaning on the rail of the yard fence, but one hand fingered the coin in her apron pocket, and the other pushed back the heavy lock of dark hair which kept falling down over her perspiring forehead.

Then Alfie cried out "Ow! Mama! You knocked sand in my eyes!" And Sandy said "Woof!" again, but it sounded more like snort or maybe even a half sneeze than a challenge.

Mama stopped when she had reached ground. She turned to peer under the porch steps. Alfie was sitting there rubbing his fists into his eyeballs. Mama said "Playing under the steps again! Lord have mercy! You come out from under there. The Watkins Man is here."

Alfie knew it was the Watkins Man because he heard him call out "Watkins Man!" But at first, when the old Ford clattered into the yard, Alfie thought it was the Gypsies. That was because of what Miss Georgia had said. And he was not going to let the old Gypsies know he was hiding under the steps. But when Sandy only pricked up his ears and said "Woof!" instead of barking and growling ferociously but staying close to Alfie to protect him from the old Gypsies, Alfie felt less fearful. Still, it was good for Mama to be standing there and saying "The Watkins Man is here, Alfie."

Even if it was the Watkins Man and not the Gypsies, it was better to stay under the steps until Mama came out of the house because even the Watkins Man might see him and say "How come you hidin' under the steps Boy? You skeered somebody'll git you an' carry you off?" And he didn't want to have to tell the Watkins Man about the Gypsies because the Watkins Man would just laugh at him and say "What would the Gypsies want with a little boy like you?"

So the sand drifted down into Alfie's eyes when Mama came down the steps, and Alfie complained about it but he didn't really mind so much. If Mama caused the sand to get in his eyes and make him cry, maybe she would buy him some candy from the Watkins Man so that his eyes would quit hurting and he would quit crying. Maybe.

Alfie didn't know about the fifty cent piece in Mama's apron pocket. Neither did the Watkins Man. But both Alfie and the Watkins Man assumed that Mama had some money, although only Mama knew this for a fact, and only Mama knew how much, fifty cents.

Mama had come to speak to the Watkins Man though, and Alfie crawled from under the porch steps and started toward the Watkins Man's car too. Sandy raced ahead of him, barking. "Woof Woof!" But the Watkins Man ignored Sandy. He considered dogs a nuisance at best and a menace at worst. Besides, dogs never buy Watkins Products and so they serve no purpose for a Watkins Man. So he ignored them in the hope that they would go away because if he kicked or scolded them he could lose a sale.

Although the Watkins Man ignored Sandy, he smiled at Mama. He also cast his eyes all about the yard to appraise the poultry running about the place, just in case Mama didn't have any ready cash. In that case she might want to trade a chicken for some spices. He hoped that wouldn't be the case though because he had a crate of chickens on the rear bumper of the old Ford and he would rather have the ready cash.

The Watkins Man did not ignore Alfie either. Alfie was not apt to have any money yet but he would grow up to be a customer some day. "How come you hidin' under the steps Boy?" The Watkins Man smiled at Alfie and spoke in a teasing voice. "You skeered somebody gonna come along and git you?"

Alfie ducked his head when the Watkins Man said that. His eyelids drooped over his eyes, then he hid behind Mama and buried his face in Mama's skirts. Sandy sat down to watch, and he swept the sand with his brushy tail and grinned at the Watkins Man as if he understood the joke. The Watkins Man saw that Alfie was not taking it as a joke though, and he said "Don't be skeered of me, Boy. I ain't gonna git you." He turned to Mama and said "I got a house fulla younguns at home. I don't need no more."

Then Mama said "Don't be afraid of the Watkins Man. He won't hurt you, and he has all sorts of good things in his car." But after she said this Mama thought it sounded too much like a promise, and she added "Now you be a big boy and don't let the Watkins Man see you acting that way."

Alfie certainly did want the Watkins Man to think he was a big boy. And Mama had spoken of the good things in the Watkins Man's car. And that meant that she might get something for him if he acted like a big boy. So he lifted his face from Mama's skirts, and he looked up at Mama. He even looked briefly at the Watkins Man to see if his face would confirm what Mama had said about the good things in his car. Then he said to Mama "Can I have some candy? Will you buy me some candy from the Watkins Man?"

"We'll see about that when I have got all the things I need." Mama was fingering the fifty cent piece in her apron pocket and figuring in her head. "I'm not promising. But you act like a big boy now so the Watkins Man won't think you don't know how to act."

Now the Watkins Man knew from what Mama had said to Alfie that she had some money, and he said "Don't be skeered of me, Boy. I ain't gonna hurt you." Then Alfie dashed away from both Mama and the Watkins Man, and he ran to the Watkins Man's car, with Sandy running alongside and bumping against his legs. Alfie climbed up onto the running board of the the old Ford and tried to look over inside where the Watkins Man had piled bolts of cloth and cans of spices and bottles of patent medicines. Then he spied the glass jar with the candy and chewing gum in it, and he became very excited.

Alfie was very little though, and he could not see over into the car as well as he wanted to. But the running board had a folding metal frame attached to it to hold the bulky items that the Watkins Man might need to carry on the running board. It was empty though because the Watkins Man didn't quite trust this method of carrying his products. He was afraid things would "jounce off on them rutty roads." So the metal frames served now only to enable Alfie to climb higher and see more, which he did. But his weight caused the flimsy metal frames to sag, then to bend and buckle, and finally to collapse. Alfie looked down at the sagging metal frames which were taking him down with them and he became frightened. He continued hanging to the Ford's door while the frames collapsed under him, and then he looked back at Mama and distress was written all over his face.

The Watkins Man was looking with growing concern too because he had paid good money for the frames and had installed them himself, and he was thinking: There go my frames. Mama saw what was happening, and quick as a flash she ran to Alfie because she was concerned for both her baby and the Watkins Man's frames, but she lifted him down and saw that he was not hurt, and when she spoke it was just to express her concern for the Watkins Man's frames.

"Now you stay down from where you have no business. You could have been hurt, and just look what you've done. You've bent the Watkins Man's luggage rack and I'll have to pay for it and then you won't get any candy for sure."

Alfie primped up his face to cry on account of the scolding he got from Mama with the Watkins Man standing there looking on and disapproving what he had done and maybe going to make Mama pay for it. Actually, the Watkins Man was eager to dismiss the subject of the bent luggage racks and get on with the business of selling something to Mama. And he didn't need anyone to tell him that charging Mama for the bent luggage rack was bad for business. So he said to Mama "Ain't no big harm done. Them cheap luggage frames was a waste of good money from the start and if they'd bend under the weight of a boy no bigger than that it just goes to show they ain't no account."

Then he went to the back seat of the Ford and hauled out a bolt of cloth with alternating red, green and white stripes in it. He held it up and shook the folds out of it for Mama's inspection and approval. "Got a bolt of good cotton cloth here," he said, trying to get Mama's mind off the luggage rack which she was trying to straighten up, and onto the bolt of cloth which he was holding up. "Make up some right pretty shirts for them boys of yours goin' back to school this Fall. Sellin' it cheap too."

The Watkins Man didn't say how cheap because he hadn't yet fully appraised Mama's ability to pay, and on an item as big as the bolt of cloth he might have to take chickens in trade, which would call for some bartering because Mama might think the chickens were worth more cloth than the Watkins Man did. The crate with the Rhode Island Red hens and the Barred Rock rooster in it already could become crowded while his pockets would be empty, and in this heat if the crate was too full some of them might smother and he would wind up losing money on the deal.

The chickens were struggling to get all the air they could and the Watkins Man didn't want them to attract Mama's attention because they might give her notions, so he said. "Make some mighty pretty shirts. Sellin' it cheap too."

Mama looked closely at the cloth and felt it to see if it had any flaws in it. She bit her lower lip and said "I guess I'll have to make their shirts from flour sacks again this year." She was thinking that this bright colored cloth would not suit Junior's taste anyway. He would say "Aw my gosh. Do I hafta go to school wrapped in a flag?"

Mama didn't say this to the Watkins Man though because it was good cloth and he might take it as an insult. She said "Times are hard and the crops don't look too good. You better just show me a spool of thread."

Disappointment spread over the Watkins Man's face at the mention of hard times, but when Mama said "a spool of thread" his hopes revived a little and he produced a spool of white thread, but with less enthusiasm than he had shown for the bolt of red, green and white striped cloth. "Genuine O.I.C." he said "Ain't none better. You need two spools?" He reached into the thread box for a second spool. "Another color?"

"One will have to do,'' Mama said. "How much is it?" She knew that thread was ten cents for a spool, but she asked anyway.

"That'll be ten cents for just one spool. I might knock off a little on two spools."

"One spool will have to do," Mama said.

Alfie's spirits had revived while Mama brought the Watkins Man down from cloth to thread, and his curiosity had grown enough for him to climb back onto the running board of the Watkins Man's car. This time he avoided the metal racks though, and pulled himself up by holding to the door so that he could peer over into the area where he had seen the candy jar. "He's got a Black Cow, Mama.Can I have a Black Cow?"

Some people would be surprised that Alfie had found a Black Cow in a candy jar but it is not surprising at all, for a Black Cow is a confection on a stick. It is chocolate colored and chocolate flavored and it possesses the consistency of taffy. For this reason it is better to suck, even to lick a Black Cow than to try to eat it, for the attempt to eat it will result in getting your teeth stuck in it and if you have false teeth this could be disastrous. Alfie still had his own teeth, many of them baby teeth and if the Black Cow pulled them out it would make room for his permanent teeth to come in. But he was still courting trouble by begging for the Black Cow when Mama was negotiating with the Watkins Man for a spool of thread. And so closely on the heels of his escapade with the luggage rack on the running board of the Watkins Man's old Ford

"You can't have a Black Cow now. I'm talking with the Watkins Man about other things that I need." Mama said this while she was examining the spool of thread to make certain that it had the O.I.C. label on it, but then she looked and saw where Alfie was.

"You get down from there. Didn't I tell you to stay off the Watkins Man's car?" Alfie had interpreted what Mama had said to exclude only the luggage racks and now the whole car was off limits. He retreated from the Watkins Man's eyes to the area where Mama's flaring hips would shield him from sight. He put his thumb in his mouth. It was a poor substitute for a Black Cow, but it met certain emotional needs which had arisen as a consequence of being ordered to get down off the Watkins Man's car. Even with a thumb in his mouth, Alfie had one free hand and he tugged persistently at Mama's apron strings with it. Mama tried to ignore what Alfie was doing; she was haggling with the Watkins Man for an eight ounce bottle of vanilla extract.

"That's pure vanilla extrack," the Watkins Man said, tapping the bottle with a forefinger. "Ain't nuthin' been added to it the way they do at the stores. And twenty five cents is a mighty good price for it when you don't hafta drive to town and burn your own gas to buy it."

Mama was studying the label on the bottle of vanilla extract but she was thinking about the price. She seemed to be about to turn it down. The Watkins Man said "Now I've got a bigger bottle that's cheaper if you want it." Mama looked up sharply into the Watkins Man's face because that did not sound right. Mama's eyes seemed to be asking if he had added water to the bigger bottle, but the Watkins Man realized that he had not made himself clear. "Same pure stuff. But if you buy a sixteen ounce bottle it's only forty cents which makes it cheaper than buying the little bottle. In the long run, that is."

Mama said "Forty cents is too much to put into vanilla extract." The tone of her voice said that vanilla extract is a luxury, not a necessity anyway, and the Watkins Man saw the imminent danger of loss of a sale. "I'll just take the eight ounce bottle for twenty five cents."

The sale was saved and the Watkins Man said "That's jest fine. Now what else?"

Mama chewed her lower lip, fingered the fifty cent piece in her apron pocket, and said "What will the nutmeg bring it all to?" Nothing had been said about nutmeg but she was thinking ahead to the final tab.

"Nutmeg's ten cents," he said, reaching into the box where he kept the spices. He picked up a little can of nutmeg, then reached into his shirt pocket for a stubby lead pencil. He wet the tip of the pencil with his tongue and began writing figures on a small brown paper sack.

Alfie tugged at Mama's skirts and whispered "Mama." But Mama gave him a hard look to indicate that he was not to disturb her while the Watkins Man was figuring. He kept tugging at Mama's skirt and she slapped his hand. Tears appeared in Alfie's big brown eyes and he pouted his lips.

The Watkins man added up the figures on the brown paper sack. "Well, let's see. There's ten cents for the spool of thread. And twenty five for the vanilla extrack. And the nutmeg is ten...That's forty five cents in all." He looked questioningly at Mama in an attempt to discern whether she had that much ready cash. Or if she had more than that.

"And a box of black pepper." Mama said it half in question and half statement. "The small one," she added, hoping to get it within the prescribed limits of the fifty cents.

"How much will a small can of black pepper bring it to?"

"I can let you have the pepper for a nickel," the Watkins Man said because he had guessed that the coin in Mama's apron pocket was a fifty cent piece, so he added five cents to the figure on the brown paper bag and got fifty. "That'll be fifty cents in all."

Mama turned to look pityingly at Alfie. "That doesn't leave anything for candy," Mama said. Alfie's lips trembled. He squeezed his eyelids shut to keep back the tears. They slid down anyway and ran down his cheeks. He wiped them away with the hand that he didn't need for sucking his thumb. This left smudges on his cheeks.

The Watkins Man saw the danger in Alfie's tears. The deal was not yet consummated. He didn't have the fifty cents in his hand. "Tell you what I'll do." He was speaking to Mama but looking at Alfie. "I'll take fifty cents for all the things you're gittin'. That's the thread and vanilla extrack an' nutmeg an' pepper an' ev'rything an' I'll throw in a Black Cow for the boy here."

The Watkins man smiled again at Alfie and reinforced the bargain by moving immediately to the candy jar. He took out a Black Cow and held it out to Alfie. "Here, Boy. Now ain't that as fine a Black Cow as you ever seen or sucked?"

Alfie reached hesitantly for the Black Cow, turning his teary eyes toward Mama. His eyes asked "Can I, Mama?" And since Mama's eyes did not say "No" he took the candy. He pulled off the wrapper and started to lick it. Tears, already flowing, ran down to mingle with the salivary juices. The Watkins Man knew that the deal was made. Mama knew it too. She reached into her apron pocket and took out the fifty cent piece. Still watching Alfie's face she said "Now what do you say to the Watkins Man?"

Alfie licked the Black Cow, smiled through the tears which had now become thoroughly mixed with the juice at the corners of his mouth; then he said "Thank you Mister Watkins Man."

Then Mama gave the fifty cent piece to the Watkins Man and he said "Much obliged." He put the thread and the vanilla extract and the nutmeg and the black pepper into the little brown paper sack with the figures on it totaling fifty cents, and held it out to Mama.

Mama took the little paper bag and folded the top of it down carefully and slipped it into her apron pocket. "You come back," she said to the Watkins Man and he put the fifty cent piece in his own pocket and prepared the Ford for departure. Standing in front of it, he turned the crank until the engine caught, because his old Ford did not have a self starter on it like Miss Georgia's. When he felt it catch, he jumped back to keep the crank from breaking his arm. He ran around to the driver's place to get control before the Ford ran off without him. He went bumping and rattling down the lane toward Pearl's house. His black hat was pulled down on his forehead to shade his eyes from the sun.

The chickens in the crate on the rear bumper raised their heads and made little noises of alarm when the engine started and the Ford began to vibrate. They drew their heads back, then stretched their necks up as high as they could reach. When the Ford was in motion they jostled one another for more of the fresh air flowing through the crate. When the Watkins Man brought the Ford to a halt again on the edge of Parker's Branch, the machine shuddered and the chickens in the crate clucked anxiously, pecked at one another, and put their heads and necks through the slats in the crate. They opened their beaks for air and looked about with glittering eyes at their new surroundings.

The Watkins Man pressed the horn. "Ah-ooo-gah! Ah-ooogah!" Then he called "Watkins Man Pearl!!"

Pearl pushed open the wooden shutter that covered the kitchen window. She leaned out through the opening, surveying with wide brown eyes and open mouth the whole scene that lay before her. She focused those sparkling brown eyes on the Ford vibrating beside the little stream which rippled merrily along towards Tobesofkee Creek. When she had seen with her own sparkling brown eyes, and heard with her own small shell shaped ears, she opened her mouth wide, exposing an impressive array of pearly white teeth while a smile spread across her smooth chocolate brown face.

The Watkins Man killed the engine. It died with one more shudder. He threw back his head and called "Watkins Man Pearl!"

Pearl's smile spread even farther across her face, and she called back in a voice that equalled that of the Watkins Man in its carrying capacity and rose a full octave in pitch. "Heah Pearl is!"

The Watkins Man stepped painfully to the running board, then onto the ground, and in a more subdued tone, like a watchdog sounding one last note after an aggressive bark, "Watkins Man."

Pearl carefully closed the shutter over the kitchen window to keep the flies out during her absence from the kitchen. She looked about her, moved a chair slightly, and prepared to go down to Parker's Branch to do business with the Watkins Man. But it took her a few minutes to gather up the baby and the hen.

Crossing Parker's Branch to meet the Watkins Man, wading ankle deep in the cold, flowing water, feeling the pebbles with her toes, and the swirl and rush of the water over her feet and about her ankles, did not bother Pearl. It made her gasp and draw in her breath and open her big brown eyes wide and flare her nostrils and even grab at her skirts, although there was no danger of getting them wet except when she crossed Parker's Branch after a heavy down pour of rain, and there had been no rain for days when the Watkins Man came and stopped on the edge of the stream and waited for Pearl to come across with her baby and the hen.

Pearl was accustomed to crossing Parker's branch. Every Saturday and at least one Sunday each month Pearl crossed. On Saturdays Pearl and her young husband Tobe went to town. Tobe was several shades darker than Pearl. His features were more classically African. He was strong and broad shouldered. With their three small children, the smallest huddled on Pearl's breast, the next smallest in Tobe's arms, and the oldest, a girl of four years wading barefoot through the water, Pearl and Tobe crossed Parker's Branch on the first leg of their weekly trip to town to buy groceries, see the sights and be entertained by mixing with others of their race who had come to town for the same purposes.

On these Saturday crossings, they would leave the shutters closed on the two room, unpainted, pine weather board shack. The door would be tightly closed, and even in Winter time the fire would be allowed to die down to a pile of coals and ashes. Tobe's black and tan coon dog would come to him, hoping to be allowed to follow, but Tobe would say "You go back to the house, Jake." And Jake would go and lie on the porch, following his family with mournful eyes, and he would even give voice to his disappointment with a mournful howl as they waded, giving out little shouts of mock surprise and genuine excitement, through the icy, sparkling water of Parker's Branch. But Jake did not attempt to follow for he did not dare to disobey Tobe.

Sunday afternoons too, on preaching days at the church. That was the fourth Sunday in each month. And when the time rolled around each year for the protracted meeting. That was every evening for a solid week. A solid week starts on Sunday and ends on Sunday, so it has eight days in it. The protracted meeting began each year on the third Sunday in August and it built to its climax on the fourth Sunday in August. Then Pearl walked each evening through the swirling waters of Parker's Branch, the cool, refreshing waters that lapped about her bare ankles, for she carried her shoes in one hand and the baby in the other. Even when she had crossed Parker's Branch, she continued carrying her shoes until she was within sight of the church house. Then she would pass the baby over to Tobe and she would slip into her shoes.

To do this she would balance herself on one foot while she slipped a shoe on the other foot, then balance again to achieve the same result with the other foot. She would not sit down on the dusty roadside to put on her shoes because that would spoil her one good dress which, like the shoes, was reserved for Sunday-Go-To-Meetin', and for that special week long religious festival in August.

The protracted meeting is a religious festival even holier than Sunday itself. It consists of non-stop preaching, singing and praying, and involves a lot of riding back and forth for those who have automobiles. Pearl and Tobe did not have an automobile, so it involved a lot of walking back and forth for them. But Pearl's face never lost its glow of health and happiness as the waters of Parker's Branch swirled about her ankles on a Sunday afternoon or on the hot days of August when she walked and waded, with her heart full of faith, hope and love, and of joy too, to the Shiloh Baptist Church.

And her face shone with that same glow of happiness on the day the Watkins Man came and stood dry shod on the bank of Parker's Branch, stood in his yellow brogan shoes from J.C. Penney's, and kept those yellow brogans dry while Pearl came tripping happily down on the other side of Parker's Branch, and walked unhesitatingly into the water with her bare feet so accustomed to its feel and to the uneven ground of its channel. Stood there, having announced his presence with the horn which sounded "Ah-ooo-gah!" and his own voice calling "Watkins Man, Pearl!!" Stood and watched her as she came with the baby in one arm and the hen in the other.

The baby was dark chocolate in color and was contentedly nursing at Pearl's breast. The hen was reddish brown, and she was not at all flustered or excited by being carried under Pearl's arm. Seemed mesmerized even by being held so close to Pearl's breast. The baby looked up trustingly into Pearl's face, then closed its eyes as it nursed. The hen looked about with small quick movements of its head as Pearl splashed through the water. But the baby seemed oblivious to the splashing even.

"Mawnin' Watkins Man," Pearl said in greeting. "I ain't got no money today but I jest got to have some seasonin' an' some thread an' things so I guess I hafta swap my ol' hen fer 'em."

At the sound of Pearl's voice the chickens in the crate on the rear bumper of the old Ford moved nervously, cocking their heads to pick up the musical notes of her voice.

The Watkins Man eyed the reddish brown hen critically, calculating her worth in seasoning, thread and things.

Alfie licked happily on his Black Cow. He had determined to make it last all day, but he was also determined to finish it before Junior learned that he had it and demanded that he let him lick it too.

Chapter Five: The Gypsies Are Comin'

It was because of what Miss Georgia said about the Gypsies coming through the neighborhood that Alfie was hiding under the front steps when the Watkins Man came. He had the Gypsies on his mind and he told Sandy to watch and be on guard in case the Gypsies came and tried to get him. And then when the Watkins Man came clattering into the yard in the old Ford he just knew it must be the Gypsies coming and that's why he was afraid; he wasn't really scared of the Watkins Man. In fact, he felt very good about the Watkins Man after he gave him the Black Cow. Well, he practically gave the Black Cow to him, Mama said, because she had spent all the money she had in her pocket for things she needed and then the Watkins Man "just threw the Black Cow in as a bonus."

"What's a bonus, Mama?" Alfie asked, with the juice running down the corners of his mouth.

"A bonus is a gift that you didn't pay for but it is just out of the goodness of somebody's heart."

"The Watkins Man is good ain't he, Mama?" And when Mama nodded her head slightly, because she really felt that after she had spent fifty cents with the Watkins Man it was the very least he could do, although she did feel badly about the luggage racks, even if they were a shoddy piece of workmanship from the beginning.

"But I hate them ol' Gypsies." Alfie's big brown eyes were troubled, even with the Black Cow sliding over his tongue.

"Well, you just don't worry your head about the Gypsies. You just go on and play with Sandy and forget what Miss Georgia said about the Gypsies."

After Alfie had gone to play with Sandy, who was hoping to get his own tongue on the Black Cow, Mama bent over the butter mold and pressed the butter into it. She talked fretfully to herself because she couldn't say things in front of the children and she didn't want to even say them to their Papa because he was apt to be intolerant of Georgia's "gaddin' about over the neighborhood spreadin' gossip." And when Papa said things like that about Mama's friends it just made matters worse.

"I do wish she had something more worthwhile on her mind, though," Mama said to herself. "The Bible says an idle mind is the devil's workshop." Mama had quoted this wisdom often when she was provoked with the boys and once Willie had teasingly asked Mama where the Bible said that.

"I can't quote you chapter and verse, but it's in there. You can take my word for it. And if you still wonder, you can read it all, starting at the beginning, until you find it, and you won't find anything that'll hurt you while you are looking for it."

Willie started in at the beginning. He took the Bible with him to the room he shared with Cliff and he found the Genesis stories pretty exciting, but when he got to the "begets" he decided that was the main activity of the Biblical heroes and he gave up on his search for the saying about an idle mind. Willie's mind was never idle anyway because he was always thinking of things to make Cliff and Junior do, and things that would be fun for Alfie to do while Cliff and Junior were doing the things that were not as much fun.

Mama's mind was never idle, but she was provoked with Georgia. "What she needs is work to do. Now that she has that colored girl there to do all the housework she's got nothing to do but run over the neighborhood in that old Ford and spread stories about the Gypsies and scare the daylights out of Alfie." Mama said all this to herself because she couldn't say it right to Georgia's face, certainly not with Alfie sitting there drinking in every word that was spoken. But she had been pretty plain with Georgia about it anyway.

"Well," Miss Georgia had shifted her considerable weight in the cane bottom chair which Mama had set in place for her, and displaying some anxiety about the chair's ability to sustain the load. This anxiety was shared by Mama, but she did not let on that she thought Miss Georgia was too heavy for the chair. "I hear tell," Miss Georgia said, taking a deep breath, "that them Gypsies will steal anything they can git their pilferin' hands on. If it ain't nailed down then it ain't safe from their pilferin' hands."

Miss Georgia paused. She took a deep breath. She shelled the pea she held in her hands and let the peas rattle in the bottom of the aluminum pan she held in her lap. Then she dropped the hull on the floor. Miss Georgia's main concern was not shelling peas. Mama and Miss Lily were shelling peas when she arrived and she only pitched in to be social. She had something more important on her mind than shelling peas. Gypsies.

She picked up the cardboard fan with Hart's Funeral Home printed on one side and a picture of Jesus cradling a lamb in his bosom on the other. She fanned herself vigorously with the fan, breathing deeply and glancing about nervously at the little boy sitting quietly at her feet and piling up the pea hulls as they fell onto the floor.

"Alfie!" Miss Georgia addressed the little boy, and he looked up into her face. His thick brown hair grew low on his forehead and seemed at times to be about to obscure his vision. But this was misleading. Alfie never missed anything. His big brown eyes gazed up unflinchingly from under the shock of hair. Bare feet extended from the legs of his overalls. From time to time a house fly would land on Alfie's bare feet. He would wiggle his toes and jerk his leg to dislodge the fly. If this didn't accomplish the desired end, he would slap at it with his chubby hands. "Alfie!" Miss Georgia said, and she breathed deeply and fanned vigorously.

"I declare I'm so hot and thirsty I'm about to burn up!" Miss Georgia clutched her throat with one hand. "My throat is plumb parched. You run and get me a dipper of cool water from the well bucket. I heard your Papa drawin' up a fresh bucket not more 'n five minutes ago and I bet it come out of the Northeast corner of the well where it's the coolest."

Alfie balanced the pea hull Miss Georgia had dropped on top of the pile he was making on the kitchen floor, watched to be sure it would not fall off, then got up and went reluctantly to fetch a drink of water for Miss Georgia. He was not eager to go because he sensed that Miss Georgia was about to say something important and he didn't want to miss it. But he went because Mama nodded her head at him and said "Run on now and get Miss Georgia a drink of water."

The well bucket sitting on the well housing was still wet because it had not been more than five minutes since Papa drew it up out of the Northeast corner of the well. He plunged the tin dipper into the bucket and drew it out, sloshing water over his own bare feet. "Ouch!" he said, but then he decided it felt good, and he sloshed some more water over his feet, and for a minute he forgot that he was missing something by playing around at the well. Mama decided that Alfie had forgotten what he went after and she called to him to hurry up, but Miss Georgia said "Don't hurry 'im. There's things to be said about them pilferin' Gypsie's that might not be good for a chile that little to hear anyway."

Thirst was not the only force that moved Miss Georgia to send Alfie to the well for a drink of cool water. But thirst was a factor. The weather was hot and Miss Georgia was a short round person who perspired a lot. She did not sweat; she insisted that only men and mules sweated. But Papa had remarked to Mama that "If that ain't sweat a rollin' off her double chin then I ain't never seen sweat." Papa also remarked that Miss Georgia was not only short and round but "if the truth was known she's probably bigger around than she is tall." But Mama told Papa that he ought to be ashamed of himself for talking that way because some people are stout by nature and there is nothing they can do about it.

"If the Lord made her that way it is not for us to pass judgment on His works." Mama said this with her mouth pursed up in disapproval of what Papa had said, but she determined not to let herself get as heavy as Miss Georgia, anyway. This decision was reinforced by Papa's parting remark that he reckoned when the Lord finished His part of the job Miss Georgia was a heap littler than what sitting long at table had done for her. Miss Georgia was sitting now, but Miss Lily had taken the floor on the subject of the Gypsies.

"Tom says they'll carry off ev'ry hen in the chicken house an' the old rooster too!" Miss Lily could talk and shell peas at the same time. The peas rattled in the dishpan like hail on a tin roof, and what Tom had to say about Gypsies also rattled off

Miss Lily's tongue. "Tom says a Gypsy can empty a hen house in two minutes and you'll never hear a squawk."

Miss Georgia made an effort to "get in a word edgewise" but Miss Lily did not pause long enough for a hen to squawk. "Tom says they'll come an' offer to shoe your mule an' you jest turn your back on 'em for two seconds an' the Gypsies'll carry off the mule. Tom says he ain't havin' no Gypsies on the place if he can he'p it. Tom says a mule don't need no shoes to plow cotton nohow an' he ruther have a barefoot mule than no mule atall."

Alfie was back with the dipper of water from the well before Miss Lily had finished quoting Tom on the dangers of having a mule shod by Gypsies, and Miss Georgia sat sipping the cool water from the dipper while Miss Lily talked. Then she handed the empty dipper back to Alfie and said "Ain't nothin' more refreshin' than well water out of a tin dipper. Some people go on about drinkin' out of a gourd but I can't see why anybody'd want to drink out of a nasty ol' gourd when there's a clean tin dipper about. Here, Alfie, you run an' take this dipper back to the well where you got it, so if your Papa comes for a drink of water he won't hafta drink out of the bucket the way I see some men doin."

Alfie said "Papa drinks outta the bucket all the time. He says it's better thataway." But Mama shooed him away and told him to go on and do what Miss Georgia had told him to do.

Miss Georgia was eager for Alfie to go too. And as soon as he disappeared the second time, she put the fan sideways before her face and leaned towards Mama, all the time watching out of the corner of her eye for Alfie's return. "Hah!" Miss Georgia said. "Chickens! Mules! That ain't all they'll carry off. I've heard tell they'll even carry off little children!"

At this point Alfie came back into the room. It had not taken him any time to return the dipper. In fact, he had almost thrown it back into the bucket and come back as quickly as possible because he didn't want to miss anything. He halted and his face blanched when Miss Georgia said that the Gypsies will carry off little children, and he sat down on the floor by his little pile of pea hulls. He studied the pea hulls for a long moment, then gazed up inquiringly into Mama's face.

Mama pursed her lips and turned a stern and outraged gaze on Miss Georgia. "Why Good Lord, Georgia!" Mama said. Mama never used any profanity but she did call upon the Lord's name in times of extremity, and now she considered it a time of extremity. "Lord! Where did you hear such a thing? What on earth would the Gypsies want to carry off children for?"

"Well, this may not be the time and place to talk about it." Miss Georgia glanced meaningfully at Alfie, but she told herself that she had tried to get him out of the room. "You know the ol' sayin' 'Little jugs have big ears'. And I wouldn't want to upset anybody. But that's what they're tellin' about over the neighborhood. I don't know what they want 'em for neither unless it's to make 'em do all the work for 'em."

Miss Georgia fanned herself vigorously, then spoke in tones so righteous that even Mama could not fault. "Lord knows you won't ketch one of them Gypsies doin' any work unless you call tellin' fortunes and playin' cards work. And I call it a sin is what I call it."

But Mama was not to be drawn away from the main issue by talk of fortune telling and card playing. "I have never heard of anyone losing their children when the Gypsies passed through," she said indignantly. "They may be lazy and sinful, and they may even be thieves, but it is ridiculous to spread a rumor like that."

Mama wanted to send Alfie out to play, but she saw it would be impossible to get him off his little pile of pea hulls without making an even bigger issue of the Gypsies. Besides, Miss Lily plunged in again with Tom's wisdom on the subject. "Tom says he don't see why the Gypsies would want to steal younguns when it's as easy as it is to git 'em without ever gittin' outta bed. Tom says he gits another youngun ever time he hangs his britches on the bed post and he don't hafta go traipsin' about over the whole countryside lookin' fer younguns to steal."

With this bit of Tom's wisdom Mama thought it was enough, and she said firmly to Alfie "You run on outside and play now Alfie. We'll put all the pea hulls in a bucket when we finish here and you can feed them to the calf your Papa let you claim."

Alfie was not easy to dismiss. He pouted his lower lip and said "I don't want to play. I want to stay here and pick up pea hulls while you an' Miss Lily an' Miss Georgia shell peas." He was on the verge of saying that he wanted to hear what they were saying about the Gypsies, but Miss Lily remembered something else that Tom had said on the subject of Gypsies and younguns.

"Tom says if the Gypsies come to our house they'll find more younguns than chickens an' it's jest a question of whether they're lookin' fer more mouths to feed or if they're lookin' fer food fer the mouths they already got."

"Well!" Mama had become exasperated, which is just one step beyond being aggravated. "Your Tom may be smarter than most of us when it comes to figuring out the Gypsies." She turned to Alfie with a tone that he recognized as the one she used when her patience was all used up. "Now you just run on and play and leave the Gypsies to us. The Gypsies are not going to hurt you. You just don't worry about them."

Alfie went under the house where he found Sandy lying in a cool place. Sandy had dug down until he reached cool dirt, and he was lying in the little declivity. His mouth was open and the saliva, or perspiration, or sweat, was dripping off his tongue. Alfie hugged Sandy and then he went to the chimney base which was about at the center of the house ,and he looked at the dominecker hen who was sitting in a corner of the chimney base. She ruffled her feathers and made a warning sound which Alfie understood, and he did not come any closer to her, but he sat down and began to figure out what to do to protect himself from the Gypsies.

Miss Georgia and Miss Lily stayed on a little longer because they had some more things to say about the Gypsies. Mostly they were the same things they had already said. Miss Lily quoted Tom at length on how clever the Gypsies are at thievery, and Miss Georgia said again that fortune telling and card playing are the deeds of the devil. The arrangement of the words was different but the essence of what they said was about the same, so Alfie didn't miss much, and he had heard a lot more than Mama wanted him to hear about Gypsies.

Mama said she would have to wash the peas and put them on the stove to cook. Miss Georgia said "I will hafta go home an' see if that nigger gal has done the jobs I gave her. They're all so lazy if you don't stay right with them all the time they won't do a thing you tell 'em."

Then Miss Georgia climbed laboriously into the Ford, causing it to sag and lean under her weight, and she set out for home to see what the black girl had done while she was bringing Mama up to date on the latest goings on in the neighborhood.

Miss Lily set out across the cotton patch. "I have got to go home and fix dinner for Tom. Tom says ain't nuthin' more aggravatin' to a man than to come in home from the field all hot an' hungry fer his dinner an' then find the dinner table all bare and empty when his woman's been off gallivantin' about an' gossipin' in other peoples' houses."

Mama was heartily in favor of Tom's sentiments, for a change. She put the peas in the pot to cook, pushed back a lock of dark hair from her damp forehead, and said "Gypsies! They better be worryin' about the boll weevil. It would be more to the point."

As she thought more about the conversation with Miss Lily and Miss Georgia, and about Alfie, she said "The very idea! Scaring the child with talk like that!"

In the late afternoon Alfie crouched under the front porch steps, watching for the Gypsies. Sandy was there with him. Sandy had dug down again to cool moist earth, and he lay with his mouth open, his tongue lolling out in the dirt, and saliva dripping from his tongue onto the freshly dug earth. Alfie's eyes were fixed on the driveway which ran from the yard gate to the big road in front of Mister Charles' and Miss maggie's house. The driveway was shaded by a row of pecan trees on each side, with branches overlapping the driveway. Peering out from under the front porch steps Alfie had a full view of the front yard, the gate, the pecan tree lined driveway which ran clear to Mister Charles' and Miss Maggie's house. If the old Gypsies came to carry him off and make him do all the work while they told fortunes and played cards and raided hen houses and rode off on stolen mules, they would have a hard time catching him.

He glanced behind him to make sure that there was no obstacle in his way if he needed to use his escape route. First he would run back to his safe place in the chimney base. He could scamper along on hands and knees to his hideout because he was a very little boy; the only advantage he had discovered yet to being very little was that he could go easily into tight places where bigger people could not go. If a fat Gypsy came for him the fat Gypsy would get stuck trying to follow him under the house. Even a little boy will forget sometimes and raise his head a little too high and bump against the floor joist. At first there will be just the numbing feeling, then the stinging, and a big lump will rise on his head. If there is nobody around to rub it and kiss it, then it will just have to go away on its own after a while, but if Mama is close by and hears him bump his head she will hold him in her arms and say "Good Lord Alfie! You bumped your head. Crawling around under the house again! What is going to become of you?!"

Alfie had thought of the chimney base when he got up from his little pile of pea hulls and left Mama and Miss Lily and Miss Georgia still talking about the Gypsies. He had made the safe place in the corner of the chimney base by scooping out a place just big enough for him. He really didn't take up any more room in his corner than the dominecker hen did in her corner, and as long as he stayed as far away from her as he could get, she wouldn't peck him.

The old dominecker hen was brooding on her eggs and Mama said that made her quarrelsome, so if he got too close she would peck him, but it is better to be pecked by the old dominecker hen than to be caught by the old Gypsies and be carried away to the Gypsy camp where he would have to work like a slave.

Gran' ma had told him about the slaves when he asked her "Gran' me, what's a slave?" Then Gran'ma took a dip of snuff and said "Lord Chile, we don't have slaves no more. Not since ol' Sherman come an' set 'em all free."

"But what is a slave Gran'ma?" he had insisted. Then Gran'ma had said "The darkies all used to be slaves. They belonged to us but after the War they was all set free."

"Don't Uncle Seeb and Aunt Hattie still belong to us?"

"In a way, Chile, but not exactly. They belong to us and they're free too. Since ol' Sherman an' the Yankees come an' set 'em all free."

"I wanta be free, Gran' ma. Will ol' Sherman an' the Yankees come an' set me free?"

"Lord, Chile! White people ain't never been slaves!"

But now the ol' Gypsies would come and make a slave of him and take him away from Mama and Papa. That's what Miss Georgia said they would do, and Miss Lily said they could do it so quick nobody would know what was going on.

If the fat ol' Gypsies came an' got him and made a slave out of him, then Papa would come and set him free the way ol' Sherman and the Yankees set the darkies free. Papa would shoot the ol' Gypsies with his Thirty Eight and make them turn him loose. But it would be better not to let the ol' Gypsies catch him because they might work him to death and make him steal chickens and mules. Gran' ma said the War lasted a long time and it might be a long time before Papa found him and set him free. He thought he might like to have the Gypsies tell his fortune, even though it would be scary, and he would like to see the cards if they had pictures on them, but he wouldn't play cards with the Gypsies because of what Miss Georgia said about it. He didn't want the ol' devil to get him for playing cards.

But the fat ol' Gypsies would not be able to crawl into his hiding place in the chimney where he had built a barricade of old bricks and shingles. They might burn the house down though and then he would have to run to the smokehouse and crawl under it. The smokehouse was so close to the ground that even Junior could not crawl under it. Junior almost got stuck under the smokehouse, but he pretended that he was not scared. "Shucks! Junior had said. "Crawlin' around under the smokehouse is for babies anyway. I'd ruther climb on top of the thing." Junior was not afraid to climb on anything, but Alfie could hide under the smokehouse until Papa came with his gun and drove the ol' Gypsies away.

Now he was sitting under the front porch steps. That was his lookout post. He could watch for the Gypsies there. Sandy was with him. Sandy would see them, or hear them, or he might even smell them. Sandy would know what a Gypsy smells like. He patted Sandy on the head and said “Good Boy Sandy!”

Sandy slobbered on Alfie’s hand and turned back to watch the gate. His ears stood up and then they flopped over at the tips. He drew his long moist red tongue back into his mouth and said “Woof!” Alfie looked in the direction of Sandy’s “Woof!” and he saw them coming.

They were coming down the driveway. It was late afternoon and the sun was setting, and the driveway was in shadows because of the pecan trees that lined it on each side. So their figures were blurred or indistinct but he could see them coming. And Sandy had said “Woof!” which meant that he had seen them too.

He could hear their voices but he could not make out what they were saying. Papa had once said that Gypsies have a language of their own that they speak when they don’t want us to know what they are saying. Alfie’s eyes were blurring too because of the fear, and his ears were stopping up for the same reason, so it was difficult to see and hear them, but when Sandy said “Woof! he was sure that the Gypsies were coming down the driveway under the pecan trees to get him and carry him off and make a slave out of him. Sandy said “Woof!” again but his “Woof!” sounded friendly.

Too friendly, for Gypsies who had come to get Alfie and carry him off. Sandy’s tail was swishing back and forth and knocking dirt in Alfie’s face, and some of it was getting into his eyes and making it even more difficult for him to see the Gypsies clearly. But there were three of them. Two big ones and a little one. A man and a woman and a boy. And they were coming right up to the front gate, talking and laughing.

“Mama! Mama! The Gypsies are comin’! Maamaa!”

Then Mama was rushing out onto the front porch. He could see her through the cracks. She was wiping her hands on her apron. She was walking quickly across the boards of the porch. And she was calling to the three at the gate. “Why, Charles and Maggie! It’s good to see you! Come on up on the porch!” Then Mama’s voice was even softer and kinder. “And Harold! I’m glad you've come to play with Alfie. Where on earth is Alfie anyway? Alfie! Alfie! Where are you?"

Then Mama was peering down through the cracks in the floor of the front porch steps. "Lordy Mercy! Hiding under the porch steps again! And Sandy with you! Come on out from under there and play with Harold."

Chapter Six: And The Hero Wore Black And White Stripes

The Gypsies came and the Gypsies went away, as Gypsies do, and have done from time immemorial. No little boy, not even any little girls, disappeared from the neighborhood along Tobesofkee Creek when the Gypsies went away.

A few chickens were reported missing, but it was never proved that the Gypsies stole them. Papa said he suspected that they mostly went into the ministry because of the protracted meeting at the Midway Baptist Church. "If the truth was known," Papa said, pouring tobacco from his little pouch of Bull Durham into a thin little sheet of paper which he held in his hand, "Them chickens disappeared back then and they jest wasn't missed till all the excitement and furor died down."

Mama nodded agreement to Papa's theory of the disappearing chickens but she thought he was bordering on sacrilege with the statement of fact that followed his theory. "It is a known fact, if it ain't actually in the Bible itself, that preachers eat more chickens durin' a protracted meetin' than a whole camp of Gypsies."

Alfie's eyes were big with wonder when Papa said this, and he thought he might be a preacher instead of a Greyhound Bus driver when he grew up. But he did not mention this to anybody, not even to Papa, because of what had happened to him at Mister Robb's house. He didn't fully trust Papa with his plans for the future any more.

But back to the Gypsies who had come and gone away, nobody knew where. Papa said that he had heard the Gypsies had elected a new king because the old one had died, but he reckoned it wouldn't change their nature any because "Human nature don't change and Gypsies are human." Papa said "Gypsies and niggers both are human but they ain't like us."

Papa had peculiar ideas about people who were not like him He was teaching Alfie to count and he gave him a little lesson in arithmetic. Drawing a zero and a nine on a scratch pad Mama had bought for Alfie to practice numbers and letters, Papa said, pointing to the zero and then the nine, "A aught's a aught and nine's a figger. It's all for the white man and none fer the nigger."

Alfie looked up at Papa uncomprehending, and Papa said "Well you see what a difference it makes when you draw a line down from the aught."

But again, back to the Gypsies. Tom did not have his mule shod. Mister Charles let the Gypsies shoe his mule, but he told Whack "Now Whack you stand right there and hold the mule while he is being shod by the Gypsies and don't you take your hand off the bridle."

Whack worked for Mister Charles in the dairy but he was almost like a member of the family, and he said "Mister Charles if it comes to a tussle I will hang onto the mule and let the bridle go." But it was a good leather bridle and Mister Charles didn't want to lose it, so Mister Charles told Whack to hold onto the bridle but to be sure that the mule's head was in it at all times as long as the Gypsies were around.

Miss Georgia's niece Rose let a Gypsy woman tell her fortune and it caused a scandal. Rose was almost thrown out of the Midway Baptist Church, but she said that they could church her if they wanted to, but it wouldn't do them any good. Rose said "I don't give a hoot. If it's my fortune, then it's my fortune and I don't reckon bein' churched will change it."

Miss Georgia said it was a sin and a disgrace for anybody in the family to go to a Gypsy to get her fortune told, and that God would punish Rose for the sin of it, but the disgrace would be a blight on the family name forever.

The Gypsy woman had read Rose's fortune in tea leaves and confirmed it in the life lines in the palm of Rose's hand. She told Rose that she was going to meet a tall, dark, handsome man and run off with him. Later Rose did, only Leon was not very tall. And God must have punished Rose the way Miss Georgia said He would because, Leon proved to be hard to live with. But Mama said that was about the run of the mill because she had never heard of a man who was easy to live with, Papa included. Rose didn't have fourteen children though, to have to keep out of jail. She had two, even though Leon was hard to live with, and it is not known whether either one of them ever saw the inside of a jailhouse, but they grew up and did about as well as common, which was the report that Whack gave them and Mister Charles agreed with Whack.

Miss Georgia continued to insist though that Rose had brought disgrace upon the family name by going to a Gypsy woman to have her fortune told, and when the word reached her ears that Leon was not easy to live with, she said "Well Rose has made her bed and she will jest have to lay in it." But all of this has nothing to do with Alfie and Tex and the Dump Truck. It all just happened at about the same time because soon after the protracted meeting was over and there had been a head count on the chickens that were left, which was not done until after the Gypsies left, the chain Gang came to scrape the Big road and plate it with yellow clay.

"How come they sent you to the chain gang, Tex?" Alfie was looking anxiously into the face of his new found friend, a face lean and brown and smooth but expressive of great pain. The dump truck was standing in the clean swept yard, the yard swept clean by Gran'ma's new brush broom made of dogwood sprouts bound together with string. The truck's engine was idling, exuding power, its body was shaking and vibrating with the motion of the powerful engine as it waited for the driver to come back and hop into the cab and roar away after another load of dirt for the county road. The driver, Tex, of the lean smooth brown face and the light blue eyes and the slightly curling light brown hair sunburned to the color of straw, was keenly aware of Alfie's eyes on him as he drank.

Tex was drinking from the well bucket, taking great gulps of the cold fresh water from the rim of the bucket where he pressed his lips. His Adams Apple bobbed up and down as he swallowed, and the water ran from the rim of the bucket, flowing around each side of his lips as he drank, running down his dust streaked chin, dropping onto the sweat stained front of his shirt. It was a black and white striped shirt, with the stripes running round and matching the stripes on his trousers. Black and white. Or white and black. Alternating. Signifying one thing, one terrible, dreaded condition. The wearer was a convict on the Georgia Chain Gang.

"How come, Tex?" Alfie's brown eyes searched the lean smooth brown face of the young man who was drinking from the well bucket. Seeking the light blue eyes which were averted, half closed while he drank. When he released the bucket and turned toward the pleading voice, his light blue eyes were remote, looking beyond Alfie's upturned, pleading face. But then they came back from wherever they had wandered, and they were misty, begging acceptance, trust, understanding from the little boy standing so close to him that he could feel the breath of his expectancy.

There had been a swagger in the way Tex had tilted the water bucket to drink from its rim. The swagger was even in the way he sloshed the water to wash away from the bucket's rim the remembrance of his own lips when he had finished drinking. Standing now on the porch floor, gripping the sides of the well bucket in his smooth brown hands, looking out over and beyond the vibrating dump truck exuding power from its throbbing engine, he was hardly more than a boy himself. In an earlier age, in a different setting, when the West was young, and young men were cowboys, or outlaws, or both, Tex might have been wearing boots and a wide brimmed hat, but no black and white stripes. He might have been standing, slouching in an attitude of relaxed but coiled readiness, rolling a cigarette from his own little sack of Bull Durham, waiting while his horse drank, snorting into the watering trough, kicking at a horse fly that settled on its underside. He might have been, but he was not; he was a convict on the Georgia Chain Gang.

It was only yesterday when he stopped for the first time at Alfie's house and asked for water. "Hi!" he said to Alfie. "My name's Tex. I'm hot an' thirsty. Is it okay with your Mama and your Papa if I git a drink of water from the well?"

Alfie was so overcome by being addressed in this manner by the handsome grownup stranger driving the big truck, that all he could do was smile and bob his head up and down in agreement. "They send a nigger boy for a bucket of water," Tex said, lowering the bucket on its chain into the well. "But by the time he gits back with it the water's done got hot and it ain't fit for a white man to drink."

So it was a one day old friendship. But Alfie had been watching the dump trucks roaring past the house all week long. Ever since the chain gang came to scrape and plate the road the powerful trucks, with their intense drivers, had roared by.

He watched by the side of the road, standing at the end of the driveway where it joins the big road. He watched the graders with their shining blades pushing dirt in front of them, smoothing out the washboard ruts. Now and then the driver of a grader would glance at him and turn quickly back to watch the blade. Once he smiled shyly and half lifted his hand to wave, but the man on the grader didn't notice, and he dropped his hand back to his side.

He watched the men with their shovels, lifting, swinging, throwing the dirt, then plunging the shovel again in the pile of dirt in front of them. The sweat rolled off their black faces, their muscles rippled under the black and white striped shirts. They opened their mouths and their eyes stood open, showing white in the heat. He did not dare to say anything to them, and they saw him watching but they gave no sign of recognition of his presence.

He watched the watchers, the armed guards, the hard eyed, leather faced men with the shotguns cradled against their shoulders, watching every movement of the men with the shovels. They chewed, working their jaws rhythmically, then spat into the dust at their feet. The spittle rolled into a little dust ball but it soon dried out in the hot dry air.

He saw all these people and their tools, the graders, the shovels and the guns. But it was the dump trucks which held him spellbound. Loaded with yellow clay from some place beyond the great cloud of roiling dust, they came out of the dust cloud, groaning and whining as they climbed the little hill past Alfie's house, beyond the little stream, Parker's Branch, where it crossed under the road, and before you get to Mister Richard's house at the top of the little hill. The dump trucks came in ordered succession, one after another on regular schedule, gears clashing and grinding, the overload of dirt spilling off onto the road as they came. With more clashing of gears, the dump trucks were put into reverse and they backed into place where the men clad in black and white stripes, and leaning on their shovels for a momentary rest, waited patiently. Somebody called out and banged the tail gate with his shovel. The dump truck stopped. The bed behind the cab raised slowly, with a hissing, whining, complaining sound. The metal tail gate flew open and the dirt cascaded onto the road surface. The tail gate was banged again with a shovel, and the great maw that had disgorged its load of yellow clay, sank slowly back into place, the tail gate swung against it with a bang, and the truck crawled forward slowly, the last remnants of its load spilling out before the bed was horizontal again.

The truck moved away, more lightly but rattling, clanging and banging its dismal signal of emptiness, and it was soon enveloped in its own cloud of rolling dust. And another truck, waiting, idling, steaming, pulled into its place as the men plunged their shovels into the yellow dirt.

So the dump trucks came, emptied themselves, and went away. One after another. From sunup to sundown. In the blazing heat of summer. But for Alfie there was now only one dump truck. Number 21. One dump truck driver. Tex. Tex, who always threw up his hand at Alfie. And smiled a faraway, lonely, fleeting smile. Friendly but not broad and easy and lingering like the smile on the face of a man who feels good about his manhood. Yet it was a smile to win the heart of a little boy standing beside the road, half enveloped in the cloud of dust. A little boy waving timidly, hesitantly, yearning to be recognized, wondering about the power in all the noise and motion, the clangor and the dust and the sweat and the haunted, fearful eyes under the hard, staring, watchful eyes with the guns.

The smile of the young man driving the dump truck caused Alfie's heart to thump inside his chest, but it made no visible impression on the man with the shotgun. He stood off to one side, out of the way of the trucks, watching the men swinging their shovels. He was not there for smiles. His hard eyes stared out from lids slitted against the sun, glared from under the brim of his dust caked hat. His hard, leathery jaws moved, chewing. Then he spat into the dust at his feet.

Tex was the only white man Alfie had ever seen wearing the black and white stripes of the Georgia Chain Gang. At least he was the only one he had seen close up, close enough to speak to. "What did you do, Tex?" Alfie said. "How come they sent you to the chain gang? I didn't know they were supposed to send a white man to the chain gang." He hesitated, then plunged ahead, driven by the demon within him demanding to know ever more and more about the strange world about him. "Did you kill somebody, Tex?"

"Did I kill somebody?" Tex gripped the rim of the water bucket in hard lean hands. "I ain't never hurt nobody in my whole life? I couldn't kill nobody if my own life depended on it."

"But how come, Tex? How come they sent you to the chain gang? What did you do?"

"I didn't do nuthin'. Not to git sent to the chain gang for."

"But how come, Tex? They ain't supposed to send a white man to the chain gang.!"

"They wasn't supposed to send me. I was framed."

"Framed? What does that mean, Tex? Framed."

"I got blamed for what somebody else done. It was somebody else done it, but his friends got together and said it was me. They ganged up and made me take the rap for it. That's the God's truth of what happened, Alfie."

The dump truck was sitting in the yard, its powerful motor idling, the giant body vibrating in the shimmering heat. He knew he would be in trouble for being late. The gang boss knew how long it ought to take him to deliver a load of dirt and get back to the loader. He could hear the gang boss giving him hell, his hard eyes boring into him, his hard mouth snapping like a turtle. One minute late and the gang boss would accuse him of loitering. Two minutes late and there would be the threat. "You can't make your load on time you can go back to swingin' a pick an' shovel with the niggers, Boy." The gang boss called him Boy to put him down in the class with the "niggers". To take him down off his high horse. The name "Tex" sounded too free, too much like the open range, like a man on horseback. Or like a real man in a dump truck, but without the black and white stripes. Without the hard faced guard with the shotgun standing over him, staring with hard eyes.

He thought: I have drunk water from the well. I have been asked by this little boy what I have done. I cannot let him believe I am a criminal. "Damn the gang boss!" he said under his breath. He turned back to Alfie, and the faraway look was in his pale blue eyes. Wonder and trust were in Alfie's bright brown eyes. "They said I broke in a store and stole some money an' cigarettes an' things. I never stole nuthin' in my life. It was another boy. His daddy is rich and powerful. They put it on me to git him off free an' clear."

A wispy smile flitted across his face. "No. I ain't killed nobody. I ain't even stole nuthin'." Alfie looked back into Tex's sky blue eyes. He saw a hero in distress, riding a sweating, lathered horse, fleeing from men with guns in hot pursuit. He knew he loved Tex and wanted to help him get away.

"How come you don't run away Tex?" Alfie' eyes, his voice, his whole trembling body pleaded for Tex's release. "You could run away and hide somewhere an' they wouldn't never know where you was at...I...I know where you could hide." He was thinking of the place in the chimney corner where he would hide himself from the Gypsies.

"Run away!" Tex's voice echoed the futility, his eyes mirrored the absurdity of Alfie's suggestion. "In these stripes? They'd ketch me before the sun come up." Tex shuddered. "They put dogs on your trail."

Alfie stared at Tex in desperation. "There was a nigger boy. He run off. They'd beat him and he run off." His mind mirrored the image of the black boy, dragged back, terror in his eyeballs, his mouth standing open, screaming silently. "They put dogs on 'im and brought 'im back."

Alfie stared back at Tex. He could see the face of the black boy dragged back to the chain gang camp. He looked like Sunshine the night of the snipe hunt. But Alfie would not give up in his attempt to set Tex free. "You could wear some diff'rent clo'es. I bet Willie's clo'es would fit you. You could wear some of Willie's clo'es."

"It ain't no use, Alfie," Tex said. His eyes and his hands were getting ready to leave. He was looking at the truck and thinking how fast he would have to drive to make up for the time he had lost talking to Alfie. "It'd jest git you an' Willie in trouble. "It ain't no use. They put dogs on you."

Tex's body shuddered at the thought,at the remembrance of the black boy, rigid with fear, terror-stricken in the face of brute power. "The nigger boy. He worked beside me. They put dogs on 'im an' drug 'im back." He turned resolutely toward the vibrating dump truck. "Well, I gotta be goin'. Gotta git rollin', Alfie...You tell yo' Mama and yo' Papa I said much obliged for the water. It was good an' cool."

He walked quickly to the truck, swung the door open, leaped into the driver's seat. The engine raced, the gears clashed, the dump truck moved forward. Tex leaned out the window. He waved one hand at Alfie. "You be a good boy, Alfie. You heah?"

Alfie's lower lip jutted out. Tears were stinging behind his eyeballs. He watched the truck until it was enveloped in a cloud of dust. With his bare big toe he drew lines in the dust at his feet. The lines signified nothing to him. They were just lines drawn in the dust with his bare toe. "Bye Tex." His voice was barely audible to himself. Tex's dump truck had disappeared beneath the banks that stand on each side of the road where it dips away from Mister Charles' house. Alfie turned and ran inside the house.

He found Mama in the kitchen. Mama was making biscuits and she had flour dust on her hands. There was just a dab of flour dust on the tip of her nose because she had touched it where it itched. It lifted his spirits a little when he saw the flour dust on Mama's nose. He almost laughed, then he remembered Tex. He looked intently into Mama's big brown smiling eyes and he said the words rapidly, as if he had to keep Mama from interrupting him and keeping him from saying what he had to say.

"I'm gonna be a dump truck driver when I git big," he said. It was as if he had made a commitment and issued a challenge.

"A dump truck driver!" Mama exclaimed and touched the tip of her nose again, leaving more flour dust there. "Lordy mercy! Whoever put that notion into your head?!" Mama remembered hearing the truck in the yard, and the sound of the movement of the well chain as the water was being drawn up. "Who's been talking to you about being a dump truck driver?"

Alfie stood looking into Mama's smiling brown eyes, but he was seeing the far away, lost blue eyes of Tex. He could hear the lonely distant words "I didn't do nuthin'." His skin prickled when he remembered the words "There was this nigger boy run away an' they put the dogs on 'im."

Then he ran to Mama and threw his arms about Mama's legs. He buried his face in Mama's apron. Then he looked up through tears at Mama's face. "But I'm not gonna be on the chain gang!" The words burst from his heaving chest. "I'm gonna be a dump truck driver but I ain't gonna let 'em put me on the chain gang!"

"Lordy mercy!" Mama held Alfie's head in her hands, getting the flour all in his hair. "Whoever put such a notion in your head?"

Chapter Seven: Sunshine Hunts The snipe

Alfie told Sunshine "You better not ever do nuthin' to git sent to the chain gang for." And when Sunshine rolled great white eyeballs at Alfie, he added "Because Tex tol' me they will put the dogs on you if you try to run away."

Sunshine's eyes became as big as saucers at this news because he knew about the chain gang and he had already made up his mind that if they sent him to the chain gang he would run away. The reason Sunshine had thought so much about it was that his Pa had told him he would probably wind up on the chain gang.

Now that Alfie had opened up a whole new dimension of threat for him, Sunshine had to think again and he said to Alfie "Shucks! I run so fas' them ol' dawgs never ketch me!"

Alfie wished that Sunshine had been there to hear what Tex said and then he would be more careful not to get sent to the chain gang, but Papa had taken Sunshine with him to pull some weeds out of the corn. Alfie would have begged Papa to let him go too if he had not been watching for Tex's dump truck.

But the chain gang stopped work at sundown and there was no use for Alfie to stand and watch any longer. Besides, Papa had come home from the corn field, and Sunshine had come with him, so Alfie and Sunshine were playing together in the corn crib when Papa called Sunshine.

"Sunshine!" Papa called. "You come here.!" Papa's blue eyes were dancing with a hint of mischief which Mama noticed with suspicion. Then Papa turned to Mama. "Where's Sunshine at? I want 'im."

Mama was feeding some day old cornbread to her hens. She crumbled the corn pone between her fingers and pitched it onto the ground where the hens, six Rhode Island Reds, four Buff Orpingtons, and eight Barred Rocks, or domineckers, were scrambling and jostling one another for the crumbs. "I sent him to the crib for two ears of corn, but Alfie went with him, so I imagine they have got up a game and forgot what they went after." Mama studied Papa's face and became certain about the mischief. "What do you want with Sunshine?"

"Never mind," Papa said, the hint of mischief becoming more distinct. "I want 'im." Then he called louder "Sunshine! You heah me. Come 'ere!"

Sunshine appeared, like a genie out of a bottle. He was holding an ear of corn in each hand. "Heah Sunshine is!" A grinning, happy, expectant black boy announced himself. He was echoed by an equally grinning, happy, expectant white boy who trotted at Sunshine's side.

"Here's Sunshine, Papa!" Alfie announced, as if he had delivered Sunshine to Papa on demand. "What do you want with Sunshine, Papa? Here he is."

Both Sunshine and Alfie stood looking up at Papa but casting glances at Mama too. Sunshine's face showed a generous expanse of white teeth and eyes contrasting with the blackness of his small pinched face. Alfie's big brown eyes were set in a round white face with a blush of pink on it that denoted recent exertions in whatever game he and Sunshine were playing in the corn crib. Sunshine's thin black wrists extended from the made-by-Mama flour sack shirt sleeves. His ankles showed below the already outgrown overalls. Mama said "Give me the corn. It took you an awful long time to pick up two ears of corn."

"Yes'm" Sunshine said, but he kept looking at Papa. Sunshine was older than Alfie. Taller. Wiser in the ways of the world. A harsh and demanding world which had taught him fast. He was skinnier than Alfie and weighed less. And he was black.Sunshine gave the two ears of corn to Mama and said "We got to playin' an' I fergot."

"Here's Sunshine, Papa." Alfie said. "I told 'im you wanted 'im." Alfie idolized Sunshine, but Sunshine was a black idol and a black idol had to do what his white worshippers wanted. Sunshine was Alfie's dark shadow. Or Alfie was the bright effulgence of Sunshine's ebullient person. Which? Maybe both. **Now Sunshine turned his ebony face up to Papa, ready to do whatever Papa commanded. Alfie turned his cherubic face up to Papa**, ready to be included in whatever Papa wanted Sunshine to do.

“Sunshine,” Papa said. “You go back to the corn crib and git me a croaker sack. Make haste now. We’re goin’ on a snipe hunt.”

Sunshine stared at Papa, uncomprehending. “Make haste!” Papa said impatiently. “Dark’ll ketch you while you’re standing there.” Sunshine turned and ran toward the corn crib. Mama looked reprovingly at Papa, then began shelling the corn for the chickens.

“Can I go too, Papa?” Alfie was torn between running with Sunshine to the corn crib to fetch the croaker sack and staying with Papa to beg permission to go with him. “Can I go on the snipe hunt?”

“You can’t go this time.” Papa reached for the two ears of corn that Mama was shelling. He rubbed them together vigorously and the corn flew in every direction; the hens ran in every direction to pick it up. “You’ll hafta wait till you’re bigger before you can go snipe huntin’.” Alfie’s face fell. “But you run an’ help Sunshine find the croaker sack.” Alfie turned toward the corn crib, but the joy had gone out of his face.

“Aw, shucks,” he said. “I wanta go snipe huntin’ too.”

When Alfie was out of earshot, Mama turned suddenly on Papa. “You ought to be ashamed of yourself. He’s just a child. Just a homeless child. It doesn’t matter if he is black. You ought to be ashamed!.”

Papa was not ashamed. “It ain’t gonna hurt ‘im.” Papa finished shelling the corn and threw the cobs on the ground. “He WAS homeless. And he IS black. But it ain’t gonna hurt ‘im.”

Sunshine was homeless. That is, he was homeless that morning when he appeared on the back doorsteps. It was only a few days after Sandy, the mostly collie dog took up at Papa’s house. It was quite early in the morning. Papa had just finished eating breakfast and he had gone onto the porch to roll a cigarette and smoke while he made up his mind about what had to be done that day. And there was the little black boy sitting on the doorsteps, with Sandy crouching happily beside him and trying to lick his face. The little black boy was trying to push Sandy away to keep him from licking his face but not trying to push him all the way away. When Papa looked at him there on the doorstep he seemed to be all elbows and knees, both of which showed through the tattered shirt and the overalls with patches on top of patches.

He was all eyes too. His eyes seemed to fill his face. Luminous, expectant, waiting, fixed on Papa. "Well," Papa said, taking out his little bag of Bull Durham. "Where'd you come from, Sunshine?"

It was on impulse that Papa called him Sunshine. But Papa was like that. Impulsive. He would look at somebody for the first time and give him a name. Always a name that fit. Because Papa seemed to know what to call somebody the first time he ever saw him. If Papa had been in the world at the time of the creation, and the Lord had run all the creatures past him the way He did Adam, Papa would have known just what to call them. He would have reeled off their names without even having to study about it. So when Papa saw a little black boy in tattered overalls and a face shining up at him, Papa said "Well, where'd you come from, Sunshine?"

"Ah run away fr'm home," Sunshine said. His big eyes searched Papa's face, pleading, wondering. "Can Ah stay heah?" Sandy's tail thumped the doorstep; his tongue dripped saliva. He turned to lick Sunshine's face.

"How come you run away from home, Sunshine?" Papa paused, sifted a thin wafer of paper from a package and started to pour the tobacco into it when he had cupped it with his fingers. "Does your Pa know where you've run off to?" Papa sat down on the top doorstep and began twisting the paper full of tobacco into a cigarette. He studied Sunshine's face closely but he didn't seem the least bit surprised to find Sunshine sitting on the doorstep, nor even surprised by Sunshine's request to stay.

"He don' keer" Sunshine dodged Sandy's tongue and looked down at his knee which was showing through a hole in his overalls. "My Pa say he don' keer wheah I goes." Sunshine hesitated, picked at the threads around the edges of the hole in the knee of his overalls. "Pa say he tard a feedin' me."

Papa struck a match on the doorstep. He held the flame to the twisted paper at the end of his cigarette. It caught. He drew in the smoke. Shook the flame from the match and threw it onto the ground. "All right Sunshine. You can stay here."

Papa drew in some more smoke and let it out through his nostrils. "You can stay here till your Pa comes for you. But you'll hafta mind me. You hear?"

Sunshine heard. "Yassuh. I minds." He was eager to please. "Ah minds you good."

Papa called Mama from the kitchen. She stood on the porch looking at Sunshine. She thought, Another stray. Yesterday a stray dog. Today a stray child. What will tomorrow bring? Papa said to Mama "This here is Sunshine. He's gonna stay. At least till he puts some meat on his bones. Or till his Pa comes to take him back."

Mama looked at Sunshine and said "He looks half starved."

"I s'pect he could clean up any biscuits you had left from breakfast," Papa said. "Only thing is, I'm skeered if he stands up them overalls'll fall offa 'im."

Mama said "You come on in the kitchen Sunshine." And she said to Papa "You'll have to fix up a place for him."

Papa said "I'll take keer of that. I can fix him a place in the smokehouse but there ain't no hurry about that. It's jest now sunup and he ain't goin' to bed till night. But you better feed 'im quick before he starves to death. He says his own Pa got tired of feedin' im. Musta not took much to make 'im tired, from the looks of 'im."

Alfie stared in wide eyed wonder at the new arrival.

Papa got together everything he thought he would need to fix a place for Sunshine in the smokehouse. Hammer, saw, nails, boards. He kept sending Alfie for little things he had forgotten, and when it was all assembled and Papa had laid out his plans, he sent Alfie for a match. "Run and tell your Mama to send me a match." Papa started rolling a cigarette, and when he had it about ready Alfie came back with a match which he held up proudly to Papa. "It takes two to make a match, Son." It was Alfie's second arithmetic lesson, Papa style. Alfie ran back to Mama who was already lighting a fire under the washpot to boil water for Sunshine's disinfection. "Did that one go out?" she asked.

"No'm. But he wont strike it till he has two. Papa says it takes two to..."

"I know." Mama had heard it before. "Here." She gave Alfie another match. "Lordy mercy!" She turned to Sunshine who was eating the last biscuit from the breakfast batch. He had made a syrup in the hole the way Alfie showed him and he had found utter contentment, but Mama put an end to it. "Get your clothes off, Sunshine. They're going in the pot and you are going in the tub." She unwrapped a new bar of Octagon soap, tore the coupon from the wrapper and stowed the coupon in her apron pocket. "Get them off!" she said to the embarrassed little black boy. "I don't guess you are any different from the four boys already running around here. Only the color of your skin."

Papa came out of the smokehouse for a board that was too big for Alfie. He scanned Sunshine quickly and said to Mama "Good idea. Better clean 'im up too. If ev'ry stray in Colaparchee County is gonna take up here we'll hafta keep the washpot boilin' in self defense." He found the board he wanted and carried it inside the smokehouse where he measured, sawed and hammered for two hours, fixing up a place for Sunshine.

He built a bed frame of two by fours, and nailed on the slats to support a mattress. He shaped a table of rough boards on four sturdy legs and fastened to the wall for extra support. A small wooden box, open at the top, would hold Sunshine's clothes and anything else he might accumulate. "I'll make a lid for it later," he said to Alfie, "if I see anything in it that needs covering up."

"Papa." Alfie said very gravely. "Is this gonna be Sunshine's room all by hisself?"

"He's come to live with us now and he'll hafta have a place of his own here in the smoke house. Till his Pa comes fer 'im anyway."

"How come Sunshine couldn't stay in the house with me Papa? How come he couldn't sleep with me?"

"Sunshine's black. That's how come. Black folks don't sleep with white folks."

Alfie was thoughtful. "Papa, will Sunshine's Pa come an' take him back?"

"I wouldn't be surprised." Papa struck the head of a nail a couple more times for good measure. "About the time we git some meat on his bones."

Sunshine had slipped in and was squatting on the floor beside Alfie. Sandy had come in too and he was thumping his tail against the floor of the smokehouse. Alfie rubbed one bare foot over the top of the other. "Papa, can I stay out here with Sunshine sometimes? Mama has done cleaned him up. Can I sleep out here with him sometime? Till his Pa comes an' takes him away from us?"

Papa sat down on the table, testing its strength. It didn't sag. He reached two fingers inside the bib pocket of his overalls, took out the little sack of Bull Durham. Then a cigarette paper. Poured the tobacco into the cupped paper. Rolled it. Twisted it at each end and put one end between his lips. Found the second match that Alfie had brought. Struck it on the table top and held the flame to the cigarette. Shook the match out and dropped it onto the floor. Drew the smoke into his lungs and expelled it.

Alfie watched, his mouth standing half open. Sunshine waited, rolling white eyeballs now at Alfie and then back at his own bare feet extending from the overalls which had belonged to Junior up until an hour ago when Mama decided to burn Sunshine's rags rather than try to get them clean. Sandy thumped the floor with his tail, looked up at Alfie and Sunshine, then fixed his eyes on Papa and smiled.

Papa had been about to repeat what he had already said about black folks and white folks sleeping together. Now he smoked and looked at Alfie and Sunshine. One white with a pink bloom on him and one black with a shine on him, Papa thought. Papa said "It'd be a mighty long way for you to hafta run in the middle of the night if you was to wake up and take a notion that you wanted to crawl in the bed with your Mama an' me." Papa stubbed out the cigarette; it had burned down so short it almost burned his fingers when he took it out of his lips. He exhaled the last of the smoke.

Alfie remembered how good it felt, how warm and safe, in the bed between Mama and Papa. Sometimes he would fall asleep there while Papa was telling him a story. Then he would awaken in his own bed alone. Afraid. Wet. He would crawl out of his bed and find his way back to the big bed. He would crawl in between Mama and Papa and he would no longer be alone and afraid. He would try to forget that he was wet. In the morning Papa would wake up when the first streak of light touched the Eastern sky. Papa would call out to Mama and say "God A 'mighty! Now how did this youngun wind up in our bed? And wet too!"

"You sure you wanta sleep out here with Sunshine instead of with your Mama an' me?" Papa waited, his eyes on Alfie.

Alfie kicked his bare feet one against the other. He ducked his head and then looked back at Papa. "I'm glad we got Sunshine, Papa, but I ruther sleep with you an' Mama."

Sunshine had stayed. He had slept alone in the little bed Papa had built for him in the smokehouse. He had put a little meat on his bones with Mama's cooking. He had become Alfie's dark shadow and his sometimes obedient idol. And now Papa had planned to take him on a Snipe Hunt. And Mama had said to Papa "You ought to be ashamed of yourself."

And while Mama was endeavoring unsuccessfully to make Papa ashamed of himself, Sunshine and Alfie had gone to the corn crib where they found a croaker sack. Then Sunshine came dragging the croaker sack with Sandy hanging to it with his teeth bared, growling and shaking it in mock battle and providing a full measure of enjoyment for both Alfie and Sunshine, but Papa called out a warning, "Be keerful you don't tear a hole in that croaker sack. If there's a hole in it the snipe will run right through it an' git away!"

Papa's word of warning brought Sunshine back to the business at hand, which was the snipe hunt. He stopped and tried to get the burlap bag out of Sandy's jaws but Sandy knew a good thing when he had sunk his teeth into it, and he sank back on his haunches and growled and shook his head from side to side. Sunshine held on, but he looked up at Papa and said "How we gon' ketch dat ol' snipe anyhow? How we gon' do it?"

"We'll run 'im in that croaker sack unless you aim to let that damn dog run off with it." Papa reached for the contested object, got a hold on it, and Sandy renewed the struggle with greater zest because now he had a real contest with a worthy opponent. But Papa was in no mood for foolishness with a dog, and he clapped Sandy on the ear with the palm of his open hand. Sandy turned loose and dodged a second blow. Sunshine, with no Sandy to offer counterforce to his own, fell over backwards with the burlap bag clutched in his hands. And Papa snatched the bag and spread it out on the ground.

"Now look here," Papa said. "You hold the sack open like this." He opened the mouth of the sack. Sunshine, Alfie and Sandy watched enraptured. But Papa addressed himself to Sunshine alone. "You'll be down in that big gully that runs through the cotton patch at the other end." Papa waited until Sunshine's face showed that he understood where he would be. "Then me an' Mister Charles will drive the snipe down the gully to you. When he runs in the sack, you close it like this." And Papa clamped the mouth of the bag shut and twisted it, making the bag jump about as if there were some living thing in it. "An' we've got 'im! Git away Sandy!" For seeing the bag jump about, Sandy had come back to renew the struggle, but Papa swatted him again. Sandy dodged the main force of the blow and stood back, his ears standing alert but drooping slightly at the tips.

"You think you can do that now, Sunshine?"

Sunshine dropped onto the ground, distended the mouth of the bag and imitated Papa's movements, even to making its contents jump about inside. "Shucks! Ah ketch dat ol' snipe f'r sho'. He ain't gonna git away fr'm me."

Alfie had stood sullen and silent throughout this demonstration of bagging the snipe. Now he turned to Mama and said "I wanta go too. I could hold the croaker sack as good as Sunshine. Make Papa let me go too."

Mama said nothing. She put her hand on Alfie's trembling shoulders and turned judgmental eyes on Papa. "Not this time." Papa said. "This time's for Sunshine. Your time will come." But seeing Mama's eyes, Papa amended this statement. "Your time may come.'' And because he saw that Alfie was about to cry, "Tell you what, son. You stay here with your Mama an' wait up for us because we'll come in all hot an' tired an' thirsty an' we'll need you to help us take the snipe outta the croaker sack. Takin' 'im out can be a bigger job than runnin' 'im in there."

Alfie still was not mollified, and he put his thumb in his mouth and clung to Mama and snuffled, but Mama said "Stop acting like a baby now. You don't want Sunshine to see you acting like a baby." But Alfie hated Sunshine at that moment and was determined never to sleep with him even if Mama and Papa did agree to it, because Sunshine was going on the snipe hunt and Papa wouldn't let Alfie go.

Then Papa remembered something. "Sunshine, you run and fetch the lantern an' don't you try to light it either. I ketch you strikin' matches an' settin' somethin' afire around here and I'll put you in a croaker sack with the snipe an' dip you both in a tub of cold water." Papa thought this ought to mollify Alfie but it didn't.

Sunshine dropped the croaker sack and ran to fetch the lantern. As soon as he dropped it, Sandy grabbed the bag again and began shaking it, but with nobody on the other end, the challenge was gone, so Sandy soon lost interest and turned to watch Sunshine, debating whether to chase after him or stay with the white folks. Alfie decided that he didn't hate Sunshine enough to let him have all the glory of bringing the lantern to Papa, so he ran after Sunshine and this settled the issue for Sandy. He ran after Alfie.

The lantern was hanging on a nail driven into one of the two by four studs holding up a partition between the milking stalls. Sunshine had to stand on tiptoe and then climb the two by four stud to get it down. "Wusht Ah had me a match," he said as Alfie drew up, breathless. "Ah' strack it an' light dis ol' lantern an' see if it give off anuff light fer me to see dat ol' snipe."

"You better not!" Alfie's hostility had returned. "You heard what Papa said about strikin' matches." But Sunshine was too elated over the prospect of going on the snipe hunt to let even the threat of being dipped in a tub of cold water dampen his spirits. He laughed wildly and dashed away, swinging the lantern.

Alfie was still concerned that Sunshine might try to light the lantern, and he ran beside him all the way back to Papa. He was going to tell Papa what Sunshine had said, but Mister Charles had arrived while he and Sunshine were at the barn, and he seemed concerned about what Mama was saying.

What Mama was saying was that she didn't approve of what Papa and Mister Charles were planning to do to Sunshine because it wasn't right and God would surely punish them for it. "If not in this life, then at the Judgement Day!" Mister Charles laughed nervously because he was a little afraid Mama was right, but he had committed himself to Papa, and he didn't want to back out now. Papa was defensive.

"It ain't gonna hurt 'im!" Papa said loudly. "I ain't never heard tell of anybody gittin' hurt on a snipe hunt." Sunshine had arrived, lantern in hand, and he stopped with his mouth open to listen to what was being said. "Here, Sunshine. Give me that lantern. What took you so long? Did you git lost between here an the milkin' barn?"

Sunshine started to defend himself by making an excuse. "Hit dark in dat ol' barn widout no light." But Papa wanted to get away from Mama's eyes, and he grabbed the lantern and shook it vigorously to determine if it had any kerosene in it. Then he opened the lantern and ran his finger along the oil soaked wick. He struck a match, giving Sunshine a warning glance to let him know that he was not to do everything he saw Papa doing, and applied the flame to the wick. It caught and flared up. Papa adjusted it and closed the chimney.

"Chimney's nearly as black as you are, Sunshine, but there ain't time to clean it now. You can do that in the mornin'. Besides, I reckon we don't need a bright light. It might skeer the snipe before we're ready to jump 'im."

Mister Charles was eager to get going and he said "You grab the croaker sack, Sunshine, and don't drag it on the ground thataway. You drag the bottom out of it and the snipe will run right through it an' git away from you."

Sunshine pushed out his lower lip and set his jaw in a determined line. "Ol' snipe ain't gonna git away frum me. Now you git away Sandy an' quit tuggin at dis yere croaker sack. Ol' snipe come runnin' down de gully at me an' Ah ketch 'im so quick he don' know who got 'im."

Mister Charles laughed, glanced back once more at Mama who had wrapped her arms about Alfie. "Well you see that he don't high ball it right past you before you can git ready for him. Looks like it might frost tonight. If that snipe gits frost on his tail feathers he's gonna be hard to hold."

"Ah hol' 'im awright." Sunshine balled up the burlap bag to keep it away from Sandy. "Don' you worry none 'bout me holdin' 'im Mister Charles. Ah hold 'im come frost or no frost. Ah ain't turnin' loose."

Sandy was still watching for a chance to grab the bag away from Sunshine, and Papa said "Here Alfie, you hold onto Sandy till we're clean outta sight, an' don't turn 'im loose even then. We don't need him skeering up the snipe before we're ready." Alfie held onto Sandy, but more to reduce his own sense of loneliness than to keep Sandy from running up the snipe before Papa was ready for the snipe to run.

Both Alfie and Sandy had been denied the happy privilege of going on the snipe hunt. Theirs was now a companionship of shared deprivation. For Sandy, being hugged by Alfie was almost as good as tugging at the croaker sack. But for Alfie nothing could heal the hurt of being left behind. Papa was taking Sunshine on the snipe hunt and he had refused to let Alfie go. Even Mama had not interceded on his behalf. Twilight faded into darkness, and a great loneliness settled upon Alfie. He sat on the doorstep, hugging Sandy and watching the dim and blurry silhouettes of the snipe hunters as they walked away into the gathering darkness. The greater darkness was inside him. The tears flowed down his cheeks.

Into the dying evening of early October the snipe hunters walked. Papa and Mister Charles and Sunshine. Papa walked with long rapid strides, swinging the lantern as he went. Mister Charles matched Papa's stride. He was breathing rapidly. His gum rubber boots clumped on the hard ground. Sunshine danced alongside, ahead of them, behind them, clutching the balled up burlap bag, the croaker sack that was to entrap the snipe.

Alfie watched them as they went away. Self pity overflowed his heart. Tears rolled down his cheeks. Sandy whined and licked Alfie's face, wiping the tears off with his tongue. Mama stood up, straightened her clothes, looked down at Alfie. "No sense sitting here all night. Come on in the house. It's getting chilly." Alfie hugged his knees and looked up at Mama. He turned back to rub the top of Sandy's head with his hand. "Sandy can come in with you," Mama said, making a big concession to Alfie's sense of desolation. "Or he can go traipsing off after the snipe hunters." For she didn't approve of dogs in the house. Mama was put out with the whole affair. Sandy came inside with Alfie and curled up on the floor near Mama's feet.

Darkness settled in over the fields where the snipe hunters walked. Dried and broken corn stalks rustled and rattled in a rising breeze. Dry, brittle grass crunched under Papa's heavy brogan shoes and Mister Charles' gum rubber boots, and rustled quietly under the light tread, the soft touch of Sunshine's ragged tennis shoes. As if by some dark work of magic, a canopy of black velvet fitted itself over a sky that had glowed with a pale rose light a short while ago. Stars appeared in the black velvet. A crescent moon hung in their midst. The light of the stars and of the moon was like distant sparklers in the black velvet canopy. On the path that led across the corn and cotton patches was the light of the swinging lantern, flickering and wavering beside Papa's rapidly moving legs.

They walked to the mouth of a large gully running across the cotton patch and into the cow pasture. Two strands of barbed wire separated the cow pasture from the cotton patch. Open, empty cotton bolls hung from the bare stalks. In the nippy autumn air their sharp points pricked Sunshine's legs through his thin overalls. "Well, here we are!" Papa announced.

He held the lantern up level with his own face. Lights and shadows played across Papa's face. "Here's the big gully, Sunshine. Here's where you're gonna ketch your snipe."

Mama lifted the tall glass chimney from the Aladdin lamp. She was careful not to disturb the fragile mantle as she put the flame of the match to the wick. The mantle heated slowly and then glowed with an incandescence that made Alfie almost glad that they had carried the old stinking lantern off with them on the snipe hunt. When she was confident that the lamp would not overheat and the flame would not run up and destroy the mantle,

Mama picked up the shirt she was making for Alfie. She looked at it and laid it down. Started to thread her needle. Her hand trembled, and it was difficult to see the eye of the needle. She drew the thread across her moistened lips. She tried again with the stiffened thread, and it went through the needle's eye. "Well!" Mama said as if she had finally accomplished a tedious task. She knotted the thread.

Alfie stood quietly at Mama's elbow. His eyes followed the jerky movements of the thread. Then they went to her face. "You reckon they'll ketch the ol' snipe, Mama?" Gazing intently into Mama's immobile face, he asked "You reckon Sunshine will ketch the snipe in the croaker sack when Papa and MIster Charles skeer it up and run it down the gully?"

Mama drew the knotted thread tight, jerked it. Her lips were tightly compressed. She started to work the buttonhole.

"They'll catch their death of cold," Mama said, "and that's all they'll catch." Her tone carried the unspoken hint that the fulfillment of her prophecy would be evidence that a righteous Providence was watching over the affairs of men, even on their snipe hunts. "You're better off right here!"

"But I wanted to go." Alfie leaned against Mama's shoulder. "I wish I could go."

He fought for control of his voice. Then, "Mama, how come Papa took Sunshine an' wouldn't let me go?" Mama laid the shirt aside. She carefully buried the needle's point in the cloth, and took Alfie in her arms.

"Don't cry about it Son. They won't even be able to see anything in the dark."

"Papa's got the lantern, Mama." Alfie snuffled and buried his face on Mama's breast.

"This is the place, Sunshine." Papa held the lantern as high as he could reach. Its movement caused the shadows to flow over the sides of the gully. "Now you stay right here and hold that sack open. You hear? Point it up the gully. That's where the snipe's comin' from. We are goin' up there an' flush him out. We'll drive him right down the gully and it's your job to ketch 'im. You do just like I showed you. Keep your eyes open. Hold still and don't make no racket." Papa studied Sunshine's upturned face. “The snipe’ll make enough racket for the both of you.”

Sunshine hunkered down in the gully. He arranged the burlap bag. By the light of the lantern he picked up a dead twig and propped the mouth of the bag open. His black face glistened as the lantern’s rays struck it, then the intense face disappeared, merged with the darkness of the night when Papa moved the lantern. “Are you ready?” Papa asked.

“Ah’s ready fer ‘im.’’ Sunshine announced. But his voice was less confident than when he was at the house.

“Well, don’t let ‘im git past you. You hear me?”

“Yassuh. Don’ you worry none bout him gittin’ away. Ah ketch ‘im.” His voice quavered slightly.

“All right. Just remember. Keep quiet. And no matter what happens, don’t move from that spot where you’re at. You hear?”

“Ah be right heah an’ Ah have ol’ snipe all bunched up in dis heah croaker sack when you’n Mister Charles come back.” Sunshine shook out the sack, rearranged it, propping it open with his arm cocked on his elbow. He thought, as Papa and Mister Charles moved away up the gully, “Wusht Alfie was heah.” He didn’t dare say it out loud.

Papa and Mister Charles walked away, the lantern swinging between them. The gully grew darker and lonelier. Sunshine watched the receding light of the lantern. Fear grew upon him. Papa and Mister Charles entered a small pine thicket at the edge of the cotton patch. The light disappeared completely.

The darkness became oppressive and Sunshine opened his mouth in order to breathe. He gripped the edges of the burlap bag and cocked his ears to the night sounds. A gust of wind stirred a dry leaf at the lip of the gully. The leaf fluttered like a bird caught in a snare. A small clod of dry dirt, loosened by Mister Charles’ boot in passing, gave way now under its own weight. It crumbled and rolled down the embankment in a delayed action. Far off, a dog barked, and finished on a howling note.

Then a new sound, unfamiliar, unidentifiable, high and keening, rose on the night air.

Sunshine raised his head at the sound, held his breath. He felt his skin prickle. His scalp tingled. His short, tightly curled hair was charged with electricity. The sound rose in pitch and volume. It was joined by a second sound. The second sound attempted to blend with the first, then pulled apart from it, moaning and transforming itself into a piercing screech.

Sunshine moaned involuntarily in cadence with the sound. He gripped the croaker sack with clenched fists. His nails bit into the flesh of his palms. The sound rolled down the gully, surrounding and engulfing him. His eyes stared into the darkness.

He became aware of his own moaning. It was now the only sound in a silent universe. He bit his lips to stop the moaning.

Raising his head, he peered over the gully's bank. A light burned in the window of the house he had left less than an hour ago. The light drew his eyes like a magnet draws an iron filing. Then the sound came again, screeching and moaning in concert on the frosty night air. It rolled down the gully toward him, then stopped. He held his breath, waiting. His eyes grew large, searching the darkness, searching for the light in the window. Cold sweat bathed his face. His hands trembled and lost their grip on the burlap bag. Tremors passed through his body, jerking him up from the ground.

The dread hovered over him silently; then the sound burst upon him again. Closer. Rising out of the darkness in the gully. Rolling along its embankments.

He bolted from the gully. His eyes found the light in the window of the house. The light gave wings to his feet. He ran with the wings of urgency, yet it seemed to him that he stood still, not moving in a world that moved past him. Suspended in the darkness, and the darkness filled with terror. In the moving darkness the stiff brittle cotton stalks, and the dry rattling corn stalks moved past him while he stood poised, elevated on the wings of time. His feet struck the floor of the front porch. He flung himself against the door. His mouth stood open. Screaming. But no sound came. The door flew open. Jerked open from within. He tumbled in at Mama's feet.

"Mama!" Alfie cried. "It's Sunshine! Mama!"

Alfie was on the floor beside Sunshine. Staring into Sunshine's distended, bulging eyes. "Sunshine! Sunshine! Is it the snipe?"

"Shet de do'!" Sunshine gasped. "Shet de do'!" He gasped again. "Fo'dat snipe git in heah!" Alfie moved toward the door, but cautiously. Sandy, bristling and barking aggressively, plunged and skittered through the open door to attack whatever might be beyond it. Sunshine collapsed onto the floor again, breathing stertorously. "Shet de do'.!"

Mama closed the door with a swift, decisive movement. She bent over Sunshine. Lifted him and cradled him in her arms. Sunshine held onto Mama for endless minutes, trembling and shaking. When the tremors stopped, he breathed deeply. He looked at Alfie and stood up. "Ah be awright now," he said. "Ah be awright." He grinned at Alfie. Sheepishly. "Dat ol' snipe. He be gone. Long gone!"

Papa and Mister Charles were on the porch now. They were stamping their feet and talking loudly. Sandy was barking a greeting to them. Alfie crouched beside Sunshine, looking into Mama's face. Papa flung the door open and the light from Mama's Aladdin lamp flowed out onto the porch. Papa raised the smoky lantern and squinted his eyes against the brightness of the lamp.

He raised the smoky glass chimney to the lantern. Ran his finger over the crusty, blackened wick. "Light went out on us right after we jumped the snipe," Papa said.

Then, "What became of you, Sunshine? I told you to hold that croaker sack. Did you see the snipe?"

Sunshine stared back at Papa. "Ah seen 'im awright. He come barrilin'' down on me lickity split an' he run clean over me. Ah hol' out my croaker sack an' he jes' run right off wid it!"

"Hunhh!" Papa said, for he was surprised and taken aback by Sunshine's response. "Musta' been a big un." Papa looked now at Mister Charles who didn't offer any help. "He was makin' a God awful racket when he come outta that pine thicket. Could you tell whichaway he went Sunshine?"

"Nassuh. He make so much racket Ah deaf an' blind. Ah cain't see whichaway he went."

Papa looked more closely at Sunshine and said "How come your overalls all tore out the way they are Sunshine? Did you git hung up in a barbed wire fence?"

Sunshine glanced down at his torn overalls. The light from Mama's Aladdin lamp glanced off his ebony cheeks. The skin was stretched tightly over the high cheek bones. The whites of his eyes stood out, dominating his whole face. "Ad didden see no bob wahr fence," Sunshine said. "Ah jes' see dat ol' snipe runnin' off thew de pasture wid dat ol' croaker sack over his head."

Chapter Eight: A Boy Needs A Goat

Mama did not let Papa forget that the Lord would punish him on Judgment Day, if not before, for what he had done to Sunshine. "Two grown men!" Mama exclaimed, thereby putting Mister Charles under God's hammer along with Papa. "Scaring the daylights out of a homeless child! Even if he is black he has feelings like anybody else!"

Papa tried to justify what he had done by saying that "Every boy needs to be took on one snipe hunt. It hep's to make a man outta 'im." But although he said this very loudly, Papa did not fully believe it, as was evidenced by his attendance at the Midway Baptist Church the very next Sunday.

The preacher chose a double text: "Let the little children come to me..." and "a little child shall lead them." He gave a very good account of himself as a preacher too, and whenever he seemed to be running out of steam on one text he would switch over to the other.

Driving home in the Dodge Papa said that he was not sure both texts came from the Bible and he suspected Mama of having put the preacher up to it and of having supplied at least one of his texts. "It don't seem right that he could dig up that much to light the fire under a fellow for jest takin' a nigger boy on a snipe hunt. He is bound to have he'p from some source."

Mama said Papa was adding a second sin to cover the first by denying the clear evidence that the Lord had laid the message on the preacher with the clear intent that the preacher would in turn lay it on Papa.

Anyway, along about Thanksgiving, Sunshine's Pa came for him and took him back home. Papa said "I reckon he will keep him to chop stovewood till he works off the meat we put on his bones." But Alfie was lonely and Papa whistled a lot which meant that he was trying to think of a way to fill up the empty spot left by Sunshine.

Papa had a special way of whistling when he was thinking and he was whistling that way when he drove up to Robb's house and saw the goat tied out on a chain. "What do you aim to do with that billy goat there, Robb?' Papa asked.

"I aim to sell 'im to you, I reckon," Robb said, spitting tobacco juice into the dirt at his feet. And when Papa didn't reply to that but kept looking at the goat, Robb said "I reckon you wouldn't a ast if you wasn't interested."

Papa wound up paying Robb fifty cents for the billy goat and he said "I reckon what the boys need is a billy goat. Especially Alfie, since Sunshine's gone."

When Papa brought the goat home, Mama said "What on earth are you going to do with a stinking billy goat?"

And Papa said "Every boy ought to have a goat at one time in his life and I reckon Alfie has come to that time." Mama was not satisfied with Papa's explanation of Billy. She stood her ground, put her hands on her hips, and drew her lips into a very firm line which let Papa know that his words of explanation had fallen upon unreceptive soil, if not solid rock. Alfie lifted pleading eyes to Mama's face, but Mama's face still did not soften.

"It won't be safe to hang the clothes out to dry on the line. That goat will drag them down and chew them to rags."

Papa said "We can keep the goat in a pen where he can't reach the clothes line."

"He will climb out of any pen you put him in," Mama replied. "You know a goat can climb like a cat."

Papa decided that the only thing to do was to temporize. "We'll see," he said.

"You'll see!" Mama said. She turned and went back into the house, leaving Papa to see.

Junior and Cliff begged Papa to let them ride the goat. Papa had said they had made him ride the goat when he was initiated into the Woodmen of the World, and Junior said "Can I ride Billy, Papa? Shucks! I can ride a goat if anybody can."

"We'll hafta see about that," Papa said, still temporizing because he had something on his mind and he was not ready to deal with the question of Junior riding the goat.

Willie said "I think Billy is just right for Junior to ride." Willie was older than all his brothers and he thought it would be great sport to watch Junior try to ride the goat. "I guess he ain't a bit too heavy for that goat."

Papa had not told anybody yet what his plans were for Billy, and if Billy had known what Papa was planning he might have taken more kindly to Junior's plan to ride him. As it was, Papa was so intent on his own plan that he didn't pay much attention to what Junior had said, and so while Papa was collecting the materials to implement his own plan, Junior said to Cliff "You hold 'im by the horns while I git on his back. Then you can turn 'im loose, once I'm on his back."

As it turned out, it wasn't necessary for Cliff to turn Billy loose. As soon as Junior jumped onto his back, Billy went berserk. He butted Cliff in the stomach and knocked the wind out of him. Then he threw Junior on top of Cliff. After that he ran about the barnlot, bucking like a wild Texas pony and butting everything in sight. Junior and Cliff climbed the fence just in time to avoid a second encounter and Billy wound up with his horns rammed between the boards of the barnlot fence. When he straightened his head up and tried to back out, he was caught by the horns and he stood there bleating angrily.

The commotion in the barnlot got Papa's attention. Alfie ran to Papa and said "Come quick Papa. Willie says the billy goat threw a duck fit and pitched Junior and cliff in it and now he's fell in it hisself."

Papa took a quick look at Billy who was impaled on the horns of his own dilemma, in a manner of speaking, and he said "Let 'im stay there. That's as good a place as any for the goat to wait while I build the goat cart."

That was the first revelation Papa had made of his plan. "You two, leave off ridin' the goat and come help me build the cart." So he put Junior and Cliff to work bringing boards and nails and tools. "Take the wheels off that ol' bicycle that's broke down anyway," Papa told Cliff. Papa had already found an iron rod that would serve for an axle.

"Shucks!" Cliff objected. "Ain't nuthin' wrong with it but a busted sprocket."

But Papa said "We don't need a sprocket for a goat cart. And after it's all over you can have the wheels back." As it all turned out the bicycle wheels got the worst part of it but that was not because of any deficiency in the goat cart that Papa built. Papa said it was because Billy was headstrong. It was a good solid goat cart and the bicycle wheels turned smoothly.

Papa cut down some old harness straps and fitted them to Billy's body. This was easy enough, the fitting, because Billy couldn't run away. He bleated, chewed, glared , and gave off a disagreeable odor, but he couldn't go anywhere because he was caught with his horns between the boards of the fence. "Best damn' goat trap in Colaparchee County!" Papa said. But it didn't keep Billy from moving his feet and when Alfie approached too near in order to rub Billy's heaving side with his hand, Billy lashed out at him with his hind foot and kicked Alfie in the stomach.

"Look out son!" Papa warned, but it was too late. "He ain't fully broke yet. But you just wait,'' Papa said because he could see that Alfie was going to be all right as soon as he got his breath back and his stomach quit hurting. "Soon as we git this goat in harness we'll hitch 'im to the cart and I'll let you drive 'im." That helped Alfie's stomach to quit hurting sooner.

When Papa had the harness on Billy, he said to Willie "I'll hold 'im and you twist his head to the side and slip it back through the fence. No sense in tearing the board off.'' Willie did it as gently as he could and Billy was glad to be out of the fence, so he submitted gracefully to being hitched to the cart. But when it began to dawn on him that something more was expected of him, he cast baleful glances over his shoulder at the contraption behind him. He stamped the ground with his front feet to let everybody know that he didn't like the developing situation. But Papa said "All aboard!" Junior and Cliff clambered onto the cart and Papa set Alfie up in the driver's position and looked to see where Willie was.

Willie was standing in the barn door and he said "I'll just watch. It'll be more fun thataway." Billy lay down on the ground and refused to get up.

Alfie said "He don't want to go, Papa." And he shook the reins but Billy lay on the ground, chewed his cud, and refused to budge.

"Never mind," Papa said. "I'll give him a little encouragement." Papa set fire to a wisp of straw with the end of his cigarette and pushed the burning straw onto one of Billy's hooves which were folded up underneath him. Then Billy leaped to his feet and leaned into the harness, and the bicycle wheels turned. The cart rolled along the driveway under the overarching boughs of the pecan trees. Alfie held the reins. Papa walked at the goat's head. Junior and Cliff dangled their feet from the back of the cart. Willie stood in the barn door, watching. And Mama, on the front porch, twisted the apron around her hands and said "Lord have mercy! I hope they don't all get killed by that stinking billy goat."

Alfie's heart swelled with both pride in his own accomplishment and tenderness for Billy. "Papa," he said. "You ought not to put the fire under Billy."

Papa said "Didn't hurt 'im. Just swinged him a little. A goat's got to know who's boss."

It was perfectly clear that Papa was the boss. For about fifty feet. Then Billy became tired. He stopped, but he did not lie down. He just stood. Papa grasped the halter and dragged Billy along. Now Papa was becoming tired, and aggravated. By the time they reached the end of the driveway, where it joins the big road in front of Mister Charles and Miss Maggie's house, Papa was about equally tired and aggravated. But he put on a good face because Mister Charles and Miss Maggie came out to see the show.

"Now that's a sight if I ever seen one," Mister Charles said. Mister Charles didn't mention the sight of Sunshine running from the snipe because it was too dark for him to see.

Miss Maggie said "And just look at Alfie driving the goat." Miss Maggie's mouth turned up at the corners when she smiled and her eyes crinkled with pleasure.

Papa released his grip on the goat's halter to throw up his hand and wave to his neighbors, and it became evident that Alfie was not really driving. He was merely a passenger holding onto the reins. Billy now found himself capable of pulling the cart without Papa's help. Even without Papa's guidance and direction. Billy whirled around in the middle of the big road, tilting the cart up on one bicycle wheel. Then he straightened up and dashed back down the driveway toward the starting gate. He was heading for the stable which had suddenly become attractive to him. It represented all that a goat could ask for in life - food, shelter, security, freedom from enforced labor, and exposure to the whims of humankind.

Alfie clung to the reins but this had little if any effect on the speed and direction of Billy. Junior and Cliff clung to the cart, and with shouts and laughter they urged Billy on in his run for the roses. Mister Charles doubled over in unrestrained mirth at the sight. Miss Maggie opened her mouth to form a large O. Then she put her hand over the O to conceal her utter amazement at this performance. And Papa, standing in the middle of the big road, watched, speechless, for a moment. Then he called to Alfie "Hold 'im Son. He's headin' for the barn."

Papa headed for the barn too but Billy was heading for the barn at a faster clip than Papa was. Papa ran as fast as he could but the distance between him and the goat cart with his offspring in it gradually increased and Papa stopped to watch because he had given up hope of catching up or doing anything to stop the runaway goat.

Willie had not moved from his place in the barn door and when he saw that Billy was going to run over him he dodged aside and grabbed the cart as it went past him. This slowed Billy down a little but it didn't stop him. Billy continued his headlong plunge toward the barn and finding the door open, he dashed inside. This might have brought the runaways to a safe landing if the cart had not been careening wildly from side to side because Willie had grabbed one side of it while it was in rapid motion.

Billy got safely inside the barn though. But one cart wheel caught in the door jamb and the cart came to an abrupt halt. Billy was brought to a temporary halt but he recovered his feet and lunged forward again, stripping the harness off him. He ran into a corner, butted his head against the wall, then turned and presented his horns to defend himself against all comers.

Alfie was catapulted by the impact over the front of the cart and onto the ground in the entranceway to the barn. His tight little fists were still gripping the reins, and he wouldn't turn loose even when Willie picked him up off the ground and dusted him off. When Willie saw that Alfie was not hurt, he said "You were the first one in the barn so I guess that makes you the winner of the race."

Cliff and Junior tumbled onto the ground behind the cart and lay there laughing hysterically, even when Mama came running from the front porch, her apron strings flapping in the wind and her eyes blazing with anger. A white ring around her mouth meant fear but she turned on Papa who had arrived out of breath and put out with the whole matter.

"Lord have mercy!" Mama exclaimed. "You're going to get them all killed fooling around with that stinking billy goat!"

Papa saw that the situation was under control though. He could tell that by the expression on Willie's face. A few scratches and bruises and a busted bicycle wheel. Cliff said "I won't never be able to fix up that ol' bicycle now." But this did not bother Papa. Instead of crying over a busted bicycle wheel he addressed himself to the real issue. He turned to his eldest son though, instead of facing Mama, and he said "Well, that does it, Willie!. We're gonna hafta do somethin' with that damn' goat."

Papa's statement to Willie that "We're gonna hafta do somethin' with that damn' goat" gave Alfie more concern than it did Willie. To Willie it simply meant that they would have to figure out an alternative to the failed experiment of the goat cart, but for Alfie it had ultimate implications because of Mama's opposition to "a stinkin' billy goat."

What Papa had in mind was an arrangement that would keep Billy from dragging the clothes off the line and trampling Mama's flower beds. He had not at this point decided to do anything about Billy's odoriferous nature. Papa assumed that Billy simply stank the way a billy goat is expected to stink. One decision had been made for Papa though. Billy would not be a cart goat. One of the bicycle wheels was damaged beyond repair and a one wheel cart was unthinkable.

The real question, then. was where to keep Billy in order to prevent him from making trouble? And as Papa looked over the outbuildings he decided upon Kate's stable. It was warm and dry and secure and the pungent odor of manure and rotting straw would offset Billy's distinctive odor, some. It had a good sturdy door that Billy could not open because the latch was on the outside. Enough light filtered in through the cracks to meet a goat's minimal needs for light. Not room enough to run about, but what was good enough for a good working mule must surely be good enough for a stinking billy goat.

Best of all, Kate's stall was actually fastened onto the corn crib. This gave ready access to the basic food supply. A small door opened above Kate's feed trough into the crib where corn and fodder were kept.

"Kate!" Papa announced, slapping her affectionately on her withers. "You are about to get a room mate." When Kate brought her large sensitive ears forward like antennae to pick up this message, Papa added "Not another mule, but a billy goat. Billy is gonna stay here with you." And studying the expression in Kate's large brown eyes, Papa also added "Till I can do somethin' with 'im."

"Papa, what are we gonna do with Billy?" Alfie wanted to reach out and touch, rub, caress the foul smelling goat. He kept his distance out of fear, remembering the kick he had received. "Is Mama gonna make us git rid of him?"

"I don't know what we'll do with him," Papa said, rubbing his hand across a stubbly chin. "Except fasten him up here with Kate. One thing's sure, his career as a cart goat has come to its end. And your Mama says his stink is rubbin' off on you boys and if you all git to smellin' as bad as the goat she's gonna put you outta the house."

Mama had been even more forceful than that in her judgment on Billy. "I'm putting my foot down on this. You have got to get rid of that stinking billy goat. I can't even hang the clothes on the line to dry. He chewed up a good shirt of yours yesterday and dragged a whole line of sheets down on the ground and I had to wash them over. And you thought you had him tied up. With a rope. Hah! He chewed it in two and came right into the house. Now I'm telling you I'm not going to live with a stinking billy goat. You either find a way to fasten him up or get rid of him."

Mama had put her foot down, and Papa had found a way to fasten billy up. In Kate's stall. With Kate. A goat and a mule sharing the same space.

Mama's final threat had turned the latch on Billy. "You keep that goat out of here or I'm putting you all out of the house."

Alfie was deeply moved by this threat. Much more deeply moved than Papa was. Papa did not take it literally. But Alfie's fear of Billy was a more powerful deterrent to his close contact with him than the dread of absorbing his odor.

Billy's sojourn in Kate's stable was not a happy one either. The goat and the mule did not get along well together. "I'd say he's about wore out his welcome with Kate," Papa observed when Billy had been in Kate's stall less than two days. "And when a goat smells too bad for a mule, it's time to do somethin' about it." Papa had not yet decided upon the next step, and it had not occurred to him that Kate might have some ideas of her own about how to deal with the crisis that had arisen in her stable.

When Willie had first raised the question of compatibility Papa had said "I've heard that all the famous race horses have goats in their stalls because it makes them more contented and easier to handle." Billy's presence had not made Kate more contented nor easier to manage. It had just the opposite effect on her. When Billy's odor was unusually strong, Kate's nostrils quivered. She snorted. Laid back her ears. Turned her head away. Got a hard, angry look in her eyes. It was a look which, to the perceptive student of mules, would indicate that she would rather have the room Billy was taking up in her stall than the companionship his presence offered. Papa was an astute mule fancier, and he knew Kate better than most mules are known by their owners. "Kate ain't takin' too kindly to that goat," Papa observed.

Papa's words were an understatement. Even so, matters got worse when Billy moved into Kate's feed trough. "That billy goat ain't gonna win no popularity contest thataway," Papa said to Alfie. "The way he's takin' over you'd think that feed trough belonged to him and Kate was po' kinfolks." Billy was standing in the feed trough and Kate was standing off watching him warily. Papa was studying the situation. He had not decided what to do about it, or even whether he would be called upon to do something more than study it.

"Son," Papa said to Alfie, "You hop up there in the crib and throw down a bundle of fodder and six ears of corn for Kate." Papa made a swipe at Billy with his hand and Billy jumped down from the trough. Alfie crawled into the corn crib.

"You can throw down one ear of corn for the goat, but pitch it on the ground. That way he won't be in Kate's way."

Kate's ears went up when Alfie threw the bundle of fodder down into the feed trough. She advanced toward it expectantly. Billy's ears went up when Alfie threw down the corn. He ignored the ear of corn on the ground and leaped in to the feed trough. At the same moment Alfie leaped down out of the corn crib and landed in the feed trough, facing the goat. "Hey! Git back you crazy goat!" Alfie grabbed the bundle of fodder and used it for a shield. He tried to push the goat, but the goat pushed back. Billy was a better pusher than Alfie and Alfie retreated.

"Look out Son! Papa called out. "Don't let 'im butt you with them horns." Alfie ran to the end of the trough where Papa reached in and lifted him into his arms. Kate came snorting to the feed trough, blowing through her expanded nostrils and making threatening sounds in her throat. She laid her ears back close to her head to let Billy know that she was not in a friendly frame of mind. Her teeth were partly bared and she swung her head at Billy in a gesture that said "Get out of my feed trough you stinkin' billy goat!"

Billy did not get out of the trough. He planted his forefeet among the six ears of corn, ignoring the one on the ground. He even ignored the bundle of fodder as being lacking in nutrients. He bleated in a plaintive but yet a belligerent voice, and presented his two long, curved horns to Kate's surprised face.

"Look out Son!" Papa warned. "There's gonna be trouble!" Alfie clung more closely to Papa now. "I think we're gonna see a fight." Kate backed away from Billy's menacing horns. Then came back, squealing with rage. Her ears were flattened against the sides of her head. Her yellow teeth were bared.

But Billy held his ground. That is, he held the trough. He jabbed Kate's sensitive nose with his sharp curved horns. He emitted a grunt which seemed to say that he had put up with about as much mule foolishness as he could tolerate.

Kate drew her head back sharply. Her big ears came forward to reassess the situation. Her eyes grew round and wondering as she stood back and studied the smelly intruder in her feed trough. Suddenly she bared her teeth again, flattened her ears against her head and stretched out her long neck, slashing at Billy and squealing in a high pitched voice.

Billy dodged the slashing yellow teeth and made a short rush at Kate's jaw with his right horn. Kate felt the prick and backed away. Billy started to nibble at a leaf of fodder but he kept his eyes on Kate, glaring balefully at her as he chewed.

They stood this way for half a minute. Billy chewing and glaring at the mule. Kate baring her large yellow teeth and screaming her outrage at the goat. Alfie clung to Papa, looking into his face. Could Papa keep the two from the final clash? Would Papa let the mule and the goat settle the matter for themselves?

"Git down Son." Papa set Alfie on the ground. "Stand behind me." Alfie stood behind Papa, clinging to his leg. Papa fumbled in his shirt pocket for the little sack of Bull Durham tobacco. He drew it out and thumbed a cigarette paper from its pack. "Looks like a standoff," he said. "But it might not be over yet." Papa poured the tobacco into the thin wafer of paper as he said "It might not be over yet."

It was not over. What happened next was totally unexpected although it was predictable, given a knowledge of the evolution of the mule and its forebears. Something primeval in Kate's genetic makeup, some instinct inherited from wild ancestors defending themselves against wild dogs or hyenas aeons ago, made the neural connection between Kate's brain and the more lethal parts of her anatomy. She whirled about so that instantly she was facing away from the goat. She lowered her head between her spread forelegs at the precise moment that she raised her hindquarters off the ground. The powerful muscles in her hind legs tightened, flexed and expanded as the weight of her body pitched forward and balanced on her forefeet.

"Crack!" Kate's hind hooves landed on Billy's horns with the sound of a pistol shot. Billy was knocked from the feed trough and went reeling against the wall of the stable. All four feet on the ground again, but with her rear end still turned toward the feed trough, Kate peered round at Billy. Billy, watching out of the corner of his eyes, was scrambling to his feet and pushing himself underneath the floorboards of the adjoining corn crib.

"Papa! Papa!" Alfie cried. "Look at Billy! He's got one of his horns on crooked!"

Papa was still holding the little bag of Bull Durham in his fingers and the thin wafer of paper was fluttering slightly because his hand was shaking. Alfie had come out from behind Papa to peer under the corn crib at Billy who was glaring back at him. Papa squatted beside Alfie and looked under the crib. Billy bleated, a whimpering, plaintive sort of a bleat. Papa said "You're right Son. I believe ol' Kate has knocked his horn wopsided."

While he was still hunkered down on the bed of manure and straw on the floor of Kate's stall, Papa tipped the little bag of Bull durham and poured tobacco into the wafer thin paper, rolled it, licked it, twisted the ends, and struck a match which he had fished from another pocket somewhere on his person. "I reckon he won't need it where he is though. Ain't apt to find nobody under the corn crib to butt with it."

Papa's match had gone out. He stood up and fumbled through his pockets, trying to find another. Kate came over and nuzzled against Papa's shoulder, nickering. "Looks like Kate and your Mama are of one mind on billy goats. Don't like 'em."He ran his fingers through his pockets again, paused and nodded toward the barn door. "You run an' ask your Mama to send me a match." Alfie's eyes brightened. He darted away. "An' don't fergit. It takes two to make a match."

Chapter Nine: Caught!

It was late Summertime again when Mama said to Papa "We need to go to Babe's and bring the children's Gran'ma home with us." It seemed to Alfie that almost everything happened in the Summertime. Except Christmas. That was because the days are longer in the Summertime which allows for more things to happen. Especially outdoors which is where most of the exciting things happen. Except at Christmas which is when the most exciting things happen at night.

Gran'ma was at Babe's because Babe was Mama's brother. Gran' ma was Papa's Mama but it never occurred to Alfie that she was anybody except Gran'ma. He knew that Uncle Babe was not Papa's brother though. It was easy enough to tell that.

Mama felt that she needed to visit her brother because of his motherless children but she was going to bring Gran'ma home, even though Babe's children were motherless. That was because Gran'ma always spent part of the year at Babe's and the other part of the year at Papa's, even if Babe's children were left to be brought up by the hair of their heads. Mama said that was the way they were being brought up. She was provoked at Babe for not remarrying so that the children would have a suitable mother to bring them up.

So on Sunday they got ready to go, and Mama said there wouldn't be room in the car for everybody so she left Margaret in charge at home. She and Papa took Alfie with them in the Dodge. "We will take the baby with us," Mama said to Margaret. "Willie can help you if the other boys get rowdy." Cliff and Junior sometimes got rowdy but Willie could soon put an end to their rowdiness in ways that they would remember the next time they felt the impulse to get rowdy.

Margaret said "Don't worry about us, Mama. We'll be all right." She hugged Alfie and told him to be a big boy and bring Gran'ma home with him. Margaret always told Alfie to be a big boy because she knew he hated being the baby.

"How much farther is it to Uncle Babe's house, Papa?" Alfie was hot and tired. Beads of sweat stood on his flushed cheeks.

His query was a whining complaint that has been heard millions of times by the parents of small children traveling. It was one that Mama and Papa had heard umpteen times since they left home shortly after sunup on that September morn. "How much farther is it?"

The sixty mile drive to Uncle Babe's house was brighter in prospect than it was on the road. For the road was dusty and deeply rutted where the rains of late summer had washed the red clay away into the ditches alongside, and then had carried it away to the nearest creek which had taken it to the next larger creek and eventually to the Ocmulgee River which was no longer the clear and shining water that had inspired the Indians to give it that name before the white man came with his cotton and his plows to turn it red like a river of blood. But the roads between Alfie's house and Uncle Babe's, the roads winding between cotton fields and cut over pines, these roads were rough. Papa said it was like driving on a washboard. "Shake a man's false teeth out if he drives more than fifteen miles an hour!" But it was Mama's duty to visit her brother and check on his children.

"The poor motherless things are being brought up by the hair of their heads." When Mama spoke of Babe's children in this way there was a note of pathos in her voice. "They're growing up there with no mother to guide them and there's no telling what could happen to them." Mama stopped just short of indicting Babe for failing to provide satisfactory moral and religious training and an admirable example for Aggie and Mutt. She stopped short of this because he was, after all, her brother, and after all, just a man, and he could not be expected to take the place of their mother who had died in childbirth, casting Mutt out upon a world full of mortal dangers, a motherless babe, to be brought up by the hair of his head. Of course, there was Aggie, but she could not be expected to take the place of a mother.

The motherlessness of his cousins who lived sixty miles away had not yet become a matter of real concern for Alfie. He had concerns of his own that were more immediate. "I'm thirsty!" he announced as the Dodge struck a very deep rut in the road.

"Just hold your horses," Papa said. "We'll soon be at the watering trough."

Alfie swallowed the saliva in his throat and added with a note of greater urgency "I've got to pee too!"

"Well now that may be harder to hold," Papa conceded. "But I reckon we'll come to a clump of plum bushes alongside the road any time now. You just keep your eyes peeled for a good place to stop and we will take keer of half your needs."

"I don't want nobody to see me." He didn't peel his eyes but he did rub them with his fists because tears of fatigue were forming behind his eyeballs. Rubbing made his eyes worse but he rubbed them some more anyway because they felt worse.

"I don't think we'll hafta worry about that. We ain't met a car in the last half hour, and there didn't nobody come by the whole while I was fixin' the flat back a ways." Papa spotted a clump of bushes up ahead. He pressed the brake pedal and the Dodge swayed and swerved onto the rough shoulder of the road. "You just hop out and run behind them bushes and take keer of your business. Your Mama and I'll sit here and see to it that nobody looks at you while you're at it."

Alfie hesitated. He squirmed and held himself. Papa said "Don't tell me you've already done it."

"I'm skeered to go by myself. You go with me Papa."

"I might see you." Papa pretended mild shock at the idea.

"Oh, go on with the child." Mama was impatient. "He might get on a snake."

Mention of the snake aroused new fears on Alfie's part and new complications for Papa. But Alfie agreed to go to the secluded spot behind the plum bushes, after Papa agreed to carry him and then to stand there with him to protect him from snakes. Also to shield him from view of passing motorists. Nobody passed, but Papa had to shield Alfie anyway.

When they came back to the car Papa said to Alfie "Now you crawl in the back seat and lay down an' sleep till we git to your Uncle Babe's." But Alfie insisted that he was not sleepy. He also insisted on sitting in Mama's lap the rest of the way.

"Well brush your hair out of your eyes," Mama chided him and she brushed his hair out of his eyes. "I don't know how you can see where you're going with your hair hanging down over your eyes that way."

Papa looked down at Alfie whose eyes were already beginning to close. "It might cover his eyes but he never misses nothin' that moves and very little that sets still. I reckon he can see right through it like a Airedale."

Alfie frowned at these remarks but he was too sleepy to protest. He was soon sleeping and Mama went back to worrying about Babe and his motherless offspring. "I just hope Babe got my letter telling him we were coming. I mailed it on Tuesday and this is Sunday. If the mail didn't run before he got off to town yesterday he wouldn't have it in time to shop for what he needs. You know how he is about wanting to put a big dinner on the table for company."

"From the looks of 'im I know how he is about puttin' a big dinner on the table whenever the table is set." Papa knew he had put his foot in his mouth with this statement but the temptation was too great for him. "I reckon if Babe has ever set down to a empty table it wasn't no dinner table."

"It runs in the family," Mama said defensively. "Being stout. All the men in my family work hard in the fields and they have to eat hearty."

Papa had some more thoughts on the men in Mama's family, and why they were all stout, but they had arrived. Babe's house loomed straight ahead. They wheeled into the yard and faced Babe's rambling weatherboard farm house with a porch around two sides of it, and Papa did not want to be in the midst of an argument with Mama when they alighted from the Dodge. Certainly not in an argument which he could see he was foreordained to lose. So he stowed the rest of his thoughts in the back of his mind and brought the Dodge to a halt in the shade of a big oak tree not far from the porch which ran along the East side of the house. Babe was sitting on the porch waiting for his sister, and Papa, and any of the younguns that they might have brought with them.

Uncle Babe's beefy red face broke into broad smiles when Mama and Papa and Alfie arrived. He heaved himself from his chair and moved toward the porch steps, hitching up his khaki trousers and pulling at the suspenders as he walked. When he had it all in place he let the suspenders fly back and they smacked against his shirt. As a small concession to comfort, he had left the top button on his trousers standing open. A large V was formed at that point where the top of his trousers met his rather impressive belly and it was obvious that the belly would win out over the trousers in any contest.

Walking in quick, short steps towards his arriving guests, he stopped and stood at the top of the steps to greet them. In his movement he had given the impression of being pushed forward by his short thick legs, and now that he had come to a halt it seemed that he might become overbalanced and tilt forward and be pulled downward by the weight of his belly, but he balanced himself at the top of the steps, smiling broadly and holding out both hands to receive Mama and Papa at the same time. Then he hugged Mama and patted her on the back and he shook Papa's hand, wringing it as if he were trying to twist it off his arm. Papa locked his elbow to keep that from happening.

Alfie was hanging back and rubbing the sleep from his eyes. Mama turned quickly to him and said in an undertone "Now you go up and hug your Uncle Babe's neck, you hear?" Uncle Babe's booming voice and Papa's hearty response drowned out what Mama was saying but Alfie realized what was expected of him anyway and he frowned, drew back and hid behind Mama's skirts. He looked down at the ground and mumbled some indistinct word of opposition to Mama's instruction that he show Uncle Babe how glad he was to be there.

"What did you say?" Mama pulled Alfie around in front of her and pushed him toward Uncle Babe, but Alfie clung stubbornly to her skirts. "Here, wipe your nose," Mama said, doing it for him with a handkerchief which she had obtained by unclasping her big pocketbook, digging briefly and then snapping it together again. To cover for Alfie's lack of enthusiasm, Mama returned to embrace her brother again, and this time, having discharged his responsibilities to Papa, Babe concentrated on Mama and crushed her in a bear hug. Mama was big enough though that Babe's short arms soon lost their purchase on her and he looked about for someone smaller to hug. His eyes fell upon Alfie.

"Here Boy come over here an' give your ol' Uncle Babe a big hug!" Alfie hung back and clung to Mama but Uncle Babe reached out and got hold of his arm and pulled Alfie to him. Then he noticed the long downy hairs growing on Alfie's plump little arms and he exclaimed "God A'mighty! This boy's got more hair on his arms than I've got on my head." He jerked playfully at the hairs and said "Sure sign he'll make a cracker jack hawg raiser when he grows up." He squinted up at Papa then and said ''Why don't you jest give this boy to me? I'll make a real farmer outta 'im. Ain't no sense in you keepin' 'im down there in a one-mule operation in Colaparchee County." Alfie pulled back from Uncle Babe who had now turned his attention to Papa because he wanted to see what effect his words would have on Papa. Papa's response was to haul out his little sack of Bull Durham and start the operation of preparing to smoke.Mutt and Aggie appeared at this time and attention shifted to them so it was not necessary for Papa to defend his one-mule operation in Colaparchee County.

Mutt was older and bigger than Alfie, and Aggie was older and bigger than Mutt. They both exuded health and happiness. Their tanned, smiling faces betrayed none of the pitiable aspects conjured up by Mama's description of them as poor motherless waifs. It was evident that Gran' ma had been doing a good job of compensating for Babe's shortcomings in that area. If they were being brought up by the hair of their heads, they had plenty of it to provide a hand hold, and it was still growing. Mutt's forelock needed pushing back as much as Alfie's did and he did this from time to time with a wide sweeping motion of his hand.

Aggie had tried, but with little success, to put curls into her heavy brown locks, and now as she ran to hug Mama she swung her head and sent her hair flying over her right shoulder. It didn't stay there, so she flung it again. "My, how you two have grown!" Mama exclaimed. "And you've both got the family build." This assurance of their genetic integrity caused a momentary clouding of Aggie's face, but it pleased Mutt.

Mutt was so pleased to learn that he looked like the family that he did handsprings on the ground. This unnerved Mama. She was inclined to frown on "showing off" on the part of youngsters, but she had not finished with her appraisal and she said "I do believe you're going to be a big man like your Daddy. And strong too." This caused Mutt to feel the necessity to show Alfie just how big and strong he was.

"Come on Alfie," Mutt said, seeing that Alfie was so little that he might,never grow up to take his place among the giants of the family. "I'll show you the airplane I built." The model airplane had been whittled from a block of wood. The wings were attached with glue. And the propeller was fastened with a small nail so that it would whirl when Mutt ran with it into the wind. Mutt demonstrated this by running into the wind with the airplane held aloft in his hand while his lips made a sound which approximated that of an airplane becoming airborne.

"I could make it fly by itself if I wanted to" And when Alfie stood openmouthed and waiting for Mutt to perform this feat, Mutt disappointed him. "But I ain't figgered out yet how to make it land once it gits goin' good and I'm skeered it will fly all the way to China, and I don't wanta lose it." Alfie had no idea how far China was but he was sure that it must be too far to go to recover the runaway airplane and he didn't blame Mutt for not wanting to risk the loss of such a valuable aircraft.

Alfie was so impressed by Mutt's airplane that he said "When I go back home I'll ask Willie to build me one. I bet Willie can build a airplane that will fly." He was about to add that he would bet that Willie could even figure out how to make it land where he wanted it to instead of letting it fly all the way to China, but Mutt didn't show any enthusiasm for the idea of Willie building a better airplane than he had built.

"Come on," Mutt said. "I'll show you the battlefield." The battlefield looked just like a corn field to Alfie, and it might have done so to any casual observer, but Mutt explained. "We had a big dove shoot here last week and it sounded like a young war."

The ground was littered with empty shell casings because Uncle Babe had invited his friends and neighbors over for the dove shoot after the birds had congregated in large numbers. The doves had been enticed by the generous outpouring of chicken feed in carefully chosen spots over the field. Alfie picked up some of the empty shell casings and started to put them in his pocket but Mutt said "You better be keerful and not put one in that's still loaded. It might blow your leg off."

Since Alfie mistrusted his own ability to tell which ones were still loaded and which ones were empty, he dropped them all back on the ground of the battlefield. He was even more impressed with Mutt's ability to produce and survive a young war than he was with his building the airplane.

But because Mutt said "Come on and I'll show you the mule barn and the hog pens," Alfie had to leave the battlefield/corn field and table the question of building planes until he got home and could discuss it with Willie. Alfie agreed to go, but he didn't actually get to see the mules, just the mule barn. The mules had been turned loose to graze in the pasture because it was Sunday. So Alfie had to settle for looking at the empty stalls, and he had to take Mutt's word for it that there was a mule for each stall, of which there were many. They stood in an endless row along each side of the mule barn. Alfie tried to count them but he lost count before he got half way down the other side of the barn.

Mutt explained his Pa's humanitarianism in letting the mules go to the pasture on Sunday, and showed that Uncle Babe's kindness extended to people. "The mules and the niggers both git Sunday off from work," Mutt said. But he pointed out the risk that one runs in being so lenient. "But you got to break 'em both in again on Monday mornin' 'cause a mule an' a nigger both'll fergit ever'thing he knows from Saturday noon 'till sunup on Monday." Although probably secondhand, this wisdom of mules and people of color made Alfie aware of the hard lot of a farmer big enough to own and work so many mules and people of color.

Alfie was on the point of deciding that Uncle Babe must be the biggest and richest Farmer in the state of Georgia although he was not sure how big the state of Georgia was. He was certain though from what Papa had said that it was bigger even than Colaparchee County. Mutt hadn't said, but Alfie thought that even Uncle Babe's farm was in the state of Georgia. He was going to ask but before he could get the question out of his mouth, Mutt was showing him the hogs in the fattening pens.

The hogs were so impressive that Alfie couldn't think about them and the mules at the same time. The hogs were already so big and fat they had difficulty getting up from the muddy, smelly "wallow" where they were reclining when Mutt and Alfie came to look at them. But when Mutt poked them with a long stick which seemed to be kept close by for that purpose,and said "Sooee!" at them, they grunted and raised themselves up and waddled over to the trough to eat some more corn. But they didn't act hungry the way Papa's pigs at home did when he threw a few ears of corn to them.

There was barely enough room for these hogs to walk more than six or eight steps~in any direction, so walking was not as important to Uncle Babe's purpose in penning them up as eating was. The trough was full of corn. Mutt explained that the idea was to get them as fat and heavy as possible before cold weather. "Soon as it gits cold anuff we'll have a hawg killin'" Mutt said. "Last winter we killed one that weighed over six hunderd pounds." He didn't attempt the mathematical task of figuring out how much sausage, hams and lard this turned out, but it was "a heap" and even Alfie could see that the lard volume must have been impressive. He was thinking about this when Uncle Babe called.

"Dinner's ready!" Uncle Babe called in a voice that could be heard distinctly above the grunting of the hogs who were being fattened for the kill. "Mutt! You boys come on heah an' wash up an' git ready to eat."

When they got to the house the first person Alfie saw was Gran'ma. She had been "seein' to the dinner" when Mama and Papa and Alfie arrived, and before she could make her way out to the porch to greet them, Alfie was off to see the wonderful world of Mutt. Now Gran'ma threw her arms about Alfie, hugging and kissing him. "Lord God Chile. How my Baby has growed! A body wouldn't know you, you've growed so!" But Gran'ma did know him in spite of his growth.

Alfie didn't mind Gran'ma hugging and kissing him. In fact, it felt good, but he wished she wouldn't call him her baby in front of Mutt who was standing there, grinning. Still, Gran' ma did make the best teacakes in the world, and for that it was all right to be called her baby. "Gran'ma," Alfie said, thinking of teacakes and muffins, "You're goin' home with us ain't you?"

"Lord God Chile, I aim to!" Gran 'ma started hugging Alfie again, and looking back over her shoulder to see if Aggie was doing all right with the dinner things, she said "I reckon these younguns here can do without me for a while." She noted with satisfaction that Aunt Hetty, the black woman Uncle Babe had hired to help with the dinner, was lifting the biscuits out of the oven, and she added "I reckon I've learned Aggie about all she needs to know about cookin'. Leastwise she can practice up on Babe an' Mutt 'till she ketches her a man of her own."

"Aw Gran'ma," Aggie protested. "You know I'm not interested in gettin' married yet."

"I know you ain't interested in nuthin' else," Gran'ma said, working her toothless gums to better position the Brewton's snuff on the back of her tongue. "But I reckon Mutt can do little light jobs like bringin' in stovewood and he'p out thataway an' they'll git along somehow."

Mutt had been at least five feet tall when he was flying his airplane to China and he had even grown some while fighting a young war in the cornfield, but he shrank several inches when Gran' ma said what she did about him being able to do little light jobs like bringing in stovewood. Alfie's appetite improved at the sight of Gran' ma and he was able to put the hogs in the fattening pen out of his mind when he saw what a good job Gran' ma had done teaching Aggie how to cook. Papa bragged on Aggie and said he hadn't eaten anything so good since he left home that morning.

Aggie blushed and said "Aunt Het ought to get all the credit. If it wasn't for her ev'rything would be a mess."

Aunt Het smiled broadly, wiped her face with her apron, and said "Miss Aggie, she jes' talkin'." But it was obvious she liked to hear that kind of talk. "Heah's mo' biskits right outta the oven," Aunt Het said. "Doan y'all want mo' biskits?"

Papa said "I'll take one, Aunt Het," and he opened it and laid a slab of butter inside it and went on bragging on Aggie. "You're gittin' pretty enough the boys will be hangin' around here like flies on the syrup pitcher, and Babe'll lose his cook before he knows what's goin' on."

Mama thought she ought to put a stop to that sort of talk because it might go to Aggie's head so she said "Pretty is as pretty does." If Mama had known about all the things Mutt had told Alfie,she would have warned him of the twin evils of boasting about what you have and lying about what you don't have. But Mutt was safe for the moment. Mama hadn't yet heard what Mutt had told Alfie. Besides, Uncle Babe had decided that Alfie wasn't doing justice to the feast that had been prepared in his honor, and he thought this called for some encouragement on his part.

"Eat Boy!" Uncle Babe admonished Alfie. "You ain't never gonna grow up and amount to nuthin' if you don't eat." Alfie had been warned earlier by Mama not to take seconds until everybody else had. Uncle Babe was holding out a drumstick to him and saying "Eat Boy!" And Gran' ma hadn't yet got half way through her first and wasn't anywhere near her second. It was hard for Gran' ma to eat chicken without any teeth.

Uncle Babe turned to Mama and said "You ain't feedin' that boy anuff at home, an' that's why he ain't no bigger'n he is now. Then when he goes someplace where they've got food he don't know how to eat. You jest leave 'im here with me and I'll fatten him up so you won't know 'im."

Alfie had a mental image of himself standing in the fattening pen like the hogs Mutt had shown him. He wondered if Uncle Babe would make him eat so much he would weigh more than six hundred pounds. Mutt smirked at him and he felt tears springing behind his eyeballs and stinging them. Aggie saw both Alfie's discomfort and Mutt's pleasure. She rapped Mutt on the head sharply with her tea spoon. "That'll do outta you Mutt!" she warned. "I know you've been tellin' Alfie a pack of lies, and you've prob'ly got him too scared to eat." She rapped Mutt again for good measure because he laughed the first time. Aggie looked at Mama for some sign of approval of her disciplinary measures, and Mutt ducked his head. The rapping hurt, but he laughed uncontrollably in an attempt to hide the fact that he felt the pain.

Mama pursed her lips and looked disapprovingly at Mutt. "Lying's a sin," Mama said, assuming that Aggie was close enough to Mutt to know what he'd been doing. A warning wouldn't hurt even if Aggie was wrong about Mutt's disregard for the truth. It might serve as a preventive measure in case he was tempted to play fast and loose with the truth in the future. "You'll never get to heaven telling lies," Mama added as a special incentive.

Uncle Babe was still holding out the drumstick to Alfie, and when Mama had finished lecturing Mutt about lying, Uncle Babe said "Eat this, Boy. I don't want nobody gittin' up from my table hungry." Mama gave Alfie the nod and he took the drumstick. Gran'ma still hadn't finished her first.

When dinner was over the table did not look nearly as attractive as it did at the beginning. Dinner plates with scraps of food and chicken bones on them do not provide the sort of setting for conversation that Uncle Babe deemed desirable. He said "Let's all go set a spell in the shade an' cool off while our dinner settles." And he pushed his chair back from the table as a signal that he was leading the way.

Mama said that she would stay and help Aggie with the dishes, but Babe said "She don't need you to he'p. She's got ol' Aunt Hetty to he'p her in the kitchen. You come all this way to visit. Now set down an' rest before you hafta start out ag'in."

Mama said that she didn't feel right about leaving Aggie in the kitchen because she hardly ever got to talk with her anyway. What Mama was hoping for was a chance to talk with Aggie, because of what had been said at dinner about her drawing boys like flies to the syrup pitcher. But Babe was aggravated by Mama's intransigence when he had made a good suggestion, and he said "Then let ol' Aunt Het do it all an' Ag can come an' set with us. Aggie don't hafta stay in the kitchen. Let Het do it all. Tha's what a nigger's for."

Aggie was embarrassed for Aunt Hettie's sake and Mama made motions at Babe in an attempt to shush him up, but Babe was only antagonized by this and he said "Tha's what I'm payin' 'er for. God knows she totes off anuff vittles inside that baggy dress she's wearin' to feed her whole crowd fer a week. Come on an' set down. You didn't come all the way up here jest to tell me what to do with my niggers, I hope."

Mama pursed her lips and became silent, which meant that she was very put out with Babe, but she realized that to say any more would only make matters worse and result in more humiliation for Aunt Hetty. But she was even more concerned than ever about the way the children were being brought up because Babe was not setting the right example before them.

Gran'ma intervened at this point. "You go an' set with 'em Aggie." She pushed Aggie toward the door and took the bowl Aggie was holding in her hands. "I'll stay with Het. Me an' her can take keer of things in here an' I'll have the next six months to jaw with them." When Aggie was gone, she turned to Aunt Hetty and said "Now Het, you jest don't pay no mind to what Babe said. He has jest got to blow off steam because he's got somebody to hear 'im and he don't mean nuthin' by it."

Aunt Het said "Yas'm" and started rubbing a bar of Octagon soap in the hot dishwater to get some suds.

Mama accepted the truce, but in her own mind she was saying that while she thought the colored should stay in their place, Aunt Het had given no cause for Babe to abuse her that way, and even if he was her brother, the Lord would surely visit judgment upon him. Apparently, the Lord had something like that in mind, but He was going to let Babe bring it on himself, which Babe proceeded to do shortly after they had seated themselves comfortably.

Babe dragged two chairs off the porch and into the shade of the oak tree in the yard. He said to Mama "I got a cheer for you too." And looking at Papa he said "You can git you one and bring it." When he was settled under the oak tree where a slight breeze was moving the leaves overhead, he unfastened the second button on his khaki trousers, enlarging the V. He blew out a great sigh of relief and remarked that it had been a hot, dry summer. "But we're about done pickin' cotton and'll start pickin' corn as soon as the weather cools."

Papa was rolling a cigarette from his little hag of Bull Durham and licking the paper to make it stick, and he hadn't got around to making a response to Babe's comment on the weather and the progress of the harvest. Mama was starting to fan herself with a recent issue of the Market Bulletin which was a publication sent out by the Agriculture Department, free. She was still considering a reprimand couched in terms of Babe's responsibility to teach his children to show respect for their elders even if they are colored. Babe looked all about him and his eyes fell upon Alfie who was standing between him and Mama. He laid a heavy, freckled hand on Alfie's head and studied him critically. Alfie looked up into Uncle Babe's face and smiled weakly.

"Now Boy," Uncle Babe said to Alfie. "When your Mama an' Papa start to go home this evenin' you jest stay right here with me." Uncle Babe displayed what he considered a winning smile. "I'll make a real hawg raiser outta you, Boy."

To emphasize his point, Uncle Babe pinched Alfie's arm where the soft blond hairs shone prophetically in the sunlight filtering down through the leafy branches of the oak. "I don't wanta stay with you." Alfie's eyes were about on a level with Uncle Babe's because he was standing and Uncle Babe was sitting. "I'm goin' home with Mama an' Papa when they go." His arm was stinging where Uncle Babe had pinched and then twisted the hairs. He could feel tears springing in his eyes, and he looked down to conceal them from Uncle Babe.

Mutt was watching and enjoying Alfie's discomfort, and probably thinking of ways he could increase it if Alfie stayed but he knew his Pap well enough to suspect rather strongly that he was teasing and had no intention of taking on the responsibility of another little boy. So he just watched and grinned. Uncle Babe, who had been tilting his chair back onto two legs and balancing himself in this position, let the front legs of the chair down and leaned forward.

"You don't wanta stay with me?" He acted as though he had made an offer that nobody in his right mind could turn down and Alfie had turned it down. Alfie drew away and stood closer to Mama. Uncle Babe turned to Papa who by now had his handmade cigarette going well, and he said to him "Now what about that? You promised to give me that boy. Now are you gonna give 'im to me or not?"

Alfie turned to Mama, his eyes pleading. Mama smiled back at him, reassuring. Papa blew out a puff of smoke and said "What about it Son? You wanta be Uncle Babe's boy?"

Alfie looked first at Papa and then back at Mama, like a cornered cat. Then he whirled about and faced Papa, his voice choking in his throat. "No! I don't wanta be Uncle Babe's boy! I just wanta be your boy!" His body trembled with emotion.

Mama laid the Market Bulletin down. She turned her eyes darkly on Babe, but he avoided them. He looked at Papa and at Alfie. "You better jest give that boy to me an' be done with it." He was fumbling in his pocket for something but having difficulty reaching it. "I ain't got no little boy no more. Mutt's about growed up." Mutt gained several inches in stature at this. "Winter's comin' on an' I need a boy to sleep with me an' keep my feet warm at night."

Papa inhaled and let the smoke out through his nostrils. "Wouldn't you like to stay here with Uncle Babe and keep his feet warm at night? I reckon he could tell you stories the way I do."

"I don't want Uncle Babe to tell me stories. I just want you to tell me stories. I WANTA GO HOME!"

"Well, I see we ain't gittin' nowhere thisaway." Uncle Babe had found what he was fishing for in his pocket. He drew out a plug of Brown's Mule. Then, leaning and straining in the other direction, he drew out his pocketknife. He cut a plug and put it in his mouth, closed the knife and put it back into his pocket, leaning and straining again.

Mama's eyes were starting to spark fire. "That'll do now Babe," she warned. "That's enough."

Babe ignored Mama. He put the package of Brown's Mule into his shirt pocket, worked the plug in his mouth down with yellowed teeth, then he said to Alfie "I reckon I'll jest hafta ketch you an' tie you up with a plow line an' make you stay here with me."

Again Mama said warningly "Babe!" But Babe kept his eyes on Alfie, who was backing away from him. Alfie said defiantly "You can't ketch me 'cause you're too fat to run fast."

Uncle Babe's body jerked forward on the chair. His face grew redder and beefier than ever. "Too fat am I?" He lurched forward out of the chair, catapulting his heavy body toward Alfie who stood paralyzed by fear and surprise at Uncle Babe's mobility.

"I'll show you who's too fat to run." He kicked over the chair as he rose, stumbled in his first few steps, then righted himself and got both feet under him again. Alfie's paralysis melted away and he ran for his life. His short legs moved like pistons. But Uncle Babe moved even faster. Hurtling across the ground, he soon closed the gap between him and Alfie. Catching him up in a bear hug, Uncle Babe exulted "I gotcha!" Then blowing for breath, "Now...who's... too fat... to run?"

"Turn me loose!" Alfie screamed, striking out at Uncle Babe with tiny balled fists. "Lemme go! Lemme go I say!"

Uncle Babe's arms pinioned Alfie so that he could do nothing but scream and kick. But Uncle Babe was already in trouble beyond his own full awareness. For while he was trying to get hold of Alfie's kicking feet and to quiet his screaming, he was puffing and blowing as if he were on the verge of apoplexy. Then he felt a very firm hand take hold upon his collar and he twisted his beet red face about, and he was staring into Mama's blazing eyes.

"That's enough Babe!" Mama's face was so close that all Babe could see was her eyes. "Put the child down and leave him alone!" Babe released Alfie who twisted violently away and ran off a short distance, then stopped to watch the contest between Mama and Uncle Babe. It was going against Uncle Babe. His eyes were bulging and his breath was coming stertorously. He opened his mouth to say something but no sound came forth. Mama said "That's enough of this foolishness now. You'll have a heart attack!"

But Mama's concern for Babe was short lived. "You've scared the child nearly to death." She turned away from Babe and approached Alfie, saying "Come here." Alfie ran to Mama and she took him in her arms and said “Now you know your Mama and Papa wouldn’t leave you here. Stop crying now and be a big boy so Uncle Babe will know you’re not afraid.”

Alfie’s screams had brought Gran’ ma on the run from the kitchen. “Lord God Het!” she said, laying aside the dish that was in her hands. “Somethin’s happenin’ to the Baby!” She rushed out onto the porch to see Alfie struggling in Uncle Babe’s arms. “Babe!” she yelled in a high pitched voice. “You turn my Baby aloose! You hear me?” Babe hadn’t heard. Or if he had, he gave no evidence of it, and Gran’ma started down the steps, putting one foot down and then the other onto the same step and holding her arms out to balance herself. “Lord God!” she said “What’s he doin’’ to my Baby?”

Before Gran’ ma could reach the struggling pair, her Baby was safe in his Mama’s arms and Babe was heaving and coughing, and his eyes were bulging, and his cheeks swelling and he was first red and then white in the face. Mama looked at him and said “Lord have mercy! You’re having a heart attack!”

But Uncle Babe wheezed and heaved until he finally got his breath and he said “I’m awright. I jest swallered my chew of ‘backy is all.” Then he wheezed and coughed some more, and it seemed that he really would be all right, but at the sound of his voice Alfie’s fears were renewed.

“I wanta go home!” Alfie wailed. “I wanta go home. Now!”

Papa moved restlessly on his chair. He got up and began moving about. He said “I guess we better git started. It’ll be sundown here before we know it and I don’t wanta be out on the road after dark.” He turned to Alfie and said. “You run and he’p your Gran’ma git her things together.” Alfie turned and seeing Gran’ma so close, he got her skirts in one hand and held onto Mama’s with the other.

Uncle Babe was breathing a bit more regularly now, and he wiped his forehead with a sweat rag that he had drawn from his hip pocket. He looked at Papa and said “You better jes’ spend the night with us.”

Papa knew that this impractical suggestion was only a concession to society’s convention of politeness, and he said

“Thank you but we better hit the road. The ol’ cows hafta be milked on Sundays same as weekdays.”

Uncle Babe was feeling a little better about everything. Even in his distress he had issued the invitation to stay. And fortunately it had been declined. He turned back to Alfie who was clinging to both Mama and Gran’ma. “Ain’t you gonna hug your ol’ Uncle Babe’s neck before you go?” He gave Alfie a gap toothed smile, but it was a bit pale around the edges because of the chew of ‘backy that he had swallowed.

“No I ain’t!” Alfie clung even more tightly to Mama’s skirt and to Gran’ma’s. “I wanta go home! I wanta go home! Now!!”

Chapter Ten: The Tramp

He came early in the day, for folks stir with morning light on the farm where men must wrest their living from the stiff red Georgia clay. The slanting rays of the rising sun fell across the doorsteps leading up to the back porch and to the kitchen door. The shadow of the well bucket, and of the chain and pulley suspended from the crosspiece at the top of the well housing, formed a dark pattern on the brightly sunlit floor. The dark pattern lay against the kitchen wall, moving slightly as the empty bucket swayed in the breeze. He was there on the steps, waiting, tapping. Sandy was barking.

He could not have walked far that early in the morning. Not on that peg leg. He must have slept in a nearby farmer's barn. Wisps of straw clung to his faded blue overalls.

Cracklings from last night's sleep were in the corners of his rheumy blue eyes. He had come unwashed to tap insistently at the doorstep where the early morning sunbeams fell with growing intensity, and where the shadows danced more lively as the breeze became stronger.

It was the year nineteen hundred and twenty eight. It was in late winter, or early spring of that year. March. Just past sunup. That was when Gran'ma heard the tapping, and Sandy barked. And Gran'ma said "Land sakes! Who could it be this early in the day?"

For it was the tapping that first caught Gran'ma's attention. And before Sandy barked. In the brief interval between the tapping and the barking, she thought there might be a loose weather board flapping in the breeze. Then Sandy barked. A sort of announcement that someone was there. And it blended in with the tapping so that Gran'ma could not make out the sound distinctly. "Run and see what all the racket is about, Baby. See who's there."

He ran, for curiosity is to the feet of a small boy what spurs are to the feet of a horse. A small boy less than six years old has a curiosity bigger than the body it resides in. "It's a tramp, Gran'ma!" Alfie called back. Then running back to Gran'ma, he whispered "It's a tramp, Gran'ma. I reckon he's hungry. He said he wants somethin' to eat." Alfie was not afraid yet. But he just might become afraid if Gran'ma's face sent him the message. Gran'ma's face was reflective but unmoved. Alfie waited, searching her face.

Nobody was at home but Gran'ma and Alfie when the tramp came. Margaret and all the older boys had gone to catch the school bus at the end of the driveway in front of Mister Charles and Miss Maggie's house. Papa and Mama had gone to town because Papa had some early peas to sell and Mama said the daffodils wouldn't keep until Saturday, so she had to take them to the doctors' offices while they were still fresh looking and their faces would make people smile when they looked at them. So it was just Gran'ma and her Baby whom she had come to believe she had rescued from his Uncle Babe's unwelcome embrace. They heard the tapping and then Sandy's barking.

"A tramp, eh!" Gran'ma was standing beside the big wood burning cook stove in the kitchen. She had just finished wiping its surface with a wet dishcloth and the steam still rose from the top of the stove. She blinked her eyes in the bright sunlight that flooded the kitchen through the open door. In his rush to deliver the news Alfie had left it standing wide open and now the sound of Sandy's barking was more distinct, but it was not threatening. "Here we are, the two of us and with a hungry tramp on our hands. Well!" Gran'ma reflected on her situation and decided that she could handle a hungry tramp. Even if she was alone with just the Baby to do the running for her.

"Well," she said again. "I ain't never turned a hungry man away from my door. Still..." For there was a question in her mind. She went and stood in the open doorway, peering sharply out at the man on the doorsteps. She was forced to blink in the bright sunlight. The tramp looked back at Gran'ma. "So that's what you was a knockin' with," she said. She motioned with the slightest dip of her head at the point where he was standing. He had a peg leg fastened with a cracked leather strap. "What's yore name?" Gran'ma asked.

"Ben Hawkins." He removed a battered greasy black hat, revealing wispy, graying hair. Not enough to cover his scalp which was lighter in color than his furrowed forehead and his sunken cheeks. A week old stubble of salt and pepper beard covered his chin and softened the sunken planes of his face. "Folks call me Peg Leg Ben, on accounta' this here."

He pointed to the rough wooden peg and the brittle leather strap about his knee. When he spoke his lips curled back and revealed yellowed and widely separated teeth. "Peg Leg Ben is what they call me." He gazed now at the wooden leg as if it were a badge, or an explanation.

"Well Ben Hawkins." Gran'ma ignored the reference to the peg leg. "The boy here says you're hungry." She waited and Peg Leg Ben dipped his head in acquiescence of Alfie's report. "Where're you from, Ben Hawkins?"

"I'm from down near the county line," Ben said evasively. Then seeing that Gran'ma was not satisfied, "Over past the Midway Church...And the boy here's right about me bein' hungry. I ain't et lately. Not a square meal nohow. If you could feed me..." Ben's words trailed off. He made a movement to sit down on the doorstep, and in doing so called attention to his crippled condition.

"If you can give me some breakfast," Peg Leg Ben said when he had achieved a sitting position, "When I start to leave here I'll tell ye a thing'll be of use to ye as long as you live." He shifted to make his stump more comfortable. "It might even save your life someday."

Alfie's curiosity was whetted by Ben's words but Gran'ma ignored the cryptic promise. She was thinking of real needs more easily defined. She wiped her hands on the dish cloth she had twisted about them while assessing the situation which Ben Hawkins' arrival had placed her in.

"I have just now cleaned up the breakfast table and there ain't a crumb left." She was talking to herself as much as to Ben Hawkins for this was her way of reaching a decision. "Fire's about out in the stove too, and there ain't enough stovewood to cook nothin' with." She turned now to Ben Hawkins. "Tell you what, Ben Hawkins. You go out there to the woodpile and chop me a turn of stovewood. The boy here'll he'p you bring it in. But you chop me a turn of stovewood and I'll fix you some breakfast."

Peg Leg Ben struggled to a standing position and appeared to be about to topple over. "A feller can't do much on one leg." He seemed to be about to slump back onto the doorstep.

"I ain't never seen a man swing a axe with his leg." Gran'ma said caustically. "Course now, you mightn't be as hungry as the boy here let on you was." Gran' ma made a motion toward the kitchen door. It was a motion of dismissal. "No choppin' no eatin' here." She was going back into the house, leaving him on the doorstep.

Peg Leg Ben straightened himself up and seemed to be fairly steady. "I reckon I can chop a little stovewood though," he said. "Even if I am crippled." He hobbled off toward the woodpile.

Gran'ma put a thin, wrinkled hand on Alfie's head. She stood watching Ben Hawkins hobbling toward the woodpile. "You'll find the axe stuck in the choppin' block," she called after him. "You send me the first few sticks by the boy."

She stood watching until Ben took hold of the axe handle and wrenched the blade out of the chopping block. Then she pressed Alfie's head with her hand and said "Now you run to the hen house an' see if you can find me two eggs. It's after sunup and the ol' hens oughtta be on the job by now if they're gonna do anything." Alfie dashed away toward the hen house and Gran' ma called after him. "You be keerful now an' don't break 'em. You hear?"

She turned back to the kitchen and engaged herself in conversation. "I'll poke up the fire in the stove first and see what's in the pantry." Gran'ma knew very well what was in the pantry. She considered a foot long sausage in its transparent casing, then laid it aside, picked up a slab of fatback. "If he ain't et in a while, fatback'll taste all right to him." She put two slices of the fatback in the skillet and began mixing corn meal with buttermilk. "Biscuits take too long," she told herself. "Buttermilk hoecakes will be good enough."

The sounds of Ben Hawkins' chopping came steadily from the woodpile. Each time he swung the axe he expelled a great huff of breath. "Hahh!" As though that might drive the axe deeper into the wood. In reality, it was to advertise the fact of his exertions. Swing. Strike. “Hahh!”

Alfie had delivered two very fresh eggs to Gran’ma. “That ol’ dominecker hen tried to peck me but I grabbed the egg out from under ‘er anyway” he reported proudly. “There’ll prob’ly be another one soon. You want me to go back and look Gran’ma? When she cackles, that’ll mean she’s laid.”

“Never mind that. Two eggs is enough. That’s all your Papa gits for his breakfast. It’s surely enough for a tramp. Now you run an’ fetch the stovewood when ol’ Ben cuts it. But mind you, don’t git in the way of the axe.”

Alfie crouched at a safe distance from Ben Hawkins, and watched him splitting stove wood. “Mister Peg...er Mister Ben. How come you ain’t got a house an’ somebody to cook your breakfast for you? Ain’t you got a Mama to cook for you?”

“Ain’t got nobody!” Ben Hawkins said, swinging the axe on a tough and springy piece of pine. “Hahh!” Instead of splitting open, the pine caught the blade and held it fast. Ben struck it twice against the chopping block before he could dislodge it. “Ol Peg Leg Ben ain’t got nobody!”

“But how come, Mister Ben?”

“Old Lady left me when I lost the farm. Hahh!” Ben brought the axe down hard in an expression of lingering anger at his old lady who had left him down on his luck.

“But don’t you have a house to live in?” Alfie squatted and set his palms against his cheeks.

“Not no more. Useta’ have a house. Hahh! Farm. Mules. Hahh! Not no more. The bank took it all away from me.”

Alfie’s face grew very grave as he considered this new revelation of evil. “But how come, Mister Ben? Why did the bank take your house an’ ev’rything away from you?”

“Bank took it all, Boy. House. Land. The whole shebang.” Ben lifted another piece of wood onto the chopping block. He swung the axe, then used the maul to drive the axe head clean through. “Hahh!” Then, “Took it all,” he repeated in a tone of utter defeat.

“But how come? Are banks bad, Mister Ben?” For Mama had told him the bank was a safe place to keep his money. He had accumulated a fifty cent piece, two quarters, a dime, two nickels, one of them a buffalo nickel, and a whole lot of pennies. One of the pennies was an Indian Head. He liked to take the coins out of the little tin can that he kept them in and play with them. If he put them in the bank he would not be able to do that. And now he was confused. Would the bank take his money and then come and get the house? His eyes searched Ben's face. "Are banks bad?"

"Banks'll take ev'rything you've got if you borry money from them, an' then hard times come an' you can't pay it all back." Ben began to push the sticks of stovewood together in a little pile with his peg...Here now, you he'p me git all this stovewood together. Grab up a armload of it an' le's go. I'm gittin' hungry from all this choppin' an' your Gran'ma's likely gittin' fidgety from waitin'."

Ben clomped up the steps and across the porch and into the kitchen, followed closely by Alfie. They dumped the stovewood into the woodbox behind the stove. Ben straightened up, dragging the peg leg across the linoleum floor of the kitchen.

Gran'ma had the fatback frying in one skillet and the cornbread browning in another, for there was enough stovewood to resurrect the fire. No need to inform Ben Hawkins of that though. "It won't be long now," Gran'ma said. "You go an' wash up and I'll call you when it's ready." Ben Hawkins looked at her questioningly and she said "You'll find a bar of soap on the shelf there beside the wash pan."

When he had gone, she resumed the conversation with herself. "And the Lord knows he'll need the soap and the water both. Never saw such a dirty neck in my born days." Alfie dashed away lest Gran 'ma decide that his neck needed washing too. On the porch he found Ben Hawkins splashing the cold water over his face, snorting as he did so, and rubbing soap on his hands and forearms. He threw out the dirty, soapy water onto the ground and a Rhode Island Red hen squawked and dodged to avoid a wetting. Ben looked around for fresh water to rinse his face, but the well bucket was empty, and he settled for wiping his face, hands and arms on a flour sack towel he found hanging on a nail driven into the wall of the porch. The towel became streaked with the dirt that Ben's efforts in the wash pan had loosened but had not removed.

"But how come you become a tramp, Mister Ben?" Alfie resumed the questioning as if there had been no interruption in order to deliver the stovewood to the woodbox behind the big iron cookstove. "Wouldn't nobody let you stay in their house?" Alfie looked expectantly into Ben Hawkins' face. "After the bank took your house away from you?"

Ben wiped his face vigorously with the flour sack towel. More dirt came off on the towel, but he didn't disturb the dirt on his neck. "Well, I ain't exackly a tramp." This was said defensively. He pointed to his peg leg. "You see, after I lost my leg, it warn 't easy to make a livin' on the farm. Then the boll weevil come, an' dry weather an' hard times." He examined his face in the mirror Papa had hung on the wall and seemed satisfied with his reflection. He turned back to Alfie. "Don't never borry no money, Boy," he warned. "Don't never borry no money."

Alfie looked steadily into Ben's face and nodded his consent not to "borry no money." Then he asked "Mister Ben, what happened to your leg? Did the bank chop off your leg?" He waited open-mouthed for Ben's reply.

Ben Hawkins laughed. It was the first time he had laughed that way in a long time, and it made him feel good. But Alfie did not know what to think about Ben Hawkins laughing. He wondered if he had done something wrong by asking him about his leg and if Ben was laughing at him for it.

Alfie had heard Papa say that if he got money from the bank to make a crop it would cost him an arm and a leg, but Alfie noticed that Ben was not missing an arm. Only a leg. But now he was afraid to ask more about it.

"No, Boy," Ben said, laughing again. Then he became serious. More serious than he had been even when he said what he did about the bank taking away everything he had.

He tapped the floor with the peg. "No, Boy. I lost that in the war." Now Alfie's eyes grew larger and rounder until they completely dominated his face. "France!" Ben added. "That's where it was. One of them Germans come at me with a bay'net.

Cut me down with it." Now Alfie's face registered new depths of concern for Peg Leg Ben. Also an anger at the German, anger equal at least to the anger he felt toward the bank.

"I fit 'im though," Ben said. "I fit back with all I had. Give 'im a good poke with my own bay'net. Wouldha' shot 'im if I hadn't run outta bullets." Ben moved the peg leg a few inches, scraping it across the porch floor boards, rasping. He reflected sadly, gazing at the peg leg and fingering the cracked leather strap about his knee. "Yep, that war cost me my leg, Boy. Cost me my leg."

Gran'ma pushed open the kitchen screen door and looked piercingly at Ben Hawkins' freshly washed face. "It's ready," she announced. "You want to eat it while it's hot you better stop the palaverin' an' come an' git it." She stood aside to let Ben Hawkins pass. He stumped into the kitchen and sat down at the oil cloth covered table where Gran'ma had set the food, a plate, a knife, a fork and a spoon.

He was surprisingly nimble about getting up to the table. And for the next ten minutes he ate without speaking a word. He applied himself with concentration to Gran'ma's hoecakes, fried fatback and scrambled eggs. From a brown and white stoneware jar, Gran'ma poured a large drinking glass full of buttermilk. Ben Hawkins drained the glass.

He was wiping the plate with the corn bread, and he nodded his head toward the coffee pot on the back of the stove. He had glanced toward the coffee pot several times. Now he spoke. "A cuppa coffee would go mighty good to stop off on."

"I reckon it would if there was any," Gran'ma said. "But there ain't none." She refilled his drinking glass with buttermilk from the stone jar. "We have got cows but we ain't got no coffee tree."

Ben Hawkins washed down the last crumbs of cornbread with the buttermilk. He pushed his chair back from the table and placing his hands on the table, pushed himself to his feet, or to his foot and peg. "I'm much obliged to ye," Ben Hawkins said to Gran' ma. Then he looked again at Alfie, whose eyes had never left Ben's face. He was now a man full of good food. He was even washed, after a fashion. He turned again to Gran'ma and repeated “Thank ye. And now I aim to repay ye, like I promised to do, by tellin’ ye somethin’ that’ll be a benefit to ye as long as ye live.” Gran’ ma squinted her eyes and held Ben’s gaze. “Might even save your life one day.”

Alfie’s expectancy rose but Gran’ma only said “What’s that, Ben Hawkins? I reckon it must be somethin’ powerful good, seein’ you carry it around with you like a rabbit’s foot.”

“It’s advice,” Ben Hawkins said. “Always cut from yourself an’ you’ll never cut yourself.” Now he laughed again, and this time he rocked back and forth on the peg leg. Then his face became sober again. “That could save your life some day.”

Gran’ma’s expression did not change, and Alfie stared wonderingly, not knowing how to react to this revelation of wisdom. Then Gran’ma laughed a little cackle and said “Now git on with you, Ben Hawkins. You tell that to the next un that cuts you a slab of fatback. Tell ‘er before she cuts it too.”

Peg Leg Ben hobbled down the steps. Sandy sniffed his wooden leg and barked at him once as he went out through the gate. Gran’ma and Alfie stood in the doorway. Her wrinkled hand was on the boy’s head. They watched Ben enter the driveway and walk along under the branches of the pecan trees, their buds just beginning to swell. When he reached the big road he turned right and after a while he disappeared where the road dipped below the rise. For a short time they could see his head with the greasy black hat bobbing up above the bank but then it was gone altogether.

Gran’ma wiped the mist from her eyes with a corner of her apron, and she said, as though holding a conversation with herself, but possibly it was for Alfie’s moral instruction. “Ain’t never turned a hungry man from the door. Black nor white. Ain’t right to do it.” She closed the screen door and returned to the kitchen where she busied herself with cleaning up the mess from Ben Hawkins’ breakfast. She glanced in the woodbox behind the stove and cleared her throat approvingly.

“Gran’ma.” Alfie looked up into her wrinkled face. “Peg.. er Mister Ben said for me not to borry no money. Never.” He stood waiting for Gran’ma’s response. It came quickly.

"Lord God Chile!" Gran' ma cackled. "Ol' Ben give you better advice for nothin' than he give me in pay for his breakfast!" She cackled again gleefully. "Lord God!"

Mama and Papa came home from town before the school bus arrived to deposit Margaret, Willie, Cliff and Junior. Alfie was glad because he was eager to tell the story of Peg Leg Ben to Papa. Mama was busy in the kitchen, getting something ready for the others so eat, but she heard what Alfie told. "I declare," she said to Papa. "I don't think it's good for Alfie to be listening to Old Ben's stories. That about the German. He can think up enough on his own without Old Ben putting ideas like that in his head."

"I don't reckon Ben's stories' ll hurt nobody." Papa started to pour tobacco from his little bag of Bull Durham into a cigarette paper which he held between the fingers of his left hand. "Cept maybe ol' Ben hisself."

Mama turned to watch Papa and warn him not to spill tobacco on the floor. She disapproved of Papa's smoking but her protests were to no avail. "Why?" Mama said. "What on earth do you mean?" She was irritated because Papa had spilled some tobacco on the floor.

"Well, don't the Bible say there'll be no liars in heaven?" Papa paused, holding the cupped paper with the tobacco in it. He looked questioningly at Mama.

"Well, yes, but..." Mama had often quoted that very verse herself in support of getting the truth out of the boys.

"Well, then, I'd say ol' Ben's in mortal danger of hell fire." Papa licked the rolled cigarette, spilled a few more crumbs of tobacco onto the floor, and brought the paper together, twisted the ends and put it into his mouth. He reached into his pocket for a match, struck it on his thumb nail and held the flame about six inches from the twisted end of his cigarette. He pretended not to see Mama's eyes on him.

Mama's aggravation was showing. "Well, I don't know why you would say such a thing." She pursed her lips. "Why do you say such a thing?"

"Ol' Ben never lost his leg in the War. He ain't never seen a German'' The flame on Papa's match was burning down towards his fingers. "Fact is, he ain't never been outside of Colaparchee County."

"Then how did he lose his leg?" Mama shot the question back because she was watching the flame nearing Papa's fingers.

"Stepped in front of a hay mowin' machine." Only then did Papa apply the burning match to the end of his cigarette. He flicked out the flame just before it touched his fingers.

"Lord have mercy!" Mama said. "You beat all." She turned to Alfie. "You go and wash up. The others will be coming any minute now." She glanced at the clock on the shelf. "Use plenty of soap and wash Ben Hawkins' wild tales out of your ears."

"Yes'm" Alfie said. He started toward the back porch and then he remembered. "Only there ain't no water in the wash pan. Peg..er..Mister Peg used it all. Papa, will you come an' draw up a fresh bucket?"

"Well thank the Lord for that," Mama said. "If he washed himself, then some good has come of it. The Bible says that cleanliness is next to godliness." She watched Papa who was rising to go to the well to draw up a bucket of water. Then she added "You may be right. I doubt that Ben Hawkins has got enough of truthfulness or godliness either to get him into heaven."

Chapter Eleven: Death Of A Guinea Chick

The Spring was advancing. Even the leaf buds on the Walnut tree were swelling, and Papa said "The walnut is the last to put out leaves in the Spring and the first to drop 'em in the Fall." The Walnut tree stood in the Southeast corner of the yard near the smokehouse. And the shrike was perched on he dead limb of the Walnut tree where it hung out over the roof of the smokehouse.

Alfie could see the shrike ruffling his feathers and looking bigger than life, cocking his head to one side so that one eye seemed fixed on the little brown chicks on the ground. Hovering protectively over the two tiny guinea chicks, Alfie scolded the shrike. "You git away, you mean ol' French Mockin' Bird!" He frowned, stamped his small bare feet on the hard ground. "You git away now. You better not bother my baby guineas!"

The shrike's unblinking eye was fixed on Alfie and on the thimble size brown balls of fluff at Alfie's feet. He preened the feathers of one wing, folded the wing against his body, and settled back on the dead branch of the Walnut tree. Watching, immobile now and inscrutable, the shrike was unmoved by Alfie's threatening words and gestures.

The guinea chicks ran about in quick, jerky motions on match stick legs. They pecked in the sand for organisms too small for even Alfie's sharp eyes to see. They stopped and looked up anxiously into Alfie's face. Then they huddled close together as a cloud passed over, throwing its shadow on the ground. Alfie felt a tremor run through his own small body. Gran'ma had a word for the feeling. "I felt a rabbit run acros' my grave," Gran'ma would say.

Alfie glared threateningly at the shrike. "You better not!" Alfie's voice trembled and he did not say what the shrike had better not do. "Papa'll git his gun an' shoot you. You mean ol' French Mockin' Bird!"

Papa had called the shrike a French Mocking Bird because of its resemblance to the Mocking Birds quarreling over the fig trees along the garden fence. The shrike was shorter, more compact though than the Mocking Bird. It's tail was shorter too, and darker black. A black streak, like a burglar's mask, ran along beneath its eyes. And the short, slightly curved beak was stout and hooked, for holding and tearing its prey. For the shrike is a bird of prey. Papa said to Alfie when he was telling him about shrikes, "You see a lizard or a grasshopper stickin' on a barb wire fence. Now that's a French Mockin' Bird's doin'. You jest watch an' he'll come back in a day or two an' eat it, when he's good an' hungry."

The shrike's predatory activities were a matter of interest to Papa, but not necessarily a matter of emotional concern. "I hear tell he ketches other birds too. Their babies anyway." Alfie's face registered deep concern when Papa told him this. "But I never saw it," Papa added.

The shrike ruffled its feathers, letting the Spring breeze flow through. He opened and closed his beak, yawning. Then he settled down on the dead branch of the Walnut tree. Waiting. Watching. Unmoving. And unmoved by Alfie's anger. "You better go away or I'll tell my Papa an' he'll take his gun an' shoot you!"

Alfie squatted on the ground near the guinea chicks. He picked up a dried, shriveled walnut, studied it closely. A weapon to use against the ol' French Mocking Bird? Once the outer hull of the walnut had been green, firm and oozing a brown juice that would stain Alfie's fingers when he touched it. Then it was heavy, round and perfectly balanced. Like a green golf ball. Cliff could have hurled it with unerring accuracy at the ol' French Mocker. But now it was blackened, crumbling and disintegrating. Prelude to the sprouting of the seed inside. Gran' ma would have held it in her thin fingers and said "Why Lord God Baby! That ol' shriveled walnut ain't no count."

It was of no account for eating. The meat inside had already begun to change into tiny leaves and roots. If Gran'ma had been interested in planting Walnut trees...But she was not. The one in the corner of the yard, with the ol' French Mocker in it, was enough of messy Walnut trees. Gran'ma was interested in keeping the yard swept clean of all litter. Such as dried up last year's walnuts. And she hadn't been able to do even that. Because of Margaret.

"Lord God!" Gran'ma would look despairingly at the unswept yard, criss-crossed with tracks and littered with the leaf and twig droppings from the walnut tree. She would work her toothless gums and work the Brewton's snuff over them to ease the pain. Then she would say to Alfie "I have got to git your Papa to go to the woods and cut me some dogwood sprouts to make a brush broom to sweep this yard with. But with Margaret layin' up there the way she is..."

For Gran'ma, sweeping the yard with a dogwood brush broom was both a labor of love and a work of art. She made the brush broom by binding the young dogwood sprouts into a small bundle, wrapping twine about the bundled stems and leaving the soft, flexible leafy ends bushed out like a horse's tail for the brush work. Then she would sweep back and forth, beginning on one side of the yard and ending on the other, always walking backwards as she worked, leaving in front of her an ever widening expanse of sand swept clean of leaves, litter and tracks. It was a perfect geometric pattern with never a foot print on the whole thing.

Then, looking back over it critically but with pride, she would gather up the leaves, litter and last year's walnuts, scooping it all up with two shingles blown off the old hay barn by the latest windstorm, and dump the lot of it into the wheelbarrow, and call to Cliff. "Here, Cliff, you rather chase a wheel better than anything. Haul this off to the big gully and dump it in. And when I'm done here I'll go in and make up a batch of teacakes for you boys. Now hurry."

It was not necessary for Gran'ma to tell Cliff to hurry. He would come racing with the wheelbarrow and she would have to caution him "Now don't you roll that wheelbarrow acros' my fresh swept yard and track it up. You hear me?" For the yard became Gran'ma's special domain when she had swept it clean and had left her perfect geometrical mark upon it.

Cliff would say "Yes'm!" and then he would race away with the loaded wheelbarrow. He would dump the load of dead leaves and dried up walnuts and other litter into the gully at the end of the cotton patch. And there it would catch and hold the moisture from the Spring rains. The dried and shriveled walnuts would sprout, swelling and bursting open, sending down roots and sending up shoots. The young trees would clog the gully. They would catch and hold the soil. And in the years to come they would slowly transform an ugly red gash in the earth's surface into a shady dell, with grass and wildflowers and walnut trees dropping more leaves and walnuts, and providing a place for small birds flitting and hopping about from branch to branch, and watching lest the shrike, the ol' French Mocking Bird,come and strike them down.

So Gran'ma planted walnut trees and created a place of beauty in the old gully, but all she had in mind was to get rid of the trash that littered the yard. And the wrinkled, dried out walnut in Alfie's hand was only a part of that trash and litter which Gran'ma would have already swept away if only Margaret were not "layin' up there and a lookin' up at us with them big soft brown eyes an' we can't do nuthin' but pray an' even ol' Doc Powers don't seem like he knows what to do fer her." Now Alfie drew back his short little arm all covered with golden hairs glistening in the sunlight, and he hurled the dried up walnut with all his strength at the ol' French Mockin' Bird, at the shrike, that black masked bird of prey sitting on the dead branch of the greening Walnut tree.

The missile fell short of its target. For Alfie was a very little boy and the shrike was high in the Walnut tree. And the withered, wrinkled, blackened walnut was no longer the deadly and accurate weapon it would have been in Cliff's hand last September when all the leaves had fallen from the Walnut tree because it is the first to drop its leaves in the Fall. So the missile, though it was hurled with all of the strength and anger in Alfie's small body, fell short. And the shrike turned its head to one side, ruffled its feathers and settled itself on the dead branch, watchful and unafraid.

The two tiny guinea chicks darted about, pecking in the sand at Alfie's feet. And Gran'ma came to the porch and looked all about for Alfie. She called "Babeee! Where are you?" Then she saw him standing under the Walnut tree and she said "Oh, there you are. Now don't go too far from the house, Baby. You stay close where you can hear me when I call. You hear? "Then Gran'ma turned and went back into the house. Alfie wanted to call to Gran'ma and tell her about the ol' French Mockin' Bird but she was gone because of Margaret.

"You jus' wait!" Alfie turned back to stare at the shrike on the dead branch. "I'll tell Papa and he'll come an' git his gun an' shoot you. You mean ol' French Mockin' Bird. Jus' sittin' up there waitin' for a chance to git my baby guineas." Alfie looked back at the house. If he saw Papa he would tell him about the French Mockin' Bird, but he couldn't see Papa.

He was hoping Papa would come out onto the back porch. But Gran'ma had closed the door behind her when she went back into the house and the porch was deserted. The water bucket was sitting on the well housing but it was dry on the outside because Papa had not taken time to draw up a bucket of fresh water when he came in such a hurry from the field. The dipper was hanging near the well bucket, It swayed and banged against the bucket, making a muffled metallic sound. The enamel wash pan was on the table against the wall. It was half full of dirty water because when Cliff had washed his hands he had left the dirty water in the pan. Papa's straight back chair leaned against the wall where Papa had left it yesterday. The porch seemed empty and silent since Papa had walked with long strides up the steps, taking them two at a time, and across the porch, making the floor boards squeak under his feet, and closing the door behind him when he went into the room where Margaret lay with her hands gripping the clean white sheet.

Alfie had waited for Papa to come back out onto the porch and call him. "You come on an' wash up for dinner, Son. Your Mama's got dinner on the table. Make haste now! You hear?" That was the way Papa would do when he came home from the field at dinner time. Kate's harness would jingle as she walked eagerly toward the barn, and Papa would be whistling a happy tune, eager for his own dinner. But not this time.

This time Papa had come with long strides and with Cliff trotting behind him, trying to keep up and being careful not to get in Papa's way. Cliff was not saying anything because he knew Papa wanted him to keep quiet. Papa had not brought Kate to the house and Alfie started to ask "Papa, where is Kate?" But something in Papa's face and in his eyes warned him not to ask. Papa's face was set in hard lines, and his eyes were different too. He did not do more than glance at Alfie as he walked past him, but even in that glance Alfie sensed the fear in Papa's eyes. But Papa walked right past Alfie and went straight to the room where Margaret was.

Alfie waited but Papa did not come back out onto the porch. Alfie wanted to tell Papa to bring his gun and shoot the ol French Mockin' Bird, but the door was still closed and he could not see Papa. Then the cloud moved over him in the sky and it cast its shadow on the ground where Alfie now sat on the ground with his two tiny guinea chicks under the Walnut tree. And the ol' French Mockin' Bird sat up there on the dead branch, waiting. And Alfie wished that Papa would come with his gun and shoot the ol' French Mockin' Bird.

Mama had sent for Papa. She had said to Cliff "You go to the field where your Papa's plowing and you tell him to come quick. Tell your Papa it's Margaret and for him to come as quick as he can."

Then Cliff had sped away on bare brown feet, right past Alfie without hardly looking at him. On past the woodpile where the axe was sticking in the chopping block. Then down the curving foot path that crossed the cotton patch where the small green plants were breaking through the ground. Cliff's face was chalky white with fear because he had seen the fear in Mama's brown eyes and he had heard it in Mama's voice which had an urgency about it when she told him to go for Papa. So Cliff didn't ask Mama any questions. He just ran to get Papa as quick as he could.

Mama had stood for a moment watching Cliff run, to be sure he was running in the right direction. Then she turned to go back into the house, and she said "I could ring the bell but it would just alarm all the neighbors this time of the morning. No use in that." She seemed to reconsider ringing the bell. But then in a despairing tone, she said "They couldn't do anything now."

Alfie looked up into Mama's face and said "How come you want to ring the bell Mama?" Then he begged, "Can I ring the bell Mama? If you hold me up so I can reach the rope I'll ring the bell for Papa." He looked questioningly into Mama's eyes, but Mama just shook her head, not looking directly at him. She turned to go up the steps to the back porch. "Never mind. I was just talking to myself. You go on and play but don't leave the yard." Alfie looked open mouthed at Mama. Then he ducked his head and looked down at the guinea chicks. He didn't feel like playing. He wanted to follow Mama into the house because he was afraid. He started to get up and run after Mama but she said "You stay here and play."

Then he remembered the ol' French Mockin' Bird sitting up there on the dead branch of the Walnut tree, watching the baby guineas. He wanted to tell Mama about the French Mockin' Bird but Mama had gone into the house and closed the door behind her. Then Papa came, with Cliff following him.

Papa had been walking so fast and putting his feet down so hard that Alfie could feel it in the ground under his own bare feet, and he thought that Papa must be mad because of what Mama had sent Cliff to tell him about Margaret. Then when Papa walked past him without pausing to say anything to him, Alfie could see what was in Papa's eyes and all over Papa's face, and he knew that it was fear. Fear and anger too. And Alfie was afraid too, and angry. He didn't know what he was afraid of, nor what he was angry at, but because Papa was afraid and angry, Alfie was too. So he turned back to the ol' French Mockin' Bird on the dead branch and tears sprang into his eyes and his voice was shrill and quavering. "You mean ol' French Mockin' Bird! I hate you!"

He sat there looking at the closed door where Papa had gone inside the house and he knew why he was afraid and angry. He knew that the French Mocking Bird was the cause of his fear and the reason he was angry was the fear of what the bird would do. He waited for Papa to come back out onto the porch but Papa did not come and he ran to the steps that led up to the porch, mounted halfway and stood looking at the closed door. "Papa! Papa!" he called but Papa did not come out to him. He ran to the door and put his hand on the doorknob and he was about to twist it and open the door when he heard Cliff.

"Git away! You turn 'im loose!" Cliff yelled. Then in a tone of discouraged resentment. "Doggone ol' French Mockin' Bird!" The shrike had flown down and seized one of the tiny guinea chicks in his hooked beak. He was flying back to his perch on the dead branch of the tree. The limp and helpless guinea chick dangled from his beak, struggling feebly.

Alfie stood motionless on the porch. Cliff ran toward the Walnut tree. He stooped to pick up a broken brick, stumbling in haste and almost dropping the brick. He quickly regained his feet and hurled the broken brick at the shrike, striking the dead limb of the tree just as the bird was alighting on it. The shrike was startled by the impact of the brick on its perch, opened its beak and the guinea chick fell toward the ground, tumbling end over end, as the shrike flew away. The chick touched the ground softly and lay limply, opening its eyes, then closing them.

Cliff ran to the chick and lifted it, a little puff of brown feathers, about the size of a thimble, and a small brown head hanging from a limp neck. Cliff held the chick by one leg and looked at it. Anger and despair were mixed in his face.

"No!" Alfie cried, running down the steps. "Don't hold 'im thataway!" He ran to Cliff, his hands outstretched. "Give 'im to me!" Alfie took the chick in his hands. He tried to make its head stand up. The lifeless head flopped over on the limber neck. He tried again. The dead chick collapsed into his palm.

"It ain't no use," Cliff said. "That ol' French Mockin' Bird's done killed 'im." Cliff bit his lip in frustration. "I wouldha killed the mean ol' thing if I couldha got to 'im in time." Then a door slammed behind them and both Alfie and Cliff looked toward the house.

"Papa!" Alfie cried. He ran toward the porch, holding the dead chick in his hands, his lips trembling. "Papa!"

Alfie thought Papa had heard and had come out to see what was happening. He ran toward Papa, holding the dead chick and calling "Papa!" But Papa was not looking at Alfie. He didn't see the dead guinea chick in Alfie's hands. He had taken his little sack of Bull Durham from his pocket and he had started to make a cigarette. Mechanically. From force of habit. But his eyes were empty. He was not looking at what he was doing. But Alfie ran toward the house, holding the lifeless chick in his hands and crying “Papa! Papa!” He was desperate for Papa to take him in his arms and hold him. And to look at the dead chick. And to hear about the Ol’ French Mockin’ Bird. He stumbled on the steps and fell forward onto his elbows. The dead chick pitched forward from Alfie’s hands. It fell onto the porch floor and scooted almost under Papa’s foot.

Papa was licking the cigarette paper and twisting the ends of the cigarette. He looked down at Alfie sprawled on the steps and his face showed some surprise. He started to move toward Alfie. “Oh Papa!” Alfie moaned. Papa was bending down, the cigarette dangling from his lips. He was lifting Alfie to a standing position. Alfie flung his arms about Papa’s neck and pointed to the baby guinea chick lying on the floor. “Don’t step on ‘im Papa! Don’t step on ‘im!”

Papa said “What?!” For he had not seen the chick lying on the floor. “What is it Son?” He looked into Alfie’s face but his eyes seemed to be looking beyond Alfie. He asked ‘‘What?” but he did not seem to hear and understand what Alfie was crying about.

Then Alfie cried “Papa, you got to git your gun an’ shoot that mean ol’ French Mockin’ Bird!” Then Papa was looking more intently into Alfie’s face and Alfie said “Papa, that mean ol’ French Mockin’ Bird got my baby guinea!” Alfie’s voice rose to a piteous wail.

Papa’s voice was breaking too. “Yes, son. I know...We got to do somethin about that ol’ French Mockin’ Bird...One a these days.” He hugged Alfie and held him until the trembling in Alfie’s body subsided to an occasional spasm. Then Papa set Alfie down and said “But ain’t you still got another one out there in the yard? You better go an’ see about him.”

Papa turned Alfie toward the porch steps. “You put ‘im back in the coop with the little ol’ Banty hen so the ol’ French Mockin’ Bird won’t git him too. Jest in case he takes a notion to come back lookin’ for ‘im.”

Alfie ran down the steps toward the guinea chick standing alone with its head raised, frightened and lonely. Papa put his hand on the doorknob to go back into the room where Mama and Gran'ma were bending over Margaret's bed, sobbing and weeping quietly. Then he turned back to Cliff who was standing under the Walnut tree, looking up into its branches. "Cliff," he said. "You run back there where I tied ol' Kate to the sweetgum saplin'. Unhitch her and bring her to the house. Put her in the stable and give her some fresh water." He watched Cliff as he turned to go back over the path that Mama had sent him on for Papa. "Make haste now," Papa said. "Bring that mule to the house and give her water and feed. You hear me?"

"Yes'r" Cliff called back, running past the chopping block with the axe blade stuck in it.

Alfie crouched beside the frightened little guinea chick. He was still holding the dead chick in his hands. He tried once more to make its head stand up but it wouldn't."

Chapter Twelve: A Nest Of Larks

Mama and Papa were never the same after Margaret died. Mama said she blamed herself for not insisting that Papa do something before it was too late. "We could have called another doctor," she said, chewing her lips. "Or taken her to the hospital."

When Mama said this, looking at Papa, it made him feel that he should have done something without waiting for her to insist. He probably felt that way anyhow, but Papa would not talk about it. Except on one occasion, he did say "If I had known then what I know now I would have done different." But there has never been anybody who knew then what he knows now. And something went out of Papa when Margaret died.

Mama and Papa bought a nice casket for Margaret's burial. They put a marble slab on her grave. Mama said it would be wrong to spend the insurance money for anything else. She had problems about this though because the boys needed things and it didn't seem right to spend everything on the dead when the living needed so much. But she could not bring herself to spend the insurance money on anything else.

Alfie would climb into Mama's lap and ask her "Why did Margaret die, Mama?" Mama told him Margaret had gone to be with the Lord but Alfie would have rather have her with him because he liked for Margaret to hold him tight. And when he asked why the Lord took Margaret Mama couldn't answer but she said "You will find something to take your mind off it."

Alfie found the baby birds when he was chasing butterflies in the tall meadow grass growing near Parker's Branch which empties into Tobesofkee Creek. But that is far away, and the four baby birds were in a nest on the ground in the tall meadow grass. Their naked bodies were bluish pink colored with little pin feathers showing and their eyes were closed, but their mouths were standing wide open because they expected their mother to put something in their mouths. Then they realized that Alfie was not their mother, and they closed their mouths and became very still and quiet.

The mama bird was not far away. She fluttered through the tall grass, dragging one wing as if it were broken. She was trying to lure Alfie away from her babies, hoping he would try to catch her and forget about the four naked, blind babies in the nest tucked away under a clump of tall grass in the meadow. Alfie stood watching the brown mother bird with yellow and black on her breast and throat.

He watched her flutter away as if she were wounded, and he stood there watching and wondering, but then he knelt to look at the babies in the nest. His hands trembled as he picked one of them up and held it against his cheek. It was the smallest of the four little birds. Papa would have called it The Runt. Then The Runt immediately became Alfie's favorite, for that reason. Alfie was the smallest of the four boys at his house and sometimes when Papa was in a teasing mood he would call Alfie "The Runt of the Whole Bunch."

Alfie could tell though that Papa was teasing him this way just because he was the baby and it was all right.

Alfie put The Runt back into the nest and raced away to the house because he wanted to tell somebody about what he had found. At first he thought of Junior but he decided he would keep it a secret from Junior because he and Junior were always laying conflicting claims to everything. And he didn't dare tell Mama because she would say "It's wrong to disturb them that way. Now don't you touch those baby birds, and don't frighten the mother bird and get her all upset."

But he could tell Willie. Willie was interested in any kind of bird or animal or anything new or strange, and what could be newer than a newly hatched bird? What could be stranger than a whole nest of them on the ground under a clump of grass in the meadow where bumble bees buzzed about the flowers in the little alder bushes that grow close to the banks of Parker's Branch where it runs away to empty itself into the Tobesofkee Creek close to where the Rattling Bridge crosses the Tobesofkee, and you can hear the bridge's floorboards slapping against the runners when Papa drives the Dodge over it with the windows all rolled down, and you can even hear the water sloshing against the pilings that support the Rattling Bridge.

He found Willie in the milking barn. Willie was getting ready to milk the cows, but Alfie said "Willie! Guess what I found! A nest of baby birds! Come and see!"

Willie went limping with him to the meadow. Willie's blue eyes were fixed intently on everything that moved or didn't move. He brushed his blond hair back from his forehead and little beads of sweat stood on his upper lip where the blond fuzz was beginning to show because Willie was getting big and almost as tall as Papa. Willie limped because he had hurt his leg jumping the bars at the cattle gap, but he did not complain much about the pain unless Cliff accidentally touched his leg when they were milking the cows.

"What are they Willie?" They were standing over the nest and Alfie's eagerness knew no bounds. He very much wanted Willie to be proud that he had found the nest of baby birds. "I found them. What kind of birds are they?"

"They're fiel' larks," Willie said, touching one gently with the tip of his index finger. "Fiel' larks build their nest on the ground. That's the mama bird over there now. She's playin' like her wing is broke. She's tryin' to git us to chase her so we'll fergit about the babies. But if we do, she'll jump up and fly away as soon as we almost ketch up with her." Willie stood watching the mama bird and said "She don't know that we won't hurt her babies."

Alfie came each day - some days he came half a dozen times - to check the nest and look at the baby birds. "I want to see how much they've grown," he said under his breath.

They grew rapidly. The pin feathers opened up as they grew out and covered the bluish skin. The three bigger ones continued to outgrow The Runt. Alfie spent so much time running to the meadow to watch the baby birds that Mama noticed. "Lordy mercy!" Mama said. "What are you doing down by the branch so much, Alfie? If you're not careful you'll get on a snake." Alfie told Mama that he was always careful to watch for snakes when he crossed the branch, but Mama said "Well there must be something awful attractive down there, for you to be spending so much time running back and forth."

Mama was busy pressing newly churned butter into the mold with the wheat sheaf imprint on it though, and she quickly forgot about Alfie's frequent trips to the meadow. The one pound butter cakes went into the wheat sheaf mold and the half pound cakes went into the pineapple imprint, and Mama went on pressing the butter into the mold, but she said "You be careful not to let a bumble bee sting you too. You know what happened to Willie when he was experimenting to see which end the bumble bee's stinger is on." Mama had the ability to let her mind run along two tracks at once until she had issued sufficient warning, and then she would put her whole mind on the task she was doing, and she did not press the matter to learn what Alfic was doing in the meadow. She went on pressing the butter into the mold, and Alfie did not tell her about the nest of larks because he was afraid she would say "You stay away from them and don't worry that mama bird about her babies. You'll worry her to death if she thinks you are going to hurt them."

Alfie wanted to keep the secret of the baby birds for himself alone, except for Willie. He thought he ought to tell Papa, but Papa was very busy because everything was growing and Papa had to keep on top of it all. He didn't know that Papa was planning to cut the meadow grass for hay. If he had known he would have told Papa about the baby birds anyway and begged him not to cut the grass because of the baby birds in the nest. But he didn't know. Sometimes Papa was so busy he didn't say what he was planning to do because it involved too much explaining, and that took up too much time that he needed for doing. Papa would say "You watch and see. That will save me a heap of time. Then you'll know what I'm doing and you'll know how to do it yourself when you get big enough."

So because Papa didn't know about the baby birds and Alfie didn't know Papa was planning to cut the tall grass in the meadow, Papa hitched Kate to the mowing machine early in the morning,and went to the meadow beside the rippling stream called Parker's Branch to cut the grass while Alfie was sleepily eating syrup and biscuits for his breakfast.

"Where's Papa, Mama? What's he doing?" Alfie poured more syrup over his biscuit, and rolled his big brown eyes at Mama.

"Your Papa went early to cut the grass in the meadow by the branch. You remember where I warned you about the bumble bees?"

Alfie dropped the biscuit with the syrup on it in his plate and cried out "Oh Mama!" He was wide awake now and running toward the sound of the mowing machine whirring in the meadow. Mama looked up in surprise, and went to the door to call Alfie back, but he was running so fast he couldn't hear Mama. He could only hear the whirring of the mowing machine in the meadow.

"Papa! Papa! Don't!" he cried, and running running running he kept crying out "Oh Papa Don't!" For Kate was arching her strong neck and straining the rippling muscles in her shoulders and flanks and placing her dainty feet one in front of the other as she approached the very spot where the lark's nest was tucked away under the clump of grass. And the mowing blade was moving back and forth so rapidly it became a blur in the sickle bar as it swept along a few inches above the ground, and the grass fell over the sickle bar as the blades cut the stems. Then the grass lay flat behind the passing bar, and even though it had not yet withered in the morning sun, the color of the grass blades was changed because the undersides were exposed. And Alfie ran toward the spot where the mowing machine was coming upon the lark's nest, and the mama bird had fluttered away from the nest and was dragging one wing and crying excitedly in her distress, and Alfie ran crying "Papa! Don't! Papa! Don't!"

Then Alfie's cries reached Papa's ears even above the whirring and the clattering of the mowing machine and the snorting and stamping of Kate as she drew the machine relentlessly on. And Papa took his eyes off the shuttling blades and looked and saw Alfie running toward the mowing machine, and Papa's face broke into both surprise and alarm, and he yelled "Whoa Kate Whoa!" And he tightened the leather reins in his hard, rough hands, and the muscles in his arms stood out like cords beneath the bulging skin, and he drew the bit down on

Kate's mouth so hard that she came to a halt with her head drawn down and her mouth open, fighting the cruel bit, and the saliva was dripping from her open mouth.

"God A' mighty Son!" Papa exclaimed. "Don't run in front of the mowing machine! It'll cut your legs off!"

And Alfie cried "Papa! Oh Papa! The lark's nest!" But it was too late because Kate had passed over the lark's nest and one of her dainty hooves had been set squarely upon the nest where the baby birds were huddled together.

"Make her move Papa! Make Kate move!" Alfie was standing too close to the mowing machine blade and Papa held the reins tight on Kate with one hand and raised the blade to a vertical position with the other.

"Git back Son! Git back outta the way of the blades!" Papa was vexed and he was shaking and trembling because he thought for a moment that Alfie would run in front of the mowing blades. "What in tarnation has got into you?"

"The lark's nest Papa! Kate's standing on it!" And then Papa got down and took Kate's bridle and coaxed her backward, saying "Back Kate. Back Girl." And the iron rimmed wheels of the mowing machine moved slowly backward while the blades in the sickle bar pointed skyward like a sword held up in the extended arm of a swordsman. And Kate stepped backwards, more daintily even than she had stepped forward, and more hesitantly, fighting the bit in her mouth, but pushing the heavy machine backwards. And Alfie, his eyes full of tears, his voice choking, looked fearfully at the spot where Kate's left front hoof had been. His face broke, his mouth twisted, and he bent down over the crushed nest and lifted one of the baby larks. It shuddered and became limp, its bulging eyes closed, its beak open. Another. And another. And at last he lifted The Runt.

The Runt was alive, untouched by Kate's hoof, for pushed and shoved aside by his larger and stronger nest mates, he had been at the very edge of the nest, and Kate's hoof had narrowly missed him. "That runty one's still alive," Papa said.

"Tell you what we'll do Son. I'll just back ol' Kate up a little more and go around the nest on the other side, and you sort of cup it up to make it look as much like it did before as you can make it without bein' a bird yourself. Then you put that runty bird back in there. Maybe its Mammy will come back and feed it and raise it and take keer of it till it can fly."

Alfie reshaped the crushed nest and he straightened up the clump of grass, and he put the runty chick back in the nest. Runt opened his eyes and beak and fluttered his wings and his little body vibrated with expectation, and Alfie said "I think he's hungry Papa." Alfie snuffled and wiped the tears and the mucus with his shirt sleeve. "He's hungry Papa. Could I catch a grasshopper and feed 'im?"

But Papa said "I reckon can't nobody feed 'im right but his own Mammy. Tell you what though Son. You run on to the house an' tell Willie I said to draw up a bucket of fresh water from the Northeast corner of the well. I'd about finished here anyway. I'll leave the rest of the grass standin' for the time bein'. Kate an' me'll foller you on to the house. A cool drink of water and a shady spot to rest will he'p us all and maybe that ol' Mammy bird' ll come back here a lookin' to see how much damage we've done, an' when she finds the runty bird all by hisself she'll feed 'im all the bugs an' grasshoppers she can rake together, and the first thing we know he won't even be a runt no more."

"Papa" Alfie said, brushing the tears again with his shirt sleeve and snuffling the mucus in his nose. "If you won't cut the rest of the grass I'll come ev'ry day an' check on Runt."

Then Papa said "You do that, Son. And I reckon I won't cut the grass till that runty bird can take off an fly to the nearest tree limb."

Chapter Thirteen: That Dog Oughtta Be Shot!!!

"Git back dog! Git back!" Alfie cringed, trembled and cowered before the big black dog, fearing that the bristling beast would charge right into his face, and not daring to turn and run because the dog would surely overtake him in two bounds and be upon his back and legs and bring him down. Better to have the menacing hound in front of him, facing him, where he could at least see him, even if he could not face him down. "Git back! I tell you! Git back!"

But the dog did not get back. Instead it charged at Alfie, barking, growling and snapping its teeth and spreading its toes apart as its feet dug into the ground by the sheer force of its stiff legged charge. He was now so close Alfie could feel his hot breath, see the saliva dripping from his hackles, see the hairs standing like bristles on his neck, see the eyes flashing in the excitement of the chase and in the elation of having cornered his quarry. For Alfie was indeed at bay. He did not dare move out of his tracks. It is doubtful that his feet would have obeyed even if he had commanded them to move. All he could do was swing the bucket between himself and the dog, pendulum fashion. The bucket, now only half full of water intended for Papa who was plowing the corn field on the back side of the farm, was all that stood, or rather swung, between Alfie and the black dog, a mixed breed of hound of indeterminate ancestry, and the dog was getting splashed or splattered by the water as Alfie swung the bucket at him because he had nothing else to swing. Oddly enough, this bothered the hound and Alfie about equally for different reasons. It disturbed Alfie to lose the water because Mama had warned "Now hurry and take this water to your Papa while it's still cold, but don't spill a drop of it!" But the water splashing out did serve to keep the dog from making actual physical contact with Alfie because some of the water splashed onto him, and each time this occurred, the dog would flinch and jump aside as if the cold water might actually hurt him, although on a purely rational basis the cold water must have felt good even to a dog on a hot summer day. But a dog that will dive into the icy waters of a lake to retrieve a stick thrown by his master does not like to have a tea cup full of water thrown on him. And so while Alfie's bucket of water might have seemed a flimsy defense against the snarling dog, it was all he had, and as the hound cane charging right up into Alfie's face, breathing his hot breath upon him and making a terrible racket, Alfie swung the bucket, and water flew out of it in all directions, and the dog jerked back onto his haunches, and it seemed that his hind legs could not get out of the way of his front legs, and he left long claw marks on the bare ground of the field road that ran past Aunt Hattie's house as he dodged the wildly swinging bucket.

Charging forward again in that interval when Alfie was trying to regain his balance after violently swinging the bucket, the dog's hind feet would then seem to run over its front feet in a frenzy to get at Alfie. The dog kept up this attack, barking, growling, snarling and scratching up the ground as he charged and drew back just out of range of the swinging bucket loaded with cold water sloshing out. And Alfie continued shouting at the dog. He was not even sure just what the words were that he shouted. Probably he repeated the same words over and over "Git back! Git back" And his cries were as much a call for help from outside as they were verbal missiles hurled at his attacker, and commanding him to cease and desist. But it seemed that the big black mongrel would not give up the attack, but would press and harry Alfie until he could no longer even swing the bucket and stand his ground in the face of the bared teeth and curling lips.

Then there was another sound, a voice calling to the dog, directed at the dog, commanding the dog's attention, demanding that the dog stop what he was doing. Alfie could not tell what this new voice was saying, what the words were, for his mind was fastened upon the attacking dog, but he knew that the voice was loud and shrill and high pitched, and he could see that the voice penetrated the consciousness of the dog, and that the dog knew and recognized that voice, realized the voice was scolding him for what he was doing, knew the voice was commanding him to stop what he was doing. And in fact the dog had already begun to lessen the intensity of his assault on Alfie when the command was accompanied by and reinforced by a terrible sensation of pain covering the major portion of the dog's body, particularly his back and hind quarters which were turned toward the house as the dog faced Alfie. And the attack on the dog came, of course, not from Alfie's water bucket and it's contents, but from the rear, from the quarter left unguarded in his headlong attack on Alfie.

The pain which the black dog felt streaking over his exposed body came from a brush broom, a bundle of small bushes or sprouts tied together with a string and comprising a large number of individual stems and twigs which altogether make up a very effective instrument for sweeping the bare dirt yard surrounding a house in the country. When the brush broom was new the twigs and stems were all covered with fresh green leaves, making the brush broom soft and pliable, and if it were brought down on a dog's back in this mint condition it might produce a severe fright but not much pain. But as the broom aged and leaves dropped off, or were worn away by usage, and the stems and twigs became bare and stiff and brittle, then the whole bundle could be wielded as effectively as a weapon as it had once served as an instrument of cleaning and neatness.

And in this case the brush broom was being wielded as a weapon and in the gnarled bony hands of Aunt Hattie, who now brought it down on the black dog' s back with force and vehemence, it was indeed a very effective weapon. The dog, caught by surprise, since his whole attention was centered upon his attack upon Alfie and the necessity for dodging Alfie's water bucket and its contents, for even the familiar voice had only penetrated his consciousness enough to distract him, but not enough to dissuade him, and suddenly feeling a thousand stings on his skin at once, whirled, snarling, teeth bared to meet this attack, and was caught again by surprise when he saw just in time, that it was Aunt Hattie, his owner, his mistress, whose authority he respected and whose anger he feared, second only to Uncle Seeb's, also his owner and his master, who usually wielded a stick of stove wood as the symbol of authority and the instrument of pain. Then, seeing Aunt Hattie, brush broom raised again for a second blow, the dog's angry snarl changed in mid air to a pitiable whine, a yelp, a plea for mercy, and a complaint that he had only been doing his assigned duty in guarding the house and its immediate environs against the intrusion of strangers, the current stranger being Alfie.

And scratching off with all four feet competing for the title of the fastest of them all, and in a vain and futile attempt to dodge a second blow of the brush broom which Aunt Hattie was already bringing down upon his head and shoulders, the cringing, cowering, yelping black dog, his tail tucked between his hind legs in a ridiculous attempt to cover and protect from injury those parts which Nature had ordained to serve the purpose of continuation of the species, the dog now obeyed unquestioningly Aunt Hattie's command: "You better git under the house, dog. Git on! Git!" When he had got under the house, he turned, looked back upon the battlefield from which he had fled, having had the glory of conquest snatched from his teeth by the blow of a worn and brittle brush broom, and transformed by Aunt Hattie's shrill voice into an ignominious and shameful retreat, he now crouched, ears alert. He started to bark but this soon turned into a mournful howl, and he turned, ears drooping, and went farther under the house, where he routed out the hens that were dusting themselves in the shade, and he lay down and licked the wounds inflicted by Aunt Hattie's brush broom.

Then Aunt Hattie was all solicitation and comfort and reassurance to Alfie who, her sharp eyes readily ascertained, had not been bitten, scratched or mauled, but only frightened out of his wits and quite possibly out of the next two weeks of growth. She then set about to repair the damage done by the dog to Alfie's ego, his psyche, his self-image, and if possible, to avert any retaliation that might come as a result of Alfie's report of the incident to his Papa, whose anger was not a thing to be taken lightly, for when it was hot it was likely to scorch everything nearby, and even as it cooled it tended to harden into acts of vengeance which bordered on the cruel and unforgiving in their execution.

Papa was known to deal very harshly with marauding packs of dogs that attacked and damaged his livestock. On one occasion he came upon dogs attacking a yearling calf in the back pasture. He waded in among them with a stick, kicking and clubbing them until they gave up the attack and fled. The calf was not dead, but it was badly injured, and he had to butcher it immediately to cut his losses. Papa recognized the dogs and he knew who their owners were, and the next morning, with the calf hanging from the hooks in the smoke house, and his anger unabated, Papa got into the Dodge and drove to the houses where the dogs belonged. He told his story, had the dogs' owners to call them out, identified them, and shot the dogs between the eyes with his .38 calibre Smith and Wesson, leaving them for their owners to bury, drag off or dispose of as seemed fitting for dogs shot for killing calves.

Papa wouldn't let Alfie go with him when he shot the dogs, but he heard Papa telling Mama about it when he came home. Mama looked worried and said she hoped there wouldn't be any trouble over it, but Papa said "Won't be no more trouble. I took care of that." But the story of Papa's shooting the dogs had reached Aunt Hattie's ears, and this was running through her mind as she consoled Alfie and reassured him that if that black dog even so much as opened his mouth again when Alfie was passing her house, she would "frail the daylights outta him, and I 'spec's when Seeb know 'bout this he'll take a stick of stovewood to 'im. Now don't you worry none bout that ol' black houn' dog an' don't you be skeered of nothin' round Aunt Hattie's house."

Aunt Hattie was a natural born psychologist, or one trained in the school of experience and hard knocks, and she not only foresaw the certainty that Alfie would report his encounter with the dog to his Papa; she also saw the inevitable demise of the dog if Papa decided that he was a threat to Alfie's safety, which demise would certainly result in fewer rabbits and 'possums to go into the big iron pot on the back of the cookstove, for without the dog Seeb was but half a hunter. And Aunt Hattie, being better than just a piddling psychologist, but worthy to be at the head of her class, said to Alfie "Now you be sho' to tell yo' Papa jes' 'xackly what happened an' you git yo' Mama 'xamine you close all over an' ef she fine even a scratch on you lef' by that dog you tell yo' Papa to come and shoot that dog, and' I drag 'im out from under the house where he hidin' so yo' Papa can shoot 'im." For Aunt Hattie knew that telling Alfie this was the surest way to safeguard the dog's life and protect the cookpot from the curse of emptiness.

And when Alfie found Papa plowing the corn on the back side of the place, and he ran to Papa crying and sobbing, for even though Aunt Hattie had dried his tears on her apron and given him a teacake to eat, when he caught sight of Papa, the tears sprang anew into his eyes and he flung himself upon Papa, saying "Papa, that mean ol' dog oughtta be shot!" He begged Papa to let him have Papa's pistol for that purpose. "I'll shoot 'im myself!" he declared. But Papa, while he was amused and pleased by Alfie's grit, and had Alfie to tell him in great detail about how the dog barked and growled at him, and how he had fought him off with the water bucket, and how the dog had turned tail and run when Aunt Hattie "flailed 'im with the brush broom" and how he left the dog hiding under the house, and Papa said he was proud of the way Alfie had handled the matter, still he thought they might give the dog another chance and not shoot him right away until they saw whether he had been cured by "the cold water and brush broom treatment" before they had Aunt Hattie to drag him out from under the house to be shot. Papa said "Lettin' you take the pistol to 'im might create more problems than it'd solve. You might scare Aunt Hattie clean outta her wits if she seen you comin' with that thirty eight in your hand and on toppa all that she'd think I had done lost my mind for lettin' you have it."

Alfie had watched Papa tilt the nearly empty bucket up and drain the last drops of water into his thirsty throat, and still unsatisfied, push the empty bucket away. "Papa" he said, "If Sandy was with me I bet he would have whupped that ol' black dog. Wouldn't he?"

"I reckon he would...if he was with you."

"Papa, where has Sandy gone to?"

"God knows, Son. He could he clear on the other side of Colaparchee County. How long's he been gone now? Two days?"

Alfie's eyes still searched Papa's face. "Mama said he might be gone for a week, but she wouldn't say why he left. How come Sandy ran off, Papa."

"I reckon he's gone a courtin' Son. Dogs do that. When a girl dog is in the heat all the boy dogs in the county go a courtin' 'er."

"What's the heat, Papa?"

"That's when a girl dog decides she wants to be a mama and have a whole litter of new puppies. That's how come all the boy dogs show up an' ev'ry one of 'em wantin' to be the papa of all them new puppies."

"Will Sandy be the papa, Papa?"

"I reckon he will. He's a strong fighter. He might git his ears cut up some, but I reckon he'll be the papa all right."

"Papa...How come Aunt Hettie's ol' black dog didn't go a courtin'?

"I don't know the answer to that Son. There are some things about a dog that a man jest can't figger out." Papa started to make a cigarette, and as he was pouring the Bull Durham into the little paper, his eyes twinkled and he said "I reckon maybe Sandy warned him to stay home this time."

"I wish Sandy'd come on back home an' whup that ol' black dog of Aunt Hattie's. Papa, will Sandy bring the new puppies home with 'im?"

"I reckon not, Son. It'd be a little early for that. And the ol' mammy dog is awful possessive about her puppies, once she gits 'em." Papa was lighting his cigarette now. He drew the smoke in, and exhaled. "But after the flailin' Aunt Hattie give that black dog of hers I don't reckon he needs another whuppin' on top of it whenever Sandy gits back home."

Papa finished his cigarette and said "I'll jest unhitch ol' Kate an' we'll go to the house early. I'm still thirsty. And I reckon Kate would like a cool drink too." He was looping the trace chains over the hames and tying up the plow lines. "Tell you what. I'll set you up here on ol' Kate's back and you can ride her to the barn. And when we go back past Aunt Hattie's house, if that black dog runs out at us, he can't reach you up there, and if he does come up close I'll haul off an' kick the daylights outta 'im an' that' ll learn him a lesson he won't soon fergit."

Alfie was so pleased with this arrangement that he did not even mind about Kate being sweaty and all lathered from pulling the plow. He thought Mama might say "Lordy mercy! Now just look at the seat of your overalls! I'll have to wash them now!" But Alfie didn't mind. He was,in fact, quite proud.

The procession, Alfie on Kate with Papa walking alongside, approached Aunt Hattie's house, with trace chains jangling and leather straps flapping against Kate's lathered haunches, and the black dog barked once from under the house, and then he was silent and didn't show his face, but it was enough to let Aunt Hattie know and she came out of the house onto the porch and she yelled at him in her high pitched, shrill voice. "You shet yo' mouth, Dawg, or I take my brush broom to you ag'in."

Then Aunt Hattie called to Alfie. "Don't you worry none 'bout that ol' black dawg, Alfie. When Seeb come home from the fiel' he take a stick of stove wood to 'im an' I bet he don't never bother you ag'in." She turned to Papa and said "Jes look at Alfie settin' up on that mule lak a little man!"

In such grandeur did Alfie pass Aunt Hattie's house, and Papa said "Well Son I reckon you won't have any more trouble outta that dog. I think you learned him a lesson."

Alfie smiled back at Papa and he clutched Kate's bridle reins in his small hands and he said "Aw Shucks! I ain't even skeered of that ol' dog no more. Come up Kate."

Chapter Fourteen: The Cyclone Shelter

Sandy came home the next day. He was lean and hungry. "He looks a bit ga'nt." Papa was staring into Sandy's eyes and Sandy turned his eyes away and pretended to be watching something off in the distance. "But I reckon he has guaranteed his immortality."

Alfie patted Sandy affectionately and stared wide eyed at Papa. "What does that mean, Papa? What did Sandy do?"

"He's made hisself the proud papa of a litter of puppies somewhere so his bloodline will live on when he's gone."

Then Papa examined Sandy for cuts and scratches and other signs of fighting. "He's got a few battle scars and he favors that right front paw. So I reckon one of 'em musta got a holt of it in the scuffle."

Mama said it was not a fit subject for discussion. "But you can't change the nature of a dog." And she drew her lips into a long thin line of disapproval.

Sandy stretched himself on the porch where a cool evening breeze would pass over him. He seemed satisfied with himself. "Papa," Alfie said. "Can I have one of Sandy's puppies? I'll take good care of it and feed it good."

"Well Son there ain't no tellin' where they're at but I wouldn't be atall surprised if the whole litter of 'em turns up here one a these days. I jest hope it won't be but one when it happens."

Alfie was thinking One Puppy. "How will he know where to come to Papa? Will he know to come to our house?"

"The puppy won't. But the man who owns the mama dog will; if he recognized Sandy he'll know where to drop them puppies when they git too expensive for him to feed."

Alfie smiled and went on rubbing Sandy. Sandy panted and slapped his tail against the porch floor to let Alfie know that he was glad to be back home, but it did not mean that he would not run off again when the same circumstances would arise again. Alfie said "I hope the puppies will look just like Sandy. Do you think the puppies will look like Sandy, Papa."

Papa said "I believe that is the general idea behind it all and I reckon he has done his job good enough that they will look enough like him that we won't have no trouble recognizin' 'em."

But Papa was reading the newspaper and his mind had moved away from Sandy and the puppies. After all, he reasoned, that was at least three months down the line and there was no need to worry about it yet. What he was reading was of immediate concern. But it was getting dark and he went inside and lit the lamp so that he could make out more clearly what the story was saying. Mama had started to iron a shirt. Papa said "You ought to hear what this says."

Papa folded thc Ocmulgee Sentinel over, shook it vigorously, adjusted his glasses by pulling them farther down on the bridge of his nose, looked again at the print, tilting his head back so that he could look down through the lenses, then looked up again at Mama, and said "We got to dig us a cyclone shelter. That's all there is to it."

"What on earth for"? Papa's words had caught Mama by surprise, and she turned from her ironing, after carefully placing the iron in its rack to avoid burning or scorching the shirt she was pressing. She stared at Papa. "A cyclone shelter for what?"

"To go in when a cyclone hits." Papa tapped the paper impatiently with his forefinger. "It says right here in the paper there'll be more cyclones to hit this part of Georgia in the next six weeks than in all the rest of the year put together." Papa shook the paper again in an attempt to bring the print into focus. "We got to have a cyclone shelter."

"The people at the newspaper don't know whether it's going to rain tomorrow." There was acid on Mama's tongue. "What do they know about cyclones six weeks from now?"

"We ain't talkin' about six weeks from now." Papa saw an argument brewing and he put himself on the side of the newspaper. "We're talkin' about what might happen tomorrow, which is when I'm startin' to dig."

Alfie dropped the funny papers he was looking at, came and stood beside Papa's chair. "Where? Where are we gonna dig it Papa?" He climbed onto Papa's lap and began examining the pictures on the newspaper. "Is that a cyclone shelter, Papa?

Which one's the cyclone shelter?" There were illustrations of the shelter, with the lid fitted closely to the ground, and with the lid propped up and showing steps leading down into the pit.

"Both of 'em's the cyclone shelter." Papa put his finger on first one, then the other. "One of 'em's shut an' the other one's open."

"Where are you going to dig it?" Mama had gone back to ironing; her lips were tightly compressed. "Have you thought about where you'll put it?"

"On the slope between the house and the hay barn. Don't want it too far from the house. When the cyclone hits there won't be no time for runnin' all over Colaparchee County tryin' to git to the shelter."

Alfie's eyes were sparkling with excitement, but Mama kept her eyes on the shirt she was ironing. She wet her finger with her tongue and touched the iron to determine if it was hot enough. The moisture on her finger turned to steam and Mama went on ironing. "You put it up there by that old hay barn and the wind'll blow the barn down on it, with us in there. You better put it in an open field."

Gran'ma worked a dip of snuff into her gums and looked severely at Papa. "You ain't a gittin' me to go in no hole in the ground. Not till I'm dead an' you put me in one. I'd a heap ruther be blowed away by the wind than shut up in a hole in the ground without no light and air." Gran'ma shook her head vigonusly to emphasize her words.

"Don't fret. We'll have a air hole." Papa spoke to Gran' ma reassuringly but with a note of impatience. "And a lantern too." To Mama. "I'll put it far enough from the old hay barn that if it blows over it won't fall on the cyclone shelter." He picked up the newspaper and reread the article. "It says right here a cyclone' ll pick up a whole barn an' carry it for miles an' then set it down without damagin' it none. One feller's barn was blowed onto another farm and now they've got a lawsuit over whose barn it is. Barn's still standin' up."

"Well that one of ours wouldn't hold together in a high wind." Mama folded the shirt and laid it aside. She compressed her lips, and her voice indicated both concern for their safety and impatience with the idea of a storm pit. "All that's holding it up is the hay you stacked in it."

Papa ignored Mama's comment on the hay barn. He went on reciting the more dramatic aspects of cyclones and the unusual events attending them. "The paper says there's a case on record of a wheat straw bein' drove through a board fence by the wind." He shook the paper and turned back to Gran'ma. "I reckon you'll change your mind when a cyclone hits us. I won't be atall surprised if you was to outrun us all a gittin' to the storm cellar first."

Gran'ma adjusted the snuff under her lip with the tip of her tongue. "Well you jest go right ahead with your grave diggin, but I wish you'd take the time off to go to the thicket and cut me some dogwood sprouts for a brush broom. That ol' last year's brush broom is plumb wore out an' stiff as a poker an' the yard needs sweepin' cyclone or no cyclone."

"Ain't got time for cuttin' brush brooms. I'm startin' in to dig first thing in the mornin'. Tell you what. You can take Alfie with you to cut sprouts for brush brooms. It ain't too far for the two of you to go."

"Aw, shoot," Alfie wailed. "I don't wanta cut brush broom sprouts. I wanta help dig the cyclone shelter."

Junior was huddled on the floor with the funny papers. He raised his head and looked condescendingly at Alfie. "Aw, you can't dig no cyclone shelter. You're too little to even pick up a shovel, let alone do any diggin' with it." Junior snorted and went back to reading the funny papers.

Alfie turned desperately to Papa. "I ain't too little, am I Papa? And I don't wanta go with Gran'ma to git brush brooms. I wanta help you dig."

But Papa said "Your Gran'ma won't rest till she's got a new brush broom because if the cyclone hits she wants to make sure the yard's been swept. Now you go with her first thing in the mornin' an' help her with the dogwood sprouts, and when you come back you can help me dig the cyclone shelter."

Morning came. Papa gathered his tools and all the boys except Alfie, and went to dig, but Alfie and Gran'ma set-out to gather sprouts for a new brush broom. Alfie wanted to get the job over with as soon as possible. He pointed to the first clump of sprouts he saw. "Look Gran' ma! Here's some good sprouts. They'll make you a good brush broom."

"Pshaw! Lord have mercy, Child!" Gran'ma was not impressed. "Them's sassafras! Ain't no good for brush brooms. We'll jest go on to where I know there's dogwood." They found the dogwood, and after much comparing and testing for flexibility and length, Gran''ma selected enough sprouts to make a brush broom. She cut them with a butcher knife she had brought with her for that purpose. Then she and Alfie dragged them home.

"You can run on to your Papa now," she said, binding the sprouts with twine. "I can finish."

"Shucks!" Alfie said. "I bet Papa and them have already finished diggin' an' I won't git to help."

"I wouldn't worry my head about that if I was you. The thing to worry about is gittin' buried alive in that hole your Papa's diggin' in the ground." She tied the string and tested her broom for flexibility. She was satisfied.

Alfie's faith in Papa's wisdom was unshaken by Gran'ma's skepticism. "Shucks, Gran'ma, Papa ain't gonna dig no hole so deep he can't jump out of it." Gran' ma was not convinced, but she released Alfie from further responsibility for the brush broom, and he ran to join Papa who was shoveling dirt into the wheelbarrow. Willie was throwing dirt into the wheelbarrow too,and it was becoming top heavy. Cliff pushed it, wobbling and weaving, then dumped the dirt about ten or twelve feet from the spot where it was loaded.

Papa looked up when Alfie came running. He saw what Cliff was doing and said "Don't dump it so close. By the time we git to the bottom it'll be slidin' hack in the hole." Papa laid his shovel aside to go and show Cliff a sinkhole about fifty feet away. "Fill up that sink hole with it," Papa said and began rolling a cigarette. He stood puffing on the cigarette while Cliff rolled the first load of dirt to the sink hole. When he turned back to the digging, Alfie had the shovel and was trying to push it into the hard red clay, but was hardly making a dent in the ground. Alfie watched Willie then, and tried pushing the shovel with his foot the way Willie did it, but the shovel flipped over and hit him in the chest. He frowned, turned down the corners of his mouth, fighting back the tears gathering in his eyes. He looked up at Papa who flipped his cigarette aside, took the shovel and said "Let me show you how it's done. You run and git your coaster wagon and you can help Cliff haul dirt." Papa then began throwing dirt like a badger, but he was interrupted by a quarrel that had broken out between Alfie and Junior.

"Make Junior give me back my coaster wagon, Papa!" Alfie tried to jerk the wagon away from Junior who responded by calling him a big crybaby.

"I told you you was too little to shovel dirt. Take your ol' coaster wagon. I'll take turns with Cliff on the wheel barrow. Coaster wagons are for babies anyway."

"Here! Here!" Papa called out. "Stop scufflin' an haul dirt. The cyclone'll be on us while you scuffle over the wagon." He turned to Willie. "Put your shovel down Willie. That ought to do it. The paper said seven feet but ain't nobody gonna stay in here long enough to grow seven feet tall. It's time to start puttin' a roof over this hole."

Laying aside his shovel and taking up his carpentry tools, Papa sawed and hammered the sturdy boards together with the biggest nails he could find. "Better toenail 'em down too, Willie. Don't want the wind to pull the nails out."

Alfie watched, open mouthed, convinced that a wind that could drive a wheat straw through a board could pull a nail out of it. "Papa, what'll happen if the wind pulls out all the nails?"

"Ain't gonna happen 'cause I'm toenailin' 'em all down." When the roof structure began to resemble the illustration in the newspaper, Papa said to Willie "Bring me that piece of eight inch stovepipe. The one with the elbow in it. That'll let the air in an' keep the rain out." He fitted it into place. "There. If your Gran'ma breathes any more air than that she'll come down with pneumonia."

But Gran'ma,impelled by curiosity, had come to watch at this point, and she allowed that the hole was big enough to let in the air but nobody would drag her into a hole in the ground ahead of her time. "Ain't nobody gonna go till his time comes, and when the Lord comes for ‘im, hidin’ in a root cellar ain’t gonna do ‘im no good.” Gran’ma worked her toothless gums vigorously to make her point, then spat a stream of snuff juice into the red clay at her feet to drive the point home.

Papa took Gran’ma’s rejection of the cyclone shelter good naturedly. “Well I hope you’re right about not goin’ ahead of time but I aim to put off my time till I git rich an’ have a chance to enjoy it, an’ if the Lord comes rappin’ on the roof of this cyclone shelter in the midst of a cyclone, I reckon I’ll let Him in but I ain’t goin’ out in the storm to meet ‘im.”

“Well if you don’t aim to go till you git rich, you’ll live to be as old as Methuselah unless the price of cotton goes up..” She reached into her apron pocket for her can of snuff, found it almost empty. “But if you go to the store before the cyclone hits I wish you’d git me a can of Brewton’s sweet snuff. I’m out.”

“Ain’t no time now to be runnin’ to the store to buy snuff. The cyclone’ll be on us before we git the job done if I go runnin’ off to the store to buy snuff. You’ll just hafta make what you’ve got last till we git the cyclone shelter finished.” Papa knew from experience that Gran’ma always declared she was out while there was still a little dab in the snuff can.

Papa turned to Cliff. “You fill up that lantern with Kerosene. And clean the chimney and trim the wick. Do it now. When the cyclone hits there won’t be no time for doin’ little things like that. The time to do it is now, not when we’re runnin’ from a cyclone.” Papa stood back and surveyed all that he had done and decided that it was good. He was ready for the cyclone. But when the cyclone approached, Papa was not near the shelter. He was plowing corn on the back side of the farm.

“Whoa Kate!” Papa called and Kate stood still in the traces, moving her great sensitive ears backward and forward nervously and flicking her skin. “Storm’s comin’ up.” Papa began unhitching. He looped the trace chains over Kate’s hames and picked up the plow lines. “Fast too,” he added, for the air which had at first been still and oppressive, suddenly began to move in gusts, whipping the corn leaves about. He and Kate started toward the house in a fast trot. When they turned into the stable

Kate's harness was slapping against her heaving sides, and the wind was getting stronger by the minute.

Papa looked toward the house and he saw Mama coming across the yard with her apron strings flapping about her body and her great brown eyes were wide with fear. The wind was gusting out of the Northwest and whipping the limbs on the big oak tree so that some of them almost swept the ground with their leaves. Gran'ma stood for a moment on the porch, squinting at the darkening sky and grabbing ineffectually at her bonnet strings which were flying about her face. Papa yelled "Git the younguns and run for the storm pit. A cyclone's comin' an' there ain't no time to waste!" He turned back into the stable, jerked the harness off Kate and flung it across the feed trough, slammed the stable door and stood for a moment scanning the sky. Dark, angry looking clouds were gathering in the West. "Make haste!" Papa shouted... "Make haste!"

Mama looked toward the storm shelter and she saw Willie standing there, holding up the cover. He was opening and closing his mouth but Mama couldn't hear a word Willie said because the wind just sucked the words out of his mouth and carried them away. Then everything became very quiet and still for a moment. Willie called "Come on ya'll! The wind's so strong I can't hardly hold the lid up. Come on!"

Alfie was running between Mama and Papa, but Mama said "You run on to Willie, Alfie. I have to go back for Gran'ma." But Gran' ma had already got down the steps and she broke into a trot, gathering up her long black skirts and moving at a remarkable clip for a lady of her age and religious convictions about storms and death.Papa went to help her anyway because he was afraid she would trip in her long skirts, and when they got to the cyclone shelter she looked anxiously into Willie's face.

"Lord God, Willie," Gran' ma declared, "You make haste an' git in there outta this storm." But Willie had to hold up the lid for everybody else and Gran'ma hobbled down the steps with Papa steadying her as well as he could. Junior and Alfie were already huddling in one corner of the pit, and when Mama and Gran'ma reached the bottom step Papa turned back to Willie who was still struggling to hold up the lid.

"Pull the lid down behind you as you come, Willie!" Willie was twisting around and getting into position to lower the lid when Mama missed Cliff.

"Where's Cliff?" Mama's eyes were big as egg yolks in the half light of the pit. Willie was wrestling with the cover, standing on the top step. Papa looked all around and bellowed for Cliff in a voice that filled the cyclone shelter, but since Cliff was not inside the storm pit, Papa's voice didn't reach him.

"God A'mighty! Wait a minute Willie!" Papa bolted back up the steps and he and Willie wrestled with the cover again outside, They looked frantically in every direction, and Papa bellowed "Cliff!" again, but Cliff didn't answer. They shoved the cover down over the storm cellar, and Papa looked at the sky again. "Look yonder in the West, Willie! That cloud's as black as my ol' hat an' shaped jest like a funnel.''

Willie's eyes were large with fright. "Come on Papa. We got to find Cliff!" They started running toward the old hay barn. Willie said afterwards that he just had a feeling about the old hay barn. Gran'ma said it was as plain as the nose on your face that the Lord was leading them in that direction because that's where they found Cliff. Anybody with knowledge of the depth of affection Cliff felt for that red bull calf that Papa had let him claim could have figured it out with or without divine guidance.

When they found Cliff he was tugging at the end of a rope and the red bull calf was hanging back on the other end. Papa said "What the hell are you doin' up here in the hay barn?" Cliff said that he was trying to get the bull calf to the cyclone shelter so he wouldn't be blown away, and Papa said "Drop that damn rope an' come on here.'' Then Papa and Willie got hold of Cliff, one on each side of him because he still wasn't willing to leave the bull calf, and they dragged him out of the old hay barn and started running toward the cyclone shelter. Papa looked once again at the black funnel cloud, and said "It's comin' closer by the second! Make haste!" Willie lifted the cover and Papa shoved Cliff inside and down the steps. Mama was standing at the bottom of the steps, lantern in hand, and the lantern's flickering light was throwing shadows on the red clay walls of the storm cellar.

Gran'ma blinked her eyes, her lips trembled, her hands were trembling too, and she said "Lord God, they found 'im and he's still alive. Git in here boy. Where was you? I'll allow you was someplace about that old hay barn jest a temptin' the Lord to blow it down on you an' take you away with it."

Willie was now inside and tugging away at the rope on the cover but the wind was pulling at it from the topside, and Willie called out to Papa, "Help me Papa! The suction's too strong for me.!" Papa got hold of the rope too and he and Willie pulled and pulled but even then the wind was stronger, but then everything became quiet. The wind let up for a moment and the lid fell into place with a loud thump.

Papa said "I reckon the eye of the storm musta passed over us, but hang on to that rope, Willie. Don't turn it loose. It might still pull the lid off an' suck us right outta here."

Mama wanted to know where Papa and Willie had found Cliff, but they were too busy holding down the cover to answer questions, and Cliff was too scared. The wind had started up again and Papa and Willie clenched their teeth and braced their feet against the cellar wall, and they hung onto the rope and the cover kept jumping up and down in spite of all they could do. Junior told Mama that he bet he could help them hold the lid down, but Mama said "You just stay out of your Papa's way. Go over there and see about your Gran'ma. But Gran'ma was praying fervently for deliverance; she was evidently counting on bigger help than Junior could offer. Then there was a noise like a freight train roaring overhead. Nobody could hear anything except the roaring of the wind, with the possible exception of the Lord hearing Gran' ma. The cover lifted off its base and went a foot or two into the air, taking Papa and Willie with it. Then it suddenly fell back into place, and Papa and Willie dropped back to the floor of the cellar, still clinging to the rope.

Gran'ma jumped from her knees to her feet when the cover slammed back into place. "Lord God!" she cried. "We're gonna be killed. And in this hole in the ground." Mama's concern about the possibility of immediate death was lessened when the cyclone shelter cover dropped back into place, but she was still upset over Cliff, and demanded to know where they had found him.

"Mama! Papa!" Alfie called out in distress. "We forgot Sandy! We got to go an' find Sandy!"

"Lord have mercy!" Mama said, "We can't go out in this storm to look for that trifling dog." Alfie was already running up the steps and clutching at Papa's leg, begging to be let out. "You come back here to me!" Mama called. But Alfie clung to Papa and he wouldn't come back to Mama.

"The very idea!" Mama said. "Wanting to go out in this storm to look for that no account dog!" Mama was still provoked at Sandy over his recent amorous excursion into whatever regions of Colaparchee County he had gone in search of immortality.

"He ain't a no count dog, Mama. He's mine!" Alfie called out at the top of his voice "Sandy! Sandy!" And there was the sound of thumping on the hard clay floor of the cyclone pit.

Papa said "Hand me that lantern." And he raised the lantern and moved it about until he saw the reflected light coming from two eyes in the Southeast corner of the pit. Papa said "There he lays. That's a damn' dog for you. When you needed him to whup that ol' black hound of Seeb's he was off runnin' after a bitch in heat, an' now I'll bet my hat he was the first one to git in here when the storm come up."

"I could have told you that," Willie said. "He run in here as soon as I lifted the top on it."

Mama was provoked. "Let a sleeping dog lie," she said. "What I want to know is where Cliff was."

"He was in the old hay barn an' hangin' to that damn bull calf by a rope." Papa hung to the rope and spoke through clenched teeth.

"In that old hay barn!" Mama echoed Papa's words. "And that old barn's going to blow away in this storm!" Mama's words were punctuated by a loud crash on the roof of the cyclone shelter, followed by heavy rain pounding on the roof, then beginning to drip and very quickly to stream into the pit because whatever had fallen on the roof had broken some of the boards.

"Lord God!" Gran' ma wailed. She was holding her little snuff can in her gnarled, trembling fingers, but she couldn't get the lid off it. "We're buried alive here and now we'll drown to death in this infernal hole in the ground." Infernal was about as close as Gran' ma ever came to using profanity but the circumstances were sufficiently extenuating to warrant this use.

The water was still streaming in and forming mud on the floor of the pit. Mama gathered up the quilts that had been placed there as protection against cold, and piled them on the steps out of reach of the water. Cliff started to help her and this drew her attention to him again. "What were you doing in that old hay barn anyway? You could have been killed!" Papa's statement that Cliff was hanging to the bull calf by a rope had not satisfied Mama's need for an explanation; at least it had not allayed her anxiety about Cliff. But Papa was no longer concerned about Cliff; he had something else to worry about.

"Wonder what's fell on the roof," Papa listened to the rain pounding and watched it streaming in. "The wind's died down some, Willie. We got to git out there an' see what's fell on the roof." He and Willie started to push against the cover but they couldn't move it. "Somethin's blowed down an' layin' on it." He pushed again but the lid wouldn't move.

Junior watched Papa and Willie trying to push the cover off the cyclone shelter and he was sure that all they needed was his help. "I bet I can move it. Lemme help." He ran to the top of the steps and tried to pry the lid up with his fingers. The lid slipped a little, Junior's fingers were caught, and he cried "Ouch! My fingers!" Willie and Papa put their shoulders against the cover and moved it enough for Junior to get his fingers out. He put them in his mouth and sucked them to relieve the pain. Tears formed in his eyes, but he said "Shucks. It don't hurt much. If I had some way to brace myself..."

Papa looked at Junior's fingers and decided he was not hurt badly. "If a frog had wings he wouldn't bump his ass ev'ry time he jumps neither. Now stay outta the way." He examined the hole in the roof where the water was still coming through, but the stream was smaller because it was not raining as hard as it had been at the height of the storm. "Well, it looks like we're trapped." He felt all about in his overall pockets for the makings of a cigarette. "Can't move it. Somethin' heavy's layin; on it."

"Lord God!" Gran'ma wailed. "Trapped in this hole in the ground and can't git out! I knowed we'd be buried alive here."

"What are you going to do now?" Mama picked up the lantern and held it so that she could examine the hole in the shelter cover. "I can see something up there." The water dripped into Mama's face and she decided she had seen enough. Papa had found his little sack of Bull Durham and he was sitting on the step, pouring tobacco into a cigarette paper which he held cupped between his fingers. He rolled the tobacco filled paper, licked the edges, then twisted the ends. The result closely resembled a cigarette Now Papa was fumbling through all of his pockets for a match, but he couldn't find one. The rain was pounding harder now on the roof and pouring through the hole into the storm cellar, but Papa was whistling tunelessly. This meant that he was thinking. Alfie crept onto Papa's lap and looked up into his face. Big tears were brimming in Alfie's eyes and his voice quavered.

"What are we gonna do, Papa, if we can't git outta here?

"We're jest gonna sit here and wait." Papa was still searching through his pockets but not finding what he wanted. "You run over there and ask your Mama to send me a match. We're jest gonna sit here and wait till the storm's over and maybe somebody'll come an' let us out. Ain't nothin' else to do."

"They'll find us buried alive and drowned to death." Gran'ma was exploring the bottom of her snuff can with her forefinger, but not finding anything. "And I'm outta snuff."

"Maybe not." Papa seemed more concerned about lighting his cigarette than getting out of the cyclone shelter. He suspected that Gran'ma's major concern at the moment was snuff, but he didn't say it. "Maybe somebody'll find us before we drown. It ain't gonna rain that much nohow. It's already beginnin' to slack up." Mama dug through a bag of soggy supplies and came up with the matches. Alfie brought them to Papa. Papa tried to strike them but the heads crumbled and fell off. "Wet!" Papa was disgusted. "The matches are all wet." And Alfie began to cry; the wet matches were the last straw. But then they heard a sound like someone stamping on the roof. Papa said "Listen. I think I hear somethin'."

"Hello. Anybody down there?" The voice came from above.

Papa threw the match stem into the water on the floor. He winked at Alfie. "Yeah. We're all down here."

"I think it's Mister Charles." Alfie sat up on Papa's lap and looked toward the sound of the voice. It was coming through the hole in the roof. "It sounds like Mister Charles."

"Charles?" Mama stared at the hole in the roof. Water was still dripping through. "Get us out of here, Charles, before these children catch their death of colds."

"Charles? Is that Charles up there?" Gran'ma returned the empty snuff can to her apron pocket. "The Lord be praised. We're saved. And jest in the nick of time. Git us outta this hole in the ground Charles before we drown to death."

Papa put his face up close to the hole in the roof, ignoring the drip. "What's fell on top of the cyclone shelter, Charles? Can you tell what it is?"

"The wind blowed the roof off that ol' hay barn and it's fell right on top of the storm pit," Mister Charles leaned close to the hole to speak. "But you jest stay right where you're at. I'll git the axe an' chop it off an' git you all outta here in no time...Right smack dab on top of it. Jest picked it up and dropped it right smack dab on top of the storm pit." Mister Charles started away toward the woodpile to get the axe. He stopped, came back, and this time he leaned close to the stove pipe vent. It carried his voice, magnified but tinny. "Stay right where you're at. I'll be right back."

"I reckon we won't go very far from where we're at." Papa ran his fingers quickly through his pockets again in search of a match. "You'll find the axe stickin' in the choppin' log. We'll wait right here for you." Mister Charles was gone when Papa observed that "A smoke sure would make it easier to wait." He turned again to Mama. "Look an' see if there ain't some dry matches somewhere." Junior felt in his pockets and drew out a dry stick match which he gave to Papa without saying a word, but watching Papa's face closely. Papa struck the match, lit his cigarette, snuffed out the match and threw the stem into the water. "What are you doin' carryin' matches in your pockets? You be careful you don't burn the house down." He inhaled the smoke and let it out in two streams through his nostrils.

Mister Charles came back and called down through the crack in the roof. "I'm gonna start choppin'. Don't worry none. I'll have this ol' rotten barn roof offa here in a jiffy."

Gran'ma praised the Lord while Mister Charles chopped and smashed and dragged the debris from the roof of the cyclone shelter. After a while Mister Charles said "Now push up from down there.I'll pull up on it from here." Papa and Willie pushed and Junior and Cliff went to help. Mostly they got in the way. Alfie watched intently, but he didn't push any except from inside himself.

Mama said "Push, Cliff, but don't get in your Papa's way. The very idea of you being up there in that old hay barn. You could have been killed. Lord have mercy!"

Gran'ma gave Cliff a disapproving look too, but she was too happy about their deliverance to worry anymore about Cliff.

"The Lord sent Charles to deliver us from a watery grave. Praise God!" Papa and the boys were pushing from below and Mister Charles was pulling from up above, and soon there was an opening large enough for Papa to crawl through. There stood Mister Charles in his gum boots and smiling proudly. He leaned down to look at everybody inside the cyclone shelter.

They all looked back happily at Mister Charles and Gran'ma worked her gums and said to him "Why Lord God Charles, the Lord sent you jest in the nick of time to save us all from a watery grave." Papa and Mister Charles moved some more of the old barn roof and made the escape hatch bigger. Alfie and Junior helped Gran'ma climb out, and Cliff helped Mama. Willie went with Papa and Mister Charles to help move the debris. Sandy didn't need any help. He had been the first to enter and he was not the last to leave. Cliff's red bull calf came over to Mister Charles and started licking his overalls. Mister Charles said he reckoned it was because his overalls smelled like milk. The bull calf was not hurt.

Papa surveyed the scene of wreckage. Leaves and broken limbs from the trees were scattered about.. Young corn stalks in a nearby field were flattened against the ground. Debris from the old hay barn lay everywhere, with rain soaked hay clinging to the barbed wire fence. "God A'mighty!" Papa said. "It was the old hay barn all right. The cyclone just took the roof right ,off it and dumped it on top of the cyclone shelter."

Mama looked as if she were about to say "I told you so!" But instead she said "Well thank the Lord the house is still standing. Come on Charles. I'll make a pot of coffee. Cliff, you busy yourself and find some dry kindling to make a fire in the stove. Land sakes, leave that calf to look out for himself!"

Gran'ma planted her feet firmly on the muddy ground. She turned her blinking eyes toward the house. "Ain't but a few shingles blowed off the roof!" she crowed. "I kep' tellin' you there wasn't no sense runnin' in a hole in the ground to git away from a storm." That was for Papa's benefit.

She turned to Mister Charles and said "Well you come on to the house Charles. The Lord sent you to git us all outta that hole in the ground and the least we can do is invite you to come in the house out of the wet."

Papa and Mister Charles started to follow Gran'ma to the house, but Alfie clutched at Papa's hand and tried to pull him away toward the slab fence Papa had built about the cow lot. The wind had knocked most of the fence flat but here and there a board hung at an angle from the sturdy posts he had sunk into the ground. "Come on Papa!" Alfie insisted."Let's go and see if the cyclone drove a wheat straw through the board fence!"

"God A'mighty!" Papa's blue eyes twinkled with merriment. "Come on Charles. The coffee can wait. Let's all go and see. I reckon there ain't a wheat straw left in Colaparchee County after that big wind passed through here. Unless it is one that's stuck in a board fence."

Chapter Fifteen: Ol' Needmo'

Daybreak on the day after the cyclone! The sun rose like a great ball of fire on a world reborn in that short midsummer night while Alfie slept. And Papa was eager. Papa always had to walk in great long strides all over the farm after a big rain, or even after a gentle shower, to see how much the corn and the cotton and everything else had grown. After the storm he had to see both the good and the bad.

"I wanta see what it's tore up." Papa said. "And what it's growed up."

But Papa looked at Alfie and said "I wonder about Seeb and Hattie. I wonder if the cyclone done any damage at their house."

"I could go an' see, Papa." Alfie's eyes grew large with the expectation of finding out what had happened there. "Uncle Seeb an' Aunt Hattie don't have no cyclone shelter, but I could go an' see if they're all right. If you'll let me go."

"You'll hafta run an' ask your Mama first." For if Alfie asked Papa he always said "You'll hafta ask your Mama." But if he asked Mama first, she would say "Ask your Papa."

"Ask your Mama and then you run up there an' check up on them two, but don't stay so long your Mama'll git worried and hafta send for you." Alfie started to run, hesitated, and Papa read the fear in his face. "Sandy can go with you to keep that ol' black dog of Seeb's offa you."

Alfie found Uncle Seeb sitting on a cane bottom, straight back chair tilted against the porch wall. He was admiring the glorious sunrise. Seeb was a ponderous man with an impressive belly that balanced him on the chair when it was tilted back against the wall. His neck was thick and the skin gathered in folds there, and the sweat ran down most of the time when it was hot; it was hot most of the time in summer. In Colaparchee County it was hot at daybreak with the sun coming up like a great ball of fire in the sky.

Seeb's face shone like the sun itself, but it was like a black shining sun, like ebony. Papa said "I don't reckon there's another face in Colaparchee County that's blacker 'n Seeb's." And Papa ought to know because he was acquainted with the people of color in Colaparchee County. Black, yellow, brown, and just pale. But he favored the ones who were black because Papa didn't approve of mixing, and when he saw a yellow face, or a pale one with reddish frizzy hair, he would say "There's been a white man in the wrong bed somewhere." You could tell that Papa didn't approve. Papa approved of Seeb though, the blackest man in the county.

Seeb smiled when he saw Alfie coming and he displayed an impressive array of ivory in his mouth matching the whiteness of his eyes, which made the blackness of his face shine even brighter by contrast. Seeb had a mouth full of white teeth, but he had one tooth that was not white. It was gold. Seeb's gold tooth caught and held Alfie's eye whenever Seeb smiled, which was whenever he looked at Alfie, and once Alfie had stared wonderingly at the great black face with its toothy smile and he had said "Uncle Seeb how come you got one yellow tooth?"

Then Seeb said "Lawd, Alfie, now you talkin' 'bout my gold tooth?"

Alfie nodded solemnly and said "How come you got one gold tooth?"

Seeb smiled again and said "Now you done ast 'bout somethin' goes way back befo' you wuz bawn, an' befo' I wuz bawn ag'in."

Alfie's wonderment grew and Seeb said "Befo' my Lawd tole me to give up my bad ways an' go preach His Name."

Six days in the week Seeb was a cotton and corn tenant farmer, but on Sunday he was a preacher. Six days a week he labored in the cotton field, but one day a week he labored in the Lord's vineyard. Six days he was black Seeb, the blackest in Colaparchee county, but on that one day he was The Rev'rend. And when he stood in the pulpit of the Shiloh Baptist Church, dressed in his black suit, and when he opened his black leatherette bound Bible, then his black face shone with the fire of the Lord. "Befo' I give up my bad ways an' become a preacher."

"What bad ways did you hafta give up when you become a preacher, Uncle Seeb? What bad ways?"

"Fightin', Alfie." Seeb was reflective. Alfie waited.

"I wuz bad 'bout fightin' in my younger days. An' there wuz this pretty little gal. She wuz a high yeller an' I thought she the prettiest gal I ever seen. But I ain't the onliest one think that. Other young fellers think it too. So we got into a big fight over that pretty little gal an' I los' mah tooth an' tha's how come I got one gol' tooth."

"Did it grow back gold, Uncle Seeb? Did it grow back thataway?"

"Lawd no, Alfie. Hit cost me a bale of cotton, this gol' sooth did. No, Alfie, hit didn't grow back lak they do for you 'cause I done got too big an' old fer that when I got to fightin' an' los' my tooth. This gol' tooth hit cost me a bale of cotton."

Seeb displayed the gold tooth for Alfie's admiration by flashing a big smile at him. "I ain't proud of how I come to have it but now I got it." Alfie could see that Seeb was proud of the gold tooth though and he wished that he could have a gold tooth to replace the one that was getting loose and Papa had been teasing him to let him pull.

Alfie sat on the doorstep to think about what Seeb had said and he forgot that he had come to see if the cyclone had done any damage. Sandy was standing on the ground near the steps, growling and with his bristles up just to let Seeb's old hound know that he had better stay under the house. The hound barked some and he even growled a little, but the growl ended up sounding more like a whine, and he backed farther under the house. Alfie sat quietly thinking about things.

Then Alfie remembered the cyclone. "That was some storm we had, wasn't it Uncle Seeb? We all run in the cyclone shelter when it hit."

"Sho'nuff!" Seeb had been able to see from a distance that the old hay barn was missing its roof, but that was all he had seen until he saw Papa and his family climbing out of the storm shelter. He had counted them then as they came out, even Sandy, and he had said to Hattie "Thank the Lawd evvybody safe 'cept the old hay barn. Hit look lak hit done lost hits cap."

Now Seeb flashed a great white and golden smile at Alfie "Ol' Massa, when he go on a rampage He sho' tear up jack! When 'at bolta lightnin' hit I said to Hattie Ol' Massa sho' th'owin' a fit. Ef you done ennything bad here lately you better be prayin'." Seeb laughed to let Alfie know that he was joking about Aunt Hattie being the one who needed to pray but Aunt Hattie appeared in the kitchen doorway at that moment. She had a little pan of bread scraps in her hand and she frowned at Seeb.

"Lawd have mercy! You oughtta be 'shamed of yo'se'f Rev'ren', sayin' a thing lak that in front of Alfie an' him jest a chile."

She pitched the bread scraps out into the yard. Eight or ten chickens came running to get them, fighting over them. There were some Barred Rocks, commonly called Domineckers, a few Rhode Island Reds and some mixed,but all of them hungry. One old Dominecker who had been moulting and hadn't yet replaced the feathers she had lost, came over to Alfie, looked up at him with her head cocked to one side, and pecked at his little toe nail. "Shoo!" Alfie kicked at her and drew his feet up under him. Turning to Aunt Hattie, he said "That ol' hen thinks my toe nail is a grain of corn."

Then Aunt hattie noticed that Alfie was sitting on the wet doorstep and she said "Law me Alfie! You settin' on nem wet do'steps an I bet you done got yo' britches wet in the seat." She lifted Alfie and felt the seat of his short pants and said "Sho' nuff! You soppin' wet an yo' Mama goan th'ow a fit an' I be the one to hafta wash an' iron 'em too. Lemme git you a cheer to set in."

"Aw, I don't mind a little wet, Aunt Hattie. It ain't gonna hurt me. You should a seen the water in the cyclone shelter yesterday."

"I bet, an' now I heah you got trapped in that ol' hole befo' it was all over. Still that ain't no cause for you to set on wet do'steps at my house an' yo' Mama think I doan know how to treat you when you come to visit."

Aunt Hattie went back into the house to get a chair for Alfie, and a fly landed on Alfie's bare knee. He slapped at it, missed, the fly lifted into the air and settled on his other bare knee. The dominecker hen came back to have another close look at his toe. Alfie said "Uncle Seeb, how come you don't screen in your porch? You could screen it in an' then nothin' couldn't git in to bother you."

Alfie didn't mention the flies and chickens by name. Mama had told him not to say things that might hurt Uncle Seeb's and Aunt Hattie's feelings, so he just said "Nothin' couldn't git in to bother you if you had a screened in porch."

But Seeb's great belly shook with laughter when Alfie asked, and his black face shone like it had been polished, and his teeth flashed white and gold, and he said "How come? On accounta ol' Needmo', Alfie. Tha's how come. On accounta ol' Needmo."

Alfie stared in wonderment at Uncle Seeb then and said "Who's ol' Needmo', Uncle Seeb?"

"You ain't never hear tell of Ol' Needmo', Alfie? Lawd! I 'lowed yo' Mama an' yo' Papa done tol' you 'bout ol' Needmo'. Jes' about evvybody know ol' Needmo."

Alfie's wonderment deepened. He had never heard of Ol' Needmo'. Gran'ma had told him about The Booger Man, and Mama had explained that The Booger Man was just the Old Devil who gets people who are bad, which is why they sometimes called him The Bad Man. And Alfie was sufficiently frightened of The Bad Man not to go out by himself in the dark. Once he had awakened from a bad dream in which The Bad Man was chasing him with a pitchfork. He was sleeping with Junior, and he raised up and cried out and jerked at the covers, but Junior said "Aw shut up and quit jerkin' the covers." But he had never heard of Ol' Needmo, and he looked solemnly at Uncle Seeb, thinking it must have been Ol' Needmo' who had made Uncle Seeb bad about fighting when he was a young man.

So Alfie looked solemnly and fearfully into Uncle Seeb's shining black face and said "Who's ol' Needmo' Uncle Seeb.? Tell me."

Then Uncle Seeb said "Needmo' flour to make biscuits to feed hungry younguns. Needmo' clo'es f'r Wintertime comin' on. Needmo' shoes f'r all our bare feet. Needmo' 'bout evy'thing so ain't no chance of buildin' no screen porch, Alfie. On accounta ol' Needmo'."

Aunt Hattie came back with a chair that matched the one Uncle Seeb was sitting on and she called to Alfie "Heah, Alfie, you set on a cheer now an' I hope you stay long anuff for yo' britches to dry 'cause I sho don' want you to go home an' yo' Mama see you been settin' on my wet do'steps."

Alfie said "Aw it don't matter Aunt Hattie. I don't mind if I git wet in hot weather; it don't matter. I don't mind."

It was hot weather and Uncle Seeb's BVD's were already wet with the sweat of his enormous body. Once Alfie had asked "Uncle Seeb, how come you wear your Winter underwears in the Summer time? Ain't they hot?"

Alfie himself pulled off everything Mama would let him pull off in hot weather. The first thing in the Spring he set in on her to go barefoot. Then he wanted to shed his underwear. Then his shirt. His back and shoulders would get sunburned and the skin would peel off and Mama would say "Lord! Alfie, you've blistered again! If you don't wear a shirt when you're out in the sun you'll burn up! Just look at you!"

But when Alfie asked Seeb about wearing his heavy knitted BVD's in the Summertime, Seeb said "Naw, Alfie. onst they git wet with sweat hit's jest lak bein' wrapped in a cool wet blanket. The mo' I sweats the cooler I gits, inside my BVD's."

But now Alfie was sitting on the straight back cane bottom chair Aunt Hattie had brought, and his feet wouldn't reach the floor, so he hooked them behind one of the rungs of the chair. He thought that would hide them from the old Dominecker hen. But then Uncle Seeb's face became very serious and he said "Alfie, whut you gon' be when you grow up?"

Uncle Seeb didn't say anything about the hairs on Alfie's arms, and raising pigs. He just said "Whut you gon'be when you grow up, Alfie?" And he leaned back against the wall, with the front feet of the chair raised off the floor and his big belly balancing him, and he waited, watching Alfie. Smiling, but serious too.

Then Alfie thought about the time he rode with Papa to Mister Robb's, and he frowned. He remembered Uncle Babe and the frown grew deeper. He thought about Tex on the chain gang, and the dump truck, and he sucked in his breath and looked fearfully at Uncle Seeb, as if he were guarding his secret.

Uncle Seeb was watching Alfie's face and seeing the frown, and he said "But you don' hafta tell me ef you don' wanta. I jest ast an' ef hit's yo' secret an' you ain't ready to tell nobody 'bout it you don't hafta tell nobody. Hit's jest yo' secret an' hit don't b'long to nobody else."

Alfie started to say something. He was going to say he didn't mind Uncle Seeb knowing but he didn't want anybody else to know. Uncle Seeb stopped him though. "Sho' now you got a secret an' you got a right to keep yo' secret an' you don' hafta tell it to nobody. I jest ast an' you don' hafta tell me lessen you wants me to know."

Then because of what Uncle Seeb had said, that he didn't have to tell, Alfie knew that he wanted to tell. He wanted to share his secret with Uncle Seeb. Aunt Hattie was standing in the doorway too. She was holding the little pan again with some more bread scraps, and she was waiting because she could see that this was a serious conversation going on between Alfie and Seeb, and she didn't want to interrupt it. And Alfie saw Aunt Hattie standing there, and he knew that it was all right for Aunt Hattie to know too, and he looked at Uncle Seeb and he flushed a little. Then he looked at Aunt Hattie out of the corner of his eye. He looked down at his bare feet which he had now taken from behind the chair rung for that purpose, so he could study them while he was making up his mind what to say to Uncle Seeb and Aunt Hattie.

He looked back at Uncle Seeb and he said "I'm gonna be a preacher like you when I grow up."

Just like that, quiet and solemn. And Uncle Seeb brought the two front legs of his chair down on the pine boards of the porch floor like twin pistol shots. "Lawd God!" he said.

"A preacher! You heah whut Alfie say, ol' woman? He gon' be a preacher when he grow up!" Seeb's great black shining face was radiant and he said "Lawd done laid His hand on Alfie. He gon' be a preacher!"

Then Aunt Hattie's face was all wreathed in smiles too, and she seemed about to hug Alfie, and Seeb gave her a restraining glance, and he said "Now you done heah Alfie too but don' you go blabbin' it to nobody. He done tol' us but ef he want ennybody else to know, he tell it hisse'f. But ain't nobody in my house goin' 'bout over the neighborhood blabbin' it."

"Sho' I know. When Alfie want ever'body to know he tell it hisse'f." Aunt Hattie 's face beamed, and she walked quickly to the edge of the porch and tossed the bread scraps into the yard. Her eyes focused on a young rooster, less than half grown. He was standing fearfully at the edge of the flock of chickens, and she said to the young rooster "You git in an' git yo' share, chicken, 'cause you goin' inta the ministry one a these days soon. Alfie gon' be a preacher an' he gon' start practisin' up on you."

She slapped her knee with the empty pan and shouted "Praise God! We gonna have us a chicken dinner heah soon as I ketch that young rooster an' wring his neck. An' we see how Alfie perfawm on a chicken leg!"

Alfie ducked his head self-consciously and he hopped down from the chair. "I reckon I better go home now," he said.

"Papa said for me not to stay so long Mama'll git worried and hafta send Junior for me."

He ran down the steps, scattering the squawking hens. Sandy barked, gave the black hound under the house a threatening glance, and then ran alongside Alfie.

"Awright Alfie. We proud you come to visit us. You tell yo' Mama I wash them britches when she pull 'em offa you...Law me, gonna be a preacher when he grow up. An' I gon' fry him a chicken to start off on."

Seeb stood up, straightening his back slowly because of the lumbago, and he said "You hurry back to see us Alfie an' we tawk some mo' 'bout things.." As Alfie raced away, Sandy racing beside him and barking like a herald of the coming of the Lord, Uncle Seeb called out again "Bye Alfie, you come back an we whup Ol' Needmo' one a these days. Praise God! Gonna be a preacher when he grow up!"

Chapter Sixteen: Alfie's Got A Sweetheart

Alfie was quiet and reserved after his visit to Uncle Seeb's and Aunt Hattie's. This was unusual and it caught Papa's attention. "What ails that boy? Solemn as a judge all of a sudden. You don't reckon his conscience is botherin' 'im?" Mama didn't respond to that and Papa went on. "He ain't big enough yet to do anything to give him a bothersome conscience. Now if it was one of the others, Cliff or Junior, I might suspect somethin'. And Willie. But Willie's quiet by nature so you can't never tell when he's been into somethin' and when he ain't, but as a rule it's a safe bet he has. But this ain't like Alfie to be so quiet."

Mama said she thought it was because he was starting school in September. "He was happy about it too until Georgia came by and said what she did about the first grade teacher. Now Alfie's been out of sorts ever since."

"What did Georgia say this time?"

"Oh, she told this wild tale about Miss Millie being moved from the sixth grade to the first grade and about her being such a terror that she had all the children scared to death of her and now Alfie's scared she'll land on him like a chicken on a June Bug when he goes in."

"What did Georgia say she done to git such a bad name?"

"She said that Millie beat them unmercifully and even threw a piece of chalk all the way across the room and nearly hit the Tidwell boy in the eye with it. But you know Georgia."

"I know Georgia and I know boys too and I guess the damage has been exaggerated by both of 'em. I'd say the boys that got a whuppin' had earned ev'ry lick and if Georgia'd talk less it'd be a powerful favor to the whole neighborhood." Papa was about as hard on gadabouts of the female gender as he was on mischief makers of the male gender.

Mama was inclined to come to the defense of anybody under attack from Papa, but she was provoked with Georgia this time. "Well, the tale on the school teacher does come mighty close on the heels of the Gypsy tale, and I'm not sure Alfie has got over that yet."

Papa was debating in his own mind whether to say something more since he and Mama seemed to be of one mind for a change, or whether to cut and run while he was still ahead. Then Mama said "Anyway, Alfie was scared out of his wits and he said he didn't want to go to school."

"Well, now he did mention that to me too. Said he'd decided not to go to school because he already knows enough without it and he wants to stay home and he'p me here on the farm."

"What did you tell him?"

"Oh, I promised 'im he could claim a pig outta the next litter the ol' sow has if he would go on an pretend not to know ev'rything. I made 'im promise not to git caught smokin' no rabbit terbaccer either while we was tradin'. So I 'specs he'll be out at the road when the school bus comes for 'im."

Mama did not think Papa was treating the subject with the seriousness it deserved. But Mama and Papa did not see eye to eye on things as a rule, where the boys were concerned, and one of the things they did not always see eye to eye on was the boys' education. Mama would fret and fuss if the boys did not do well in school and if they presented behavior problems for Miss Florrie and the other teachers, but Papa had a quick fix for both bad grades and bad conduct reports.

"If I hear about you gittin' a whuppin' at school I'll give you another one when you git home." This was a powerful incentive to suppress any reports of Miss Florrie's wielding of the orange wood paddle.

"And if you can't study your books and behave yourself I will put you between the plow handles and you can study the rear end of the mule all day and I reckon then you might find arithmetic more interestin'."

Neither Mama nor Papa had plumbed the depths of Alfie's troubled waters. He was in love, and as is always the case with the first bout of infection, it was a virulent case, and having built up no immunity through previous exposure, he had succumbed to it, and he had found himself helpless in love's coils as a bird in the coils of a chicken snake.

But he was not talking about it. He was not telling Papa, for he had learned that secrets of such a personal nature were not to be shared with Papa. Nor Mama. For she would say he was too young to even think about such a thing.

And not Junior. But Junior had already guessed the truth.

"Alfie's got a sweetheart. Alfie's got a sweetheart." Junior sang the taunting ditty to the universal tune and in the tone of children everywhere whenever they wish to torment one of their own kind, especially if the one being tormented is littler than his tormentors.

Alfie lay on the porch floor near the swing and he stared hard at the funny papers. If he stared hard enough at the funny pictures he could keep the tears from coming into his eyes. He began cutting the pictures from the funnies with his little blunt nosed scissors, and pretended that he did not hear what Junior was saying, or did not care, was not aware that he was being teased about Fay. But the tears came into his eyes anyway, salty, stinging his eyeballs, and he wanted to ball up his little fists and hit Junior, but Junior lay on the porch floor beyond the swing, at a safe distance. If Alfie jumped up and ran at Junior, then Junior could easily dodge, or fend him off, or even catch Alfie's hands and hold him prisoner to Junior's greater size and his superior strength. Powerless and frustrated then, there was nothing left for Alfie to do but cry out for Mama to come and make Junior stop teasing him.

Then Mama was there, for Mama could smell trouble brewing. Had she not smelled it often enough with four boys underfoot all the time, fighting and squabbling among themselves? "Stop teasing the baby about Fay." Mama's big brown eyes held Junior in their grip. "If he wants to play with Fay it's all right for him to play with her. It doesn't mean anything. Now stop teasing him."

Alfie glanced with liquid eyes at Fay, who was standing up now shaking the paper scraps from her red and white checked gingham dress, clutching the pictures Alfie had cut out for her. He would not let her use his scissors but he cut the pictures and gave them to her, the ones he wanted her to have, which were the ones he did not want for himself more than he wanted to give them to Fay. She held them tightly in her little hands, her lips trembled and she turned and ran down the steps and crossed the yard under the big oak tree that stood close to the house, its branches hanging out over the scuppernong arbor, and her little bare feet kicked up the sand as she ran. Alfie turned back to the funny papers. He was glad Mama had come to scold Junior for teasing him, but it was not altogether true that it did not mean anything. Fay was special simply because she was available and nobody else was, and he liked to play with Fay much better than he liked playing with Junior because he always had to do what Junior said, and when they played Fox and Hound Alfie always had to be the Hound and he could never catch Junior because Junior could run away fast on his long legs and leave Alfie struggling along and puffing and panting and about to cry.

But Alfie could run as fast as Fay could, almost, and sometimes Fay would let him catch her. Sometimes she would even fall down as they ran, so that Alfie would tumble onto the ground with her and she would laugh, panting for breath, and she would say "You caught me Alfie. I couldn't outrun you. You can run too fast."

When Mama had gone back to her work inside the house where she was making a shirt on the Singer Sewing Machine, Junior pretended to be reading the comics and he glanced at Andy Gump in his funny car with the motorcycle policeman throwing a hook on a rope to catch the rear bumper of Andy Gump's funny little car, but then Junior cut his eyes at Alfie and said "And she's a towhead too. Alfie's sweetheart is a towhead." Then he sang the taunting ditty, but not loudly enough for Mama to hear him. "Alfie loves a towhead. Alfie loves a towhead."

And what is so undesirable about loving a towhead? Indeed, what is a towhead? A towhead is, usually, a small girl child with blond hair bleached white by constant exposure to bright sunshine. And there is plenty of bright sunshine in Colaparchee County where red clay farm land lies along both banks of the Tobesofkee Creek which flows through the heart of Georgia. In the summer time the sunshine is both bright and hot and it is to be found by small children playing outside the farm houses. It can be found for as many as sixteen hours a day on those days which closely precede and follow the twenty first day of June. And on many of those days Alfie and Fay played in the hot bright sunshine, so that Fay's blond hair was burned white above her cornflower blue eyes. Even Alfie's dark locks showed the effect of the sun, but mostly they grew down heavy over his forehead and threatened to cover his big brown eyes, so that when Papa would look at Alfie he would say "God A'mighty! If I don't cut that boy's hair soon the dog catcher'll git 'im. Mistake 'im for an airedale as sure as gun barrel's iron." But Mama always changed the subject when Papa spoke of cutting off Alfie's hair. And Fay only smiled shyly and brushed her own sun bleached blond hair aside with a grimy little hand which she swiped across her face, leaving a dirty streak in its wake, and her cornflower blue eyes sparkled as she smiled at Alfie and she would say "Let's play, Alfie." But if Junior was watching, Alfie was reluctant to go and play with Fay, and she would say "Aw come on Alfie and play with me." For Fay was not aware that there is anything strange about a boy and a girl playing together, lost in the world of make believe, a wonderful world created out of the innocence of child hood and peopled with the fancied creatures that Alfie and Fay had fashioned as they played together in the sand under the big oak tree that stood in the corner of the yard near the house where Alfie lived with his Mama and his Papa and all his brothers, and sometimes even his Gran'ma.

Fay had many brothers too in the house where she lived across the cotton patch, that bordered the cow pasture and all her brothers were bigger than she was. Except for the baby. He was so little that sometimes Fay's Mama would say "Fay you hold the baby while I cook dinner. Your Pa'll come in from the field and he'll want his dinner and if I ain't got it ready for him to eat he'll want to know what I've been doin' all mornin' when I ought to be cookin' his dinner. Now you hold the baby and keep him from cryin' so I can have dinner on the table when your Pa comes in from the field." And that was why Fay's Mama had called her and she had straightened up and shaken the paper clippings from her red and white checked gingham dress, and holding the pictures Alfie had given her, turned to go.

"Ma's callin' me." Fay said. "I better go." Then she ran with her towhead lifted to the slight breeze and pointed toward the house across the cotton patch, but because there was a short cut through the pasture Fay darted under the barbed wire fence and started to run, but that was when the Holstein bull raised his head, saw Fay's running figure, shook his head up and down with the sunshine glinting on his horns, pawed the red clay earth with his right forefoot, switched his tail to knock the flies off his flanks, raised his ears to a horizontal position, and emitted a sound which began as a low moaning but grew until it became a loud bellowing which caused Fay to freeze in her tracks.

The bull was black and white, and not very large for he was a young bull, but he had begun to be aware that he was a bull in a pasture full of cows and heifers, and he was ready to challenge any intruder on his territory. His horns were about ten inches long and they pointed outward at an angle from his broad face, and they shone in the sunlight as if they had been polished, and indeed they had been for he had rubbed them against the bark of the trees in the pasture and shoved them into the hard red clay under his feet in the exhilarating discovery that he was a bull. Now he tossed his head, feeling the presence of the horns as his weapon and as if he were testing them for balance and effectiveness against a target.

And now there was the target, a small towheaded girl child in a red and white checked gingham dress that barely came to her sun browned knees and now swished and fluttered about her rapidly moving body as she raced toward home. But then the target stopped moving, stood frozen in its tracks, for Fay had heard the moaning sound that had grown and become a bellowing, and she stared in the direction of the sound, and her big blue eyes became even larger with fright, for she saw the bull shaking his head and pawing the red clay earth and swishing his tail with the dark coarse brush at the end of it and starting toward her in a trot the way the bulls in the bull rings in Spain begin to move when the bull fighter gets their attention, and although Fay had never even heard of bull fighters in Spain, she stopped and stood staring at the bull, for she was paralyzed with fear of the bull. And the bull stopped too because his target was no longer moving, for it is not true that bulls are angered by the color red; they are lured to attack by the movement of the object they attack. And so the bull stood, staring at Fay with wide bulging eyes, and sniffing the air with wide flaring nostrils, and swishing his tail and tossing his head, and moaning low until the moaning grew in volume and intensity and became a bellowing, and it was this bellowing that signalled to Fay that the bull was about to charge, and at the same time it unfroze the frozen muscles in her tiny body, and she turned and ran as fast as her little sun browned legs could carry her.

She did not run toward the house where she lived with her Ma and Pa and her many brothers though, and where her Ma was waiting for her to come and hold the baby while she cooked dinner for Fay's Pa. She turned and ran back toward the house where she had been playing with Alfie and looking at the funnies with him. And now she was running running running and making little noises in her throat and some of them were even coming up from her heaving chest, for she was like a frightened animal squeaking out the sound of her fear, giving to her terror a voice that knows no particular language such as English or Greek or Latin or any other language that man has fitted into a system to express his thoughts, his hopes and his fears, but it is the language of animal fear and it is understood by all living creatures in this world and if there are other worlds where other creatures live, then it is possible, even quite likely, that they too recognize and understand that language. At any rate Alfie, who was scrambling up from the porch floor and from the midst of the funny papers, heard, and he understood and for a moment,he too was frozen with fear. Sandy, the mostly collie dog, who was lying in a cool place under the steps that lead up to the porch, heard and understood and his ears raised up and his sharp eyes focussed on the running girl child, and then on the bull.And Alfie's Papa heard, for he was coming out of the barn where he had been forking some hay into the mule's feed trough, and he stood alert with the pitch fork in his hand and his tall lean body was tense as he turned toward the sound that had come from the small fleeing target, the tow headed girl child in the red and white checked gingham dress, and with the cornflower blue eyes dilated in terror, and the round red mouth open to breathe and to cry out, and the small sun browned legs flashing as she ran toward the place where she had left Alfie amidst the funny papers on the porch, back toward the place where she had crawled under the barbed wire fence to take the short cut home from Alfie's house because she had heard her Ma calling her.

Sandy the mostly collie dog was the first to move, to break the trancelike motionlessness in which he and Alfie and Papa were frozen for one moment as by the closing of the camera's shutter. It was Sandy, whose sharp ears perceived first the meaning of that little cry of terror, and associated it with the moaning which had become a bellowing. Sandy, whose keen nose picked up the scent of fear in the air that hung over the whole scene and drifted invisibly to him on the slight breeze as his sharp nose lifted and pointed toward the fleeing towhead running before the black and white bull whose pace had increased to a fast trot, for the young bull was now running tentatively, questingly, toward the running girl child, his ears standing out from his face and his eyes staring brightly and the sunlight glancing off his polished horns. It was to the trotting bull that Sandy's attention turned; it was on the bull that his whole tense and quivering being was focussed.

Alfie heard the sound, his small body absorbing the impact of the sound.He heard the squeal of terror and he heard the bull's bellowing. He heard, or perhaps he felt the vibrations in the earth as the bull quickened his pace and advanced toward the tow headed girl child as she raced to the barbed wire fence, clutched at the strands of wire in desperation, stared beyond the fence toward the house and was drawn irresistibly to look behind her at the charging bull, tried to slip between the strands of barbed wire, but finding her red and white checked gingham dress caught in the barbs, or the barbs caught in the cloth, she could not get between the strands and, staring, panting, squealing, she flung herself onto the ground and tried to crawl under but this only made matters worse for her because the barbs held in the cloth and she only managed to get part way under, but she was unable to rise and run because the barbs held her dress, and it was this that Alfie saw as he stood staring at the spectacle, and holding in his hand the little blunt nosed scissors with which he had been cutting pictures of Mutt and Jeff from the funny papers which Miss Maggie had given him when she and Mister Charles had finished reading the Sunday edition of the Ocmulgee Sentinel.

It was Papa whose flashing blue eyes took in the whole scene at once, the running, terrified girl child and the trotting, questing bull with the sunlight glinting off his polished horns, and the sudden movement of Sandy, and the frozen figure of Alfie holding the scissors on the thumb and the first two fingers of his right hand. And Papa's grip tightened on the handle of the pitch fork, and he said "God A'Mighty" and he moved in great sweeping strides toward the pasture where Fay was struggling desperately to disentangle herself from the barbed wire fence,and where the bull was advancing in ever quickening paces toward the moving, twisting target of his brightly polished horns, and where Sandy was now racing with both head and tail close to the ground, racing toward the charging bull, and Alfie was starting to run toward Fay who was caught in the barbed wire fence and, squealing in terror, her cornflower blue eyes dilated and turned to dark pools of fear, her little round mouth drained of its redness and opened to seek breath for screaming.

Papa was swinging his long legs over the barbed wire fence and with the pitch fork held out before him like an Athenian warrior's spear, and Sandy was racing close to the ground with his dark eyes fixed on the bull's staring, bulging eyes and a low growl rising in his chest and turning into a snarl on his lips as he braked suddenly to a smothering halt in the bull's face, and his lips were curled back in a snarl as his canine teeth fastened into the bull's flaring nostrils, and Alfie was rushing rushing rushing to the little bundle of towheadedness and blue eyes and sun burnt cheeks and red and white checked gingham cloth entangled in the barbed wire fence, and the bull, startled by Sandy's attack, planted his forefeet in the red clay about three paces from Fay and tossed his tormented head upward on bulging neck muscles, with Sandy clinging, snarling, to his nose and Papa thrusting the tines of the pitch fork into his shoulder, and Alfie on the ground beside Fay, tugging and pulling at her and at last hearing her scream "Cut me loose Alfie. Cut me loose. Quick." And at first Alfie could not understand, for he was not even aware of the scissors in his hand, and he did not realize that he had in his hand the instrument of Fay's deliverance, but Fay's own quickly darting, desperately pleading eyes had seen the scissors in Alfie's hand, and even though it had not occurred to him, her wildly pleading eyes drew the realization from him as she cried "Cut me loose Alfie." And while Sandy sank his canine teeth into the bull's nostrils and hung on, even though the bull shook him from side to side like a rag doll, and while Papa jabbed powerfully at the bull's muscular neck and shoulders with the pitch fork bellowing almost as loudly as the bull himself, Alfie finally reached with the little blunt nosed scissors held in a small and trembling hand, and he cut the cloth that was hung in the barbs. Cutting, tearing, jerking at the gingham cloth, and first one, then another, and the third gave way under Fay's frantic struggling and Alfie's desperate cutting and jerking, and Fay rolled free, tumbling Alfie over on the ground as she rolled under the bottom strand of the barbed wire fence, and both Fay and Alfie looked up amazed and joyful, amazed to be suddenly free of the barbed wire fence, and flooded with joy and wonder at their escape. They looked up to see Sandy still holding the bull's nose, and Papa still jabbing the pitchfork and roaring at the bull while the bull, having lost all interest in the original target, was now mainly concerned with shaking Sandy loose from his nose and getting beyond the reach of Papa's pitchfork. And the bull, tearing the turf and the red clay soil with his sharp, slashing hooves, turned in a desperate attempt to shake Sandy off and to escape Papa's thrusting fork. Papa gave the bull a parting jab in the flank and the bull raised his head and bellowed in pain and rage. He shook his head mightily and this time he dislodged Sandy who rolled on the ground and, rolling, leaped frantically to his feet because he expected the bull to turn his sharp polished horns on him, or to trample him with his slashing hooves. But the bull bucked and kicked like the rodeo performers do, and with his tail in the air and blood streaming from nostrils, shoulders and flank, he bucked away to a safe distance where he stopped, kicked, bucked and bellowed again, but he did not return to the fray. Instead, he trotted away with head and tail raised aloft, toward a little thicket of sassafras saplings.

And Papa, his blue eyes flashing over flushed cheeks, threw his long legs over the barbed wire fence and shoved the tines of the pitchfork into the hard red clay so that it stood there vibrating like a tuning fork. Sandy chased the bull for a short distance, just for good measure, but being careful to stay well clear of the bull's kicking heels. Then he came back to stand beside Alfie, with his tongue lolling out between the long white canine teeth that were still dripping blood from the bull's nostrils. He was hassling and dripping saliva and sweat from his mouth and he turned his eyes up to Papa's face in pride and in expectation, for he was proud of his triumph over the bull and he expected Papa to praise him. Then Papa said "God A'mighty". And he looked at Sandy and his eyes told Sandy all that Sandy needed to hear. Then Papa said to Alfie "Son, you an' Sandy better walk Fay home across the cotton patch. An' be keerful with them scissors. If you was to fall down an' jab 'em in your foot you might hurt yourself."

Then Alfie looked down at his bare brown feet and said "Aw Papa." For he knew Papa was just talking that way to keep him and Fay from bursting into tears, and he added "Didn't ol' Sandy do good though Papa?"

"He done good," Papa said. "An' I reckon you didn't do too bad for a boy that ain't never fought a bull before. Now you run on an' hurry back. I expect your Mama's about got dinner ready." Alfie and Fay trotted away along the narrow twisting path that runs across the cotton patch, with Alfie trotting in front and Fay following and looking down ruefully at the tears in her red and white gingham dress, and fingering the torn material, but she did not say anything about it to Alfie.

Papa turned back to the barn where he found Willie setting milk cans in the cooler. "Willie" Papa said. "The first time you can git that bull in the stall you better git the tar bucket an' dab some on 'im. He's sorta cut up from his run in with Alfie's sweetheart, and if the blow flies git to 'im he might not live to chase no more red an' white skirts nor nuthin' else, I reckon."

"Yess'r." Willie chuckled softly as he lifted the last can of milk into the cooler. "I saw it all. Not in time to do nothin' about it but I saw it all from the barn door." Willie chuckled again and said "I reckon Alfie's a goner over that little towhead now."

"He's young yet." Papa leaned the pitchfork against the wall of the barn and prepared to roll a cigarette from the makin's in the Bull Durham sack. "Las' time we talked man to man he said he was gonna marry his Mama when he grows up but you can't tell what effect a run in with that Holstein bull will have on 'im. Might've changed his plans."

Chapter Seventeen: But Gran'ma's Already Washed My Feet

To fall in love, and then to be teased about it, and at last to see one's beloved threatened by grave danger, is a terrible thing. But the worst of it is soon over, if a boy is not yet six years old, so in spite of having shared his funny paper cutouts with Fay, in spite even of having used his own blunt nosed scissors to cut the cloth of her red and white gingham dress to set her free from the barbed wire fence while Sandy and Papa stopped the charge of the young Holstein bull and even turned him back and sent him bucking away to escape the sharp fangs of Sandy and the equally sharp tines of Papa's pitchfork, Alfie did return to those activities which had been the substance of his daily play before he fell in love with Fay. And those activities did involve Junior, whose taunts had added to the pain of being in love with a towhead and robbed the experience of that easy joy which goes with childhood's innocence.

So Alfie and Junior were playing again, and the game was Fox and Hound. It is a game in which the one who is the Hound chases the one who is the Fox, and the one who is the Fox attempts to outrun the one who is the Hound. And there are safe bases, sometimes certain trees with a magic ring drawn about them, and if the Fox can attain the safety of that magic ring, he is immune to the Hound who is in hot pursuit and whose one object is to touch the Fox before he enters the safety of that magic ring.

"Tick-alock! Can't get in!" Alfie shouted and clung to the trunk of the walnut tree.

"I touched you before you got here!" Junior accused. "You're caught!"

"I'm not caught!. I said Tick-a-lock".

"Don't matter if you did say Tick-a-lock. I touched you before you touched the tree."

Yes, it was the game of Fox and Hound, and Alfie was the Fox, Junior the Hound. And it was evening, dusk, of a summer day. The heat of the sun was replaced by cooling breezes. Long shadows crept across the ground, and the geometric patterns in the sand, made by Gran'ma's dogwood sprout brush broom, were crisscrossed by the tracks of bare feet. For in the cool of the evening Junior and Alfie got a new burst of energy, the urge to run. Could it be the dying of the day, the sensing of night's approach, the realization that soon the opportunity for running and playing and shouting would be no more, and they would be called into the house, to be caged by the walls of the house and by the darkness of the night, to be tamed by the demands of the code of behavior which governed the supper table, to be muzzled into silence by the family's preparations for bed?

A foretaste perhaps, a premonition, an ernest of that time of life when a strong man sees his image in the silvered glass and hears the tolling of the years and grows anxious that his youth is slipping away,that his play time is coming to an end, that darkness and the summons of the Night will put an end to childhood's games.

For Alfie, it was far simpler. A very small boy is not a philosopher. In the evening he simply wanted to run. Twilight gave the wings of Mercury to his feet. He could run and it was as if his feet did not touch the ground.

It was not so in the long hot Summer afternoons. In the Dog Days, even a small boy's energies are drained from his body, his spirit sags into fretfulness, and drowsiness overcomes him. His eager, inquiring mind rejects the challenge of learning something new. His driving wish to be at the center of all that is happening in his world succumbs to a lethargy and he turns his face away from the smiling, coaxing face that seeks to gain a smile in return.

Until the setting of the sun. Until cool evening breezes stir and rustle among the leaves of the trees. Until the long shadows stretch and fall across the earth. Until Day is fading into Night. Then the eyes grow large and wide and expectant nostrils flare with excitement. Voices rise in pitch. It is the time for running.

But twilight is fleeting; the darkness comes and chases the twilight away.

"Alfie!" Gran'ma called. "Come here Child. It's time for me to wash your feet." It was a Summer ritual, an evening rite that closed the eyelids of the day. The inescapable penalty that is paid for the joyous freedom of going barefoot. When Winter's echoes are cast aside, to grow stiff, and smaller, so that they will never again stretch over the feet that have rejected them, and bare feet touch the earth and tingle with the joy of that touch, that pleasure is bought with a price, and the price is footwashing. "Alfie! You hear me?" Gran'ma called. "Come right this minute!"

"Aw, Gran'ma," Alfie wailed, his face contorted with the pain of freedom lost. "Can't I play just a little longer?"

"No, it'll be dark soon. Come on now."

"But.I want to play Fox and Hound. I'm the Fox and Junior's the Hound. I don't never get to be the Fox. Junior makes me be the Hound all the time, and this time I'm the Fox."

"I know, but it's time to wash your feet and get ready for bed."

"But I don't want to go to bed. Please Gran'ma... Aw shucks my feet ain't very dirty nohow. It won't take long."

"You come on while the water's still warm. It'll get cold while you're runnin' all over the place."

The footwashing was for Gran'ma a labor of love. Dipping each dirty little foot into the basin of sudsy water, she soaped and she scrubbed and she examined for cuts and bruises and thorns. "Ouch, Gran'ma, that's my sore toe!" "Land sakes Child, what happened to it?" "I stubbed it on that ol' tree root that sticks up out of the ground." She touched the water, tepid from sitting in the afternoon sunshine - for she had anticipated and prepared for the ritual as carefully as the priestess of some Aegean shrine - to take away the shocking chill. She let the water run from the squeezed wash cloth, over the sore toe too sensitive to be touched. And then she toweled Alfie's feet dry, or if she had forgotten to bring a towel, she dried them with her apron. Thus did Gran'ma, High priestess in the Temple of Love, perform her litany, her evening rites.

Gran'ma was old. How old? She was the oldest person Alfie knew. She was much older than Mama and Papa. Gran'ma was gray haired and her face and hands were wrinkled, She walked slowly and never ran, not even to catch up with Alfie when he ran ahead of her on the path to the woods where they went to gather dogwood sprouts for a new brush broom because the old one had worn stiff and would no longer sweep gently over the sand and leave the pretty pattern she wanted because it was "plumb wore out."

Sometimes Gran'ma was "plumb wore out" too, especially after she had completed the job of sweeping the yard with the brush broom made from green dogwood sprouts, for when the broom was new and covered with the green leaves, it was heavy, and Gran'ma's arms grew very tired. And Gran'ma's strength did not come bounding back the way Alfie's did. She could not eat the solid foods that she said would give her strength because she had lost all of her teeth and she had to "gum" the soft foods she could eat, and her jaws moved and her lips worked but it was not the same. It was as if the jaws and the lips were searching for the teeth that were no longer there.

Gran'ma got far more pleasure from cooking good things for Alfie. She would make tea cakes and sometimes she would make one that was shaped like a man and it was something very special, but even more special than the tea cakes was the blackberry pie, for when she made the blackberry pie, the pleasure was doubled. There was first the excitement and the adventure of going into the pasture where the blackberries grew along the banks of the little stream there. "Watch out and don't step on a snake," she cautioned Alfie, and she rubbed kerosene on his arms and legs to keep the chiggers away. And then even this pleasure was topped by the aroma of the blackberry pie being lifted from the oven with the juice bubbling up through the crust, and droplets of sugar being deposited on the crust itself. "You have to wait until it cools." But Alfie could never wait until the blackberry pie cooled, even if it meant burning his lips as he touched the berry laden spoon with them.

And now Gran'ma sat on the steps that led up to the back porch. Before her was the basin of luke warm water and the bar of Octagon soap, and the wash cloth made from a flour sack, and the task that must be done to mark the end of day.

But for Alfie it was the end of play. Once his feet were washed, he could not set them on the ground again. He must sit on the doorsteps beside Gran'ma until his feet were entirely dry.

Until the last light of day had faded from the sky. And then inside the house.

"Come on Alfie!" Junior called. "I'll race you to the gate post." Junior could wash his own feet, for he was older and bigger than Alfie, and although he wouldn't do a very good job of it, he was left free to run a little longer.

"You know I can't!" Alfie wailed, looking longingly at the last shred of light in the sky. "Gran'ma's already washed my feet!"

Chapter Eighteen: The Lunch Box

All little boys in Colaparchee County were required to go to school on, about, or shortly after their sixth birthday. Whether they knew everything already or not. That is, the parents of all little boys - and little girls too - in Colaparchee County were required to send their progeny to school to be educated, even though some of them would rather stay home and help their Papas run the farm.

This rule applied to all citizens of Colaparchee County, regardless of color, but it was not applied with equal vigor. It was more strictly enforced on those who were white than on those who were black. The reason it was applied to whites more forcefully was not punitive. Simply put, nobody cared a great deal whether the blacks went to school or not since it was assumed that education would serve no useful purpose in their lives and might even cause them to become "uppity", a state of being frowned upon by whites.

But Alfie was white and he had attained the age of six years, that is, of eligibility for schooling, and in spite of what Miss Georgia had said about Miss Millie being a terror, in spite of Alfie's confidence that he already knew all that he needed to know in order to help his Papa run the farm, Alfie had to go to school, come September. But he did not give in to authority unconditionally. He did not surrender without a price. He must have his price. But he did not name the price until he had put up his protest against going to school. And even so, Mama was so busy getting his clothes ready for him to go to school that she had almost forgotten that Alfie did not intend to go.

"Lordy mercy!" Mama shook a lock of dark hair from her face and pumped the Singer Sewing Machine vigorously with her foot. "School starts next week and I don't know where the Summer has gone to." She glanced at Alfie who was standing beside her and digging the toes of one foot into the top of the other. His big brown eyes were swimming in tears, and his lips trembled, and his face was on the brink of imminent collapse.

"Here you'll be starting to school next week and I don't have this shirt finished for you to wear."

"I don't want to go to school!" Alfie wailed. "I hate school!"

"Hate school? Good Lord! You've never even been yet. How could you hate school?" She lifted the little shirt waist she was making for Alfie, bit the thread off and shook the loose threads from the nearly finished product. "Well, there's nothing to cry about. Come here and try on this shirt to see if it fits before I sew the buttons on. I want my baby to look good for his first day in school."

"But I don't want to go to school an' I ain't goin'." Mama's calling him her baby had caused Alfie to abandon all caution and to defy the authority vested in parents and on the elected officials of Colaparchee County, which authority required him to go to school. "I ain't no baby neither."

Mama laid the shirt waist down and fixed Alfie firmly with her big brown eyes. "What on earth! Why, you know you want to go to school!There's not a thing to what Miss Georgia said about Miss Millie. You're going to like school!" Mama had no intention of caving in to Alfie's rebellion, and when Alfie pouted his lips Mama hauled out the big gun that had always worked when persuasion failed. "Now you just straighten up your face, Young Man, and tell me what's got into you. If you're too sick to go to school, you just need a dose of castor oil."

Alfie had not liked being called Mama's baby, but when she called him Young Man he realized that the wind was changing around and coming from a potentially dangerous angle. And the threat of a dose of castor oil meant that the worst possible cure was being planned for what ailed him. He collapsed onto Mama's lap and buried his face in her apron. "I ain't got no lunch box!" he wailed. "I can't go to school without a lunch box!"

"No lunch box!" Mama exclaimed, somewhat relieved to discover that there was nothing wrong with Alfie that might require dosing him with castor oil this close to the start of school. "Lordy mercy! That's nothing to primp up and cry about." But upon further reflection Mama realized that what was wrong might cost money to set it right. And money was in very short supply. “What’s wrong with carrying your lunch in a brown paper sack the way the other boys do? Then you wouldn’t have to keep up with a lunch box all day long.”

Mama’s argument missed the point with Alfie. He wanted to keep up with the lunch box. “ I don’t wanta carry my lunch in no ol’ brown paper sack! I want to carry my lunch in a lunch box. I hate ol’ greasy paper sacks.” Alfie had seen a lunch box advertised in the Ocmulgee Sentinel among all the other school supplies and it had become the one thing he could not go to school without. “I hate ol’ greasy paper sacks. I want a lunch box.”

Junior appeared in the doorway at this point. He was holding a “syrup in the hole” in his hand, and between his slirruping attacks upon this confection he expressed himself on the relative merits of brown paper bags and lunch boxes. “Shucks! I like carryin’ my lunch in a paper sack. Nobody but a cry baby would wanta carry a lunch box to school.”

“I ain’t no cry baby!” Alfie turned his tear stained face on Junior and was ready to lash out at him with his harmless fists. “And I don’t wanta hafta carry my lunch to school in a greasy ol’ paper sack!”

“Shucks!” Junior smirked at Alfie’s tears, regarded his balled up fists with contempt, and licked the biscuit loaded with syrup now running over the edges onto his dirt smeared hand. “I can throw the paper sack away after I eat and I ain’t bothered with it no more.” In fact, Junior had at times eaten his lunch before he even got to school and thrown away the sack through the window of the school bus. “I wouldn’t carry a ol’ lunch box around all day if Sandy Claws brought it.”

Mama’s eyes were on Junior. She was watching the syrup dripping onto his hands and threatening to drop onto the floor. “You just run along and finish pulling the weeds out of the zinnias the way I showed you. And don’t drip that syrup on the floor.” She studied Junior’s face more closely. “Good Lord! you must have a tape worm! Always got something to eat in your hands. That’s why you can’t get any work done.”

“Aw Shoot!” Junior licked his fingers, then passed them across his forehead to brush his hair back. “I always hafta do all the hard work an' it's hot out there in that ol' flower garden in the hot sun." The taste of the syrup was so good that it was difficult for him to frown as deeply as he wanted to do.

"Hard work never hurt anybody." This was one of the pillars of Mama's faith and practice, and she stated it without a trace of humor. "Now you just get on with what I told you to do." Her eyes bored into Junior disapprovingly.

Junior turned, grumbling. The screen door slammed behind him as he went out. Mama opened her mouth to call after him and make him come back and close the door quietly, but she stopped, glad to have the encounter with Junior over. She could now give her attention to Alfie and the lunch box and school. "Your Papa and I are going to town Saturday. I'll see if I can find you a lunch box for school at Woolworth's."

Alfie's tears dried to a dirty smear on his reddened cheeks. His despair changed to hope. Miss Millie became kind and beautiful. Mama was good. Going to school was attractive.

"Can I go with you an' Papa to pick out the lunch box, Mama? Can I go an' pick out the lunch box I want? Can I?"

"You'll have to ask your Papa." When Mama wanted more time to decide whether to give her permission she would say "You'll have to ask your Papa." And when Papa was not sure whether he wanted to be bothered he would say "You'll hafta ask your Mama." This kept Alfie running between the two while they made up their minds. In this case it gave Mama time to think about how much the lunch box would cost and how many bunches of zinnias and marigolds she would have to sell in town on Saturday to raise the money to buy the lunch box.

Alfie found Papa currying and trimming Kate the mule under the oak tree where he also curried and trimmed Alfie and the other boys when he decided they would either get a haircut or be picked up by the dogcatcher. "Papa, can I go to town with you and Mama Saturday? Mama's gonna buy me a lunch box to take to school an' I wanta go an' pick it out. Can I Papa? Mama said to ask you." All in one breath.

Papa clipped a little more off Kate's mane just behind her ears. He was not concentrating on what Alfie was saying but he was fully aware that it was a request. "You'll hafta ask your

Mama." He stepped back to see his work from a little distance. "Hold still Kate." Kate shook herself vigorously, flicking the skin on her neck and withers.

"But I already ast Mama an' she said to ast you. Can I, Papa? Can I go? I want to pick out my own lunch box."

"Well, you ask your Mama if she thinks there'll be room enough for you with all the tubs of zinnias she haulin' to town on Saturday." Papa now saw that he would have to give some of his attention to Alfie's request, but trimming Kate's mane was a work of art and he didn't like to be disturbed when he was concentrating on something so he wanted to put the decision onto Mama. "You run on now and ask your Mama an' don't let Saturday ketch you standin' there in your tracks."

Saturday found Alfie perched among the tubs of zinnias and marigolds in the back seat of the Dodge. Mama said "Now you stay right here in the car while I deliver these flowers to Doctor Thompson's office and when I'm done we'll see about your lunch box." Alfie wanted to know why they couldn't get the lunch box first so that he could look at it while Mama and Papa were making deliveries.

"The doctors' offices close at noon," Mama said. "Then they'll take the flowers home with them." The people in the offices got double duty out of the flowers. Besides, Mama had to sell the flowers before she could buy the lunch box. But at last the zinnias and marigolds were all gone, and Mama said "You come on now and go with me to Woolworth's. We'll get your lunch box before your Papa comes back to the car to meet us."

There was quite an assortment of little tin lunch boxes at Woolworth's but one of them caught Alfie's eye and he could no longer see any of the others. Peter Rabbit sat on the yellow lid of the box and he peered out at Alfie from behind a giant parsnip. Alfie's face was all smiles as he clutched the little tin box and looked up at Mama. "This is the one I want Mama. Can I have this one?"

Mama looked closely at the price tag on the lunch box and when she saw that it was twenty cents she checked several more to make sure that this one had not been improperly tagged. Then she remarked to the clerk "A little tin box ought not to cost more than a dime. Ten cents would be plenty for it."

"Yes'm," the clerk smiled apologetically. "Ev'rythings awful high this year. I was tellin' Buford just last night that it costs so much to live these days an' then we have to buy things for the kids startin' to school...I reckon Alfie's startin' to school this year. Who's your teacher Alfie?"

Alfie ducked his head and opened and closed the lid on the lunch box but he wouldn't say anything. He was smiling shyly though and Mama said "Tell Miss Sadie who your teacher will be." But Alfie wouldn't tell and Mama said "Miss Millie is teaching the first grade this year and she's awful good to the little first graders." Mama wanted to counteract Miss Georgia's word on the school teacher without mentioning Miss Georgia or what she had said.

"He looks big for the first grade," Miss Sadie said, and Alfie thought he liked Miss Sadie better after that, but he still wouldn't say anything to her. He held the Peter Rabbit lunch box and smiled into it.

Mama explained that Alfie's sixth birthday would come before school started and she guessed the lunch box would have to be his birthday present; then she didn't feel too badly about paying twenty cents for it since it was serving for two occasions. Miss Sadie said "Alfie's grown so I wouldn't recognize him." And when she said this Alfie felt so good he was almost ready to say something to Miss Sadie, but Mama said they would have to go because Alfie's Papa would be back at the car by now and they had to go to the Birdsey store and get their groceries. Alfie was eager to go too so that he could show the lunch box to Papa. Mama just wanted Miss Sadie to know that they had other expenses besides the lunch box that ought not to cost more than a dime, so she mentioned Birdsey's.

At the Birdsey's store Alfie hid his lunch box behind his back because he didn't want the clerk to see it and say "What have you got there Boy? Lemme see it." So while Mama and Papa were shopping for meal and flour and grits Alfie kept his lunch box behind him, but the clerk noticed and said to Papa "What's the boy got in his hands?"

"Let me see what you've got there Son." And when Alfie reluctantly brought the lunch box out for Papa to see, Papa said to the clerk "God Almighty! Did you think the boy was about to make off with a hunderd pound sack of chicken feed?" The clerk laughed and Papa laughed and they took all the purchases to the Dodge and started home. Mama was thinking about something that she dreaded to mention to Alfie because she didn't want to upset him, but she knew it had to be done. Instead of bringing it up though, she said "I guess we got everything. Flour, meal, and everything we had to get today."

Papa said "I can't remember anything I've forgot. But we'll have to stop for gas and oil." So he stopped at the Sinclair Station and bought two gallons of gas and a quart of oil. "It won't hurt it none to drive it without gas," Papa said. "But if you let it run out of oil it'll burn up the engine." He never explained to Alfie why running the Dodge without gas wouldn't hurt it, but he always got little crinkles behind his ears when he said it.

Mama recited the conversations that took place between her and the people in the doctors' offices and the insurance agents' offices and Papa pretended to be listening but he was thinking ahead to what he would do when he got home. They drew up close to the back steps and Papa called to Junior and Cliff and said "You carry ev'rything in the house for your Mama. I'm goin' to the milk barn to see if Willie has got ev'rything done."

Papa knew that Willie would have everything done, but he always came and said "You get ev'rything done Willie?" Willie would be whistling or singing in his fine tenor voice, and he would just wave his hand at the row of clean milk cans and buckets and bottles, and Papa would see and know.

"Alfie git his lunch box?" Willie asked and when Papa confirmed it Willie said "I'm glad. It's all he talked about for three days. I reckon he's all set up for school now."

Inside the house, the reign of happiness had ended though because Mama had said what she knew she would have to say. "We'll have to put some air holes in the bottom of your lunch box so it will breathe and not get to smelling bad." Alfie was startled and alarmed, but Mama said "You run and tell your Papa he'll have to bring his ice pick and punch some holes in the bottom of your lunch box."

Alfie appealed to Gran'ma to intercede on his behalf. Clutching the little lunch box so tightly his knuckles were white, he cried "No Mama! No! I don't want no holes punched in my lunch box. That'll ruin it!"

Gran'ma said "Lord God, Child! If your Papa don't punch some holes in the bottom of that tin box the scent of them salmon patties your Mama'll put in there for your lunch'll run ev'rybody outta the school house."

Papa came back from checking on the milking barn and he said "What's all the racket about? It sounds like Peter Rabbit's got hisself caught by the Tar Baby." Papa was always getting the stories about Br'er Rabbit and Peter Rabbit mixed up that way and then Alfie would have to straighten it all out and make him tell the stories all over again. But this time Alfie was not amused because when Papa found out what all the racket was about he agreed with Mama and Gran'ma that they ought to punch some holes in the bottom of the lunch box. "There's more room outside than there is inside."

"Punchin' holes in my lunch box will just ruin it!" Alfie wailed, but Papa punched five little holes in the bottom of the lunch box with the point of the ice pick. He pushed the ice pick through from the inside so that the rough edges would be on the bottom.

"See!" Papa said. "All the rough edges are on the outside where you won't scratch your fingers when you reach inside to get your lunch. An' not a hole in Peter Rabbit! He's still a grinnin' from Farmer Brown's garden. I jest hope he don't go an' git hisself stuck on that Tar Baby you was tellin' me an' your Mama about last night."

Alfie took the lunch box back and he fitted the lid on tightly so that nobody could see the holes After a while the tears stopped but his eyes were still red, and Junior said "I guess punchin' them holes in Peter Rabbit's bottom oughtta make 'im jump clean outta the cabbage patch!"

Alfie hugged the lunch box and said "It wasn't no cabbage patch and you know it! You mind your own business!" He made up his mind that he would go to the milking barn and tell Willie about Junior teasing him, because he could usually count on Willie to take his side and make Junior quit teasing him. But then when Junior got him off to himself where Willie could not see or hear what was going on, Junior would tease him again and call him a Cry Baby for running to Willie and getting Willie to take up for him. That was all because Junior was older and bigger than Alfie, and he had already been going to school before Alfie even started.

There were bigger boys than Junior on the school bus when Alfie climbed aboard that first day of school. And this meant trouble for that little lunch box with Peter Rabbit smiling from behind the giant parsnip. Alfie clutched the lunch box in one hand and a box of crayons in the other, and the first thing the big boys on the school bus noticed was Alfie's lunch box. Then the big boy named Sidney said "Well, looka here! If it ain't Peter Rabbit in person!"

Alfie looked up in alarm, but Sidney just reached to take hold upon the lunch box, saying to all the others who were now watching with interest and anticipation of some excitement, "Now le's jest look inside this Peter Rabbit lunch box an' see what's in there." But Alfie jerked back and clung to his lunch box with all his strength. He even dropped his box of crayons and held onto the lunch box with both hands. And when it seemed that Sidney would wrest the lunch box away from him, Alfie looked desperately toward the bus driver who was already staring into the rear view mirror and looking like a giant snapping turtle because he had noticed the commotion in the back of the bus.

Sidney hadn't noticed the bus driver's eyes on him though, and he kept pulling at the lunch box. Then Alfie cried out "You leave my lunch box alone!" And he looked desperately at the bus driver's eyes in the rear view mirror, and he called out to the bus driver "Make 'im leave my lunch box alone!"

Alfie didn't wait for the bus driver to take action on his behalf though. He jerked the lunch box away from Sidney so violently that Sidney lost his hold on the smooth surface of the little tin box and Sidney's fingers were raked across the bottom where the sharp edges of the holes Papa had punched in the lunch box stood up like tiny rasps, and Sidney's fingers raked across those five tiny rasps. Then five white streaks appeared instantaneously on Sidney's fingers. Then the five white streaks began to turn red as the blood started flowing.

Sidney's face blanched for a moment too when he felt the pain and saw the blood. But he glanced for one moment at the eyes of the bus driver in the rear view mirror, and he looked around him at the other big boys who were watching him, and Sidney said "Why, that there Peter Rabbit has got claws on his hind legs like a tiger!" He watched the blood gathering and beginning to drip from his fingers, and he squeezed his fingers tightly with his other hand. The pain and even the fear were in his eyes but Sidney tried to keep up the farce. "Just look what he done to my hand!"

This drew so much admiration from the other big boys, and even squeals of concern from the girls, that Sidney pretended that it hurt even more than it actually did. He said he wouldn't be surprised if he bled to death, or at least got blood poisoning and lost his whole arm as a result of it all. "And Alfie'll be to blame for it all because he brought that dangerous Peter Rabbit on the school bus and you can see what he done to me."

But Alfie's heart was not melted by Sydney's plight. He held his little lunch box even closer than ever. "It serves you right!" he said. "Cause you got no business grabbin' my lunch box!" Then he gathered up his crayons and edged farther away from Sidney, mumbling "It ain't my fault neither. It ain't nobody's fault but your own. Grabbin' my lunch box when it wasn't none of your business!"

The bus driver's eyes were still fixed on the rear view mirror, and he watched until Sidney looked up and saw him watching him. "One more stunt like that outta you, Sidney, and you'll hit the ground." He stared at Sidney for five seconds longer, then lowered his eyes to the road in front of him, clashed the gears of the big yellow bus, and they all rolled forward, gaining speed and leaving a roiling cloud of dust behind them.

As they entered the school house and Alfie headed for the first grade class room, with Junior showing him the way, he reached inside his pocket and felt the fifty cent piece. It was still there. He had not lost it in the scuffle with Sidney over the lunch box. But because of the fifty cent piece he would have to face Miss Millie and find out if Miss Georgia was right about her.

"Now you give this fifty cents to Miss Millie," Mama had instructed him. "It's to pay for the chalk and things. Everybody has to pay fifty cents. Don't lose it now. Give it to Miss Millie and tell her it's your fee."

Miss Millie had blue eyes and curly blond hair and a smile for the boys and girls in the first grade, but Alfie was still scared, and when Miss Millie said "Now I will call your names from my roll book, and as your name is called, you stand up and walk down to my desk with your fifty cents." She smiled again and called the first name "Mary Adams." Then Mary Adams rose and went to Miss Millie's desk with her fifty cents in her hand; she held it out to Miss Millie and Miss Millie checked it off in her roll book. This went on until she had called four or five names and each time Alfie thought it would be his name and he was scared because of what Miss Georgia had said. All of the names Miss Millie had called belonged to girls and he thought Miss Millie was just waiting for a boy to show that she could do all the things Miss Georgia had said.

Then there was a knock on the door and Miss Millie went to see who it was. It was Miss Florrie, the principal and Miss Millie stepped out into the hall to talk with Miss Florrie. While Miss Millie was out of the room Alfie saw his chance to escape her wrath and he slipped out of his desk and walked timidly down to Miss Millie's desk and laid his fifty cent piece beside her record book, and went back to his desk. Miss Millie came back, looked all around at the children, took her seat at her desk and found the next name on the roll. It was Alfie's name. "Come up here and bring your fifty cents, Alfie."

Alfie looked down at his lunch box and tried to escape Miss Millie's gaze. Peter Rabbit smiled back at him but he was no **help to Alfie because Alfie no longer had the fifty cents. "Don't you have your fifty cents, Alfie?" Miss Millie fixed her blue eyes** on Alfie with concern.

"No'm." Alfie's voice choked and he could hardly frame even this one syllable response to Miss Millie's question.

"Didn't your Mama give you fifty cents to bring to school?"

"Yes 'm" Alfie croaked.

"Then what did you do with it, Alfie?"

Alfie tried to hide his face, then croaked again. "I put it on your desk."

"You put it on my desk?" Miss Millie looked for the fifty cent piece but she said "I don't see it."

"I put it on your desk." Alfie's voice was coming back now because he had to defend his honor.

"Well, I just don't see it anywhere Alfie. Are you sure?"

"He did, Miss Millie." Mary Adams spoke up. "I seen 'im when he done it."

Now Miss Millie turned to Mary Adams and corrected her grammar before resuming the search for the missing fifty cent piece. "You saw him when he did it."

"Yes'm. I saw him when he did it." Mary Adams smiled proudly at her mastery of the English language.

"Well you come up here and help me find it Alfie." Alfie rose to his feet, trembling. "I'm sure it's here somewhere. Come up here and help me find it."

Alfie moved on reluctant feet until he stood beside Miss Millie, and looked into her face. Miss Millie smiled at Alfie and said "Now where did you put it Alfie?"

"I put it right here beside your record book." Alfie pointed to the spot where the fifty cent piece should be.

"Well, let's just look for it together." Miss Millie started to lift the record book and there lay the shining silver coin. She and Alfie saw it at the same time. "There it is!" Alfie exclaimed. And Miss Millie's hand reached for it at the same time Alfie's did, and their hands touched. Miss Millie's hand was warm and soft and dry and it felt good to Alfie's hand which was small and clammy with fear. Then he looked into her face because he was so surprised by the way her hand felt, and when he looked he saw smiling blue eyes and he heard her voice. It was full and kind, and she said "Why, I must have laid my record book on top of it. But we found it right where you put it Alfie. Thank you for helping me find it."

That evening Alfie said to Mama "I like Miss Millie. She's real pretty." And when Papa asked him if Miss Millie was the prettiest in the whole world, Alfie looked up at Mama and blushed and said. "Almost. 'Cept for Mama."

Chapter Nineteen: The Haircut

Alfie had been in school three days when Mama noticed. "Lord have mercy!" Mama exclaimed. "The child needs a haircut." Junior came to see what Mama had found to exclaim about and she saw that he was in the same condition.

Papa said "They are beginnin' to look like a pack of sheep dogs but they are still recognizable." Mama did not doubt that everybody at school would recognize her boys, nor that anybody would fail to pass judgment on the parents of boys who were allowed to start school needing a haircut.

"You will just have to take a day off and cut their hair." Mama looked despairingly at Papa, but Papa was busy harvesting the crops and he was short handed in the fields because the boys were in school.

"I'll do it Sunday," Papa said. Mama did not approve of hair cutting on Sunday, but she admitted that the ox was in the ditch, and Papa said "The better the day, the better the deed." Upon reflection, he amended the old adage slightly. "The better the day, the better the haircut." And Papa was a perfectionist when it came to cutting hair.

Mama said it was a shame that Papa couldn't cut the boys' hair before they went to school another day, but Papa said "They have been seen now. Seein' 'em again before I clip 'em ain't gonna damage nobody's eyes."

Cutting the hair of four boys was a major operation and when he undertook it Papa wanted to have time to finish. "Four heads," Papa calculated. "If they have got as much inside them as they have got on top of them there'll be so much brightness we'll hafta turn washtubs over 'em so the sun can come up in the mornin's."

Papa planned the operation in advance. "I will start at the top and work my way down." That means that Willie would be first and Alfie would be last, with Cliff and Junior in between. He would set up the chair under the oak tree so that he could work in the shade. He oiled the clippers and worked them vigorously to test them. He made sure that the scissors were where he could lay hands on them when he was ready to begin the hair cutting operation.

"I'll start Sunday mornin'. While the preacher's shearin' the sheep at church I'll clip the goats here at home."

The operation went fairly well with Willie and Cliff. Willie was stoical about pain anyway, and Cliff was afraid to complain lest he make matters worse. It was when Papa got to Junior that the trouble started.

Junior's hair was thick and heavy. He was in the habit of wetting it thoroughly to comb it, but wetting with water was a temporary measure because in the hot dry air, the water soon evaporated. In the Wintertime it would freeze and hold the hair in place longer. But Junior had found that by adding vaseline his heavy locks could be held in place almost all day. In the absence of vaseline, lard would do the same job. The result was that Junior's hair was a bit greasy and stiff.

"Hold still!" Papa said. "Quit your fidgeting!" Papa stepped backwards two paces and cocked his head to one side, surveying his handiwork. He might have been a Rembrandt looking at his brush strokes before going on with his work of art. He decided to take a little more off the left side to even it up.

Junior sat huddled, desolate, sullen, on the stool. Tears streaked his freckled cheeks, reddened now by the heat of summer and of passions agitated. The tears mingled with clipped hairs, smeared where he had swiped at them angrily with his fist. His eyes glared at Papa, and at that small part of his world that was in his limited field of vision, limited because he did not dare to turn his head, for Papa had commanded him to hold still.

Alfie watched. His eyes were big with wonder at the change being wrought in his brother's appearance. The unruly shock of dark brown but somewhat sunburnt hair that had given Junior a slightly top heavy, look, had indeed made the wearing of a cap unnecessary in cold weather even, was gone. Not all gone, but greatly reduced in length; it didn't even seem to be as thick as it had been. In fact, it was not as thick, for some of it had been pulled out, leaving small bare spots on his scalp. But it was around the edges that the greatest change was apparent. Here Junior's scalp, hidden for weeks beneath a thick covering of hair, now shone white because the hair had been clipped close, except in one area behind Junior's left ear. And it was here that Papa had decided a little more had to come off, to even it up.

"Gosh, Junior!" Alfie exclaimed. "Your head looks skinned!" Junior scowled and glared at Alfie, and Alfie added. "But it don't look too bad. It's just white where Papa cut all the hair off."

"Well, it ain't funny!" Junior said, because Alfie was beginning to titter, and trying hard not to. "And you'll soon find out for yourself what it's like."

Alfie knew too that he would soon find out for himself. For he was next in line. And to see in our predecessors our own fate is an experience not limited to those who wander through cemeteries and make a pastime of reading epitaphs on the tombstones of those who once walked the earth with firm and steady tread. A mixture of dread and apprehension filled Alfie as Papa neared completion of the task on Junior. When Papa called "Next!" the bell would toll for Alfie.

"Ouch!" Junior yelled. "That hurts."

"Now what's the matter with you?" Papa demanded of Junior, who was snuffling and wiping his shirt sleeve across his nose. Papa stepped back for a moment to get a better perspective and to decide just how much more hair had to come off behind the left ear.

"It hurts" Junior said. "Them ol' clippers pull my hair out!" He tried unsuccessfully to brush the clipped hairs from his neck; they clung to his damp skin, irritating, stinging, itching, adding to his discomfort.

"Well hold still!" Papa said, not visibly moved by Junior's discomfort. "I've just got to even it up on one side. "Hold still and the clippers won't pull so bad." Papa laid one hand heavily on the top of Junior's head and flexed the clippers rapidly with the other. "Hold your head still and you won't hardly feel it."

Whether Junior held still or not, the old clippers pulled his hair because two teeth were broken out of them and they caught the hair, chewed away at it while Papa worked them rapidly, vexedly, until his patience had worn thin, at which point Papa would jerk the clippers loose bringing a hank of Junior's hair with them. And this was the cause of Junior's pain and anger. It was also the cause of Alfie's anxiety, his dread, his premonition of impending pain, as he anticipated his own session on the stool.

Papa ran the clippers behind Junior's left ear again for good measure. The clippers hung up. Papa squeezed and clipped furiously but the clipper teeth hung onto Junior's hair. Papa's patience reached the end of its string. He snatched the clippers, pulling with them another hank of Junior's hair from his tormented scalp. "Ouch!'' Junior cried. "That hurts!" Holding both hands to his head, Junior jumped down from the stool Papa had decided would serve his purpose better than a chair for the little ones. He brushed angrily at loose hairs on his shirt front, ran one hand over the back of his neck, and fled the scene of his torment. Stomping along blindly toward the house, and still batting at the hairs that stuck to his neck, Junior collided with Charles Earl.

Charles Earl was Miss Lily's boy who was nearest to Junior in age and size. Miss Lily said that no matter what age or size a boy might be, she had one to match him. "Tom says they come like doorsteps," Miss Lily told Mama on one of the frequent occasions when her brood was the subject of discussion. "And Tom says he don't mean no doorsteps for no long legged man."

Tom had marked Charles Earl well. He was towheaded and red faced. There was a goodly thatch of tow on his head, and his red face usually bore a good natured expression which was capable of breaking into a smile easily. He grinned at Junior and found the normal amount of pleasure in seeing a fellow traveler in pain. Charles Earl himself had come to escape the pain of being assigned some job of work to disturb his Sunday morning rest. He had chosen this particular place because it was the nearest house to his own where he might escape Tom's eye. Or maybe just to find a shady spot where a growing boy with a normal amount of curiosity and sociability could sit down and watch what was going on. Being generously endowed with both of these qualities, Charles Earl sat down happily under the oak tree and waited, brushing his own sun bleached hair out of his eyes with his hand, and watching to see what would happen next.

"Next" Papa called, motioning to Alfie, who climbed hesitantly, tremblingly, onto the stool. Then, adjusting his dime store glasses, Papa caught sight of Charles Earl who at that moment was adjusting his back comfortably to the trunk of the oak tree. Papa stood' clippers poised in hand, looking at Charles Earl. Charles Earl looked back at Papa, peering out from under his sun-bleached forelock like an overgrown Airedale. "My God, Charles Earl!" Papa said. "If somethin' ain't done about you soon you'll go blind from tryin' to see out from under all that hair. When's the last time your Papa cut your hair?"

"I don t remember exactly," Charles Earl said. "Pa told Ma to cut it an' Ma said I'm gittin' too big an' Pa ought to do it an' Pa said..."

"Well, that's enough of that," Papa said. "I'll settle that family argument right here an' now."

"Hop down, Alfie" Papa said. "You can wait. Charles Earl, you climb up here on this stool. If you are left to run loose in the neighborhood much longer the dog catcher'll have you."

Alfie was glad to have his own sentence postponed and he leaped eagerly from the stool. Charles Earl did not dare to offer resistance to what Papa clearly intended to do; besides, he had no clear idea of what he was in for because he had not witnessed Junior's ordeal on the barber stool. He climbed onto the stool, grinning at Papa's dire prediction about the danger that faced him in his unshorn state. Papa set himself to the task of saving Charles Earl from the dog catcher's net, whistling happily as he worked. On those frequent occasions when the clippers hung in Charles Earl's matted locks, Papa disengaged them by flexing them furiously and then when this failed, by jerking them free. Charles Earl winced, grimaced, and made little whistling noises to express his discomfort, pain or distress, but otherwise made no complaint.

Papa was half way around Charles Earl's head, going counter clock wise and working with complete concentration and commitment to the job under his hand. He had cut the hair close to the skin, thus accentuating the stark contrast between the shorn and the unshorn halves of Charles Earl's scalp, when a strident female voice split the sultry noon time air, carrying clear and volubly across the cotton patch that lay between Papa's house and the place of origin of that high pitched, keening sound. "Charles Ear-rel!" The voice called, making two syllables of Charles Earl's second name. "Dinner's ready! You come on here!"

Charles Earl started to raise his head to answer, but Papa's big rough hand was pressing down on Charles Earl's head. Papa had got the clippers hung up, and in an attempt to get them free, he was working them rapidly and vigorously with his right hand while matching this effort by pressing and squeezing the top of Charles Earl's head with his left. "I think Ma's callin' me to come to dinner," Charles Earl managed to squeak from under Papa's hand, and tried to slip down from the stool.

"Hold still!" Papa commanded Charles Earl in a tone that clearly was to be obeyed above the high shrill voice of his Mama, especially considering the position of Papa's hand. "Hold still. I'll be done in a minute." The fact that Papa was only half way around Charles Earl's head had no bearing on his estimate of time required to finish the job.

"Charles Ear-rel! You hear me?" Miss Lillie's voice rang out again, this time more insistent than before. "You better git on home if you know what's good for you!"

"I think Ma means bizzness," Charles Earl said, his voice cracking under the tension building up inside him because his Mama was calling him to come home and Papa's heavy hand was pressing down on his head. "When she yells thataway she means bizzness."

"Well, you better answer her," Papa said, stepping back to get a better look at his half finished Job. "But sit still. I ain't done yet." Papa could see Charles Earl's foot slipping off the rung of the stool. "Don't move. Just answer your Mama."

"Comin' Ma!" Charles Earl yelled. "In just a minute!" he added, looking, pleading, into Papa's face, but Papa was oblivious to Charles Earl's plight. Papa had meat to eat that Charles Earl and Lillie knew not of.

"You come on here right now, young man," Miss Lillie screamed back at Charles Earl who, she assumed was dilly dallying and shilly shallying around and ignoring her order to come home.

Charles Earl looked up desperately at Papa. Evidently, when Charles Earl's Mama called him "young man" things were reaching the danger point. "I think I better go," he said.

"I think you better go too," Papa conceded. Miss Lillie's screams had penetrated Papa's consciousness. "Your Mama's callin' you...You can come back after dinner and I'll finish the job."

Charles Earl hopped to the ground and ran for home, following the footpath across the cotton patch and occasionally leaping two rows at a time to reduce the time lapse between Miss Lillie's call and his bodily appearance at the dinner table. Halfway across the cotton patch Charles Earl yelled at the top of his voice "I'm comin' Ma!", but he did not slow down in order to do it. Papa stood watching Charles Earl disapprovingly because he regretted leaving anything half done, but he decided the matter was out of his hands, and now that work had lost its iron grip on him, he decided he was ready for his dinner too. "Well," Papa said. "We might as well all take out and eat. Go wash up, Son." And Alfie, relieved at this further extension of his reprieve, said "Yes'r, 'cause I'm hungry too."

Junior was still in a bad humor when he answered the call to dinner, and he plunked down sullenly on the bench beside Alfie, bumping against him and causing him to protest loudly, but the unpleasant experience on the barber stool had not had any bad effect on Junior's appetite for Mama's fresh vegetables and cornbread; he even drank two glasses of buttermilk to wash it all down. Papa looked hard at Junior's head, but he didn't say anything about touching it up so he must have been pretty well satisfied.

The fact was that Papa had lost interest, for the time, in barbering, and when Charles Earl came back, Papa had not only finished dinner, but he had assumed his favorite after dinner position of relaxation on the front porch. He had tilted a cane bottom chair against the wall, placed a pillow against the chair and, with his head resting against the pillow, he had stretched his long body on the floor. "Alfie," Papa instructed, "You keep the flies shooed away, you hear? Don't let a fly light on me while I'm gettin' my nap."

Alfie was willing, even eager. The longer Papa slept, the longer he could put off the dreaded ordeal of the barber stool, and the less Papa was disturbed in his nap by pesky flies, the better mood he would be in when he awakened. But Papa's nap was not destined to be undisturbed because Charles Earl came back and stood under the oak tree where the stool was, yelling "I'm back! I come back!"

Papa was just drifting off to sleep when he heard Charles Earl. He shook his head as if a fly had landed on him, and said "Alfie, you run an' see what all that racket's about. If that ain't Lillie come here in the yard an' yellin' for somethin' its bound to be one of her younguns with a voice just like hers."

Alfie came back just as Papa was drifting off again to tell him it was Charles Earl and that he'd come back to get the rest of his hair cut. "Charles Earl's back, Papa," Alfie said, waving his newspaper fan at a fly that seemed about to land on Papa's head. "You gonna finish 'im now?"

"Not right now," Papa said sleepily. "I'm gonna take a little nap an' let my dinner settle." Papa shifted and settled himself in a more comfortable position. "You go an' tell Charles Earl he can go home.and come back tomorrow an' I'll finish 'im up then." Papa twisted again on the hard floor and began to snore.

Alfie scooted away but he was back again before the fly could find a place to land on Papa. "Papa," Alfie said.

"Huh? What is it?" Papa sounded irritated.

"Charles Earl said his Mama said for him not to come back home again 'till you finish cuttin' his hair all the way 'round his head. He said she said she never seen anything like it in her life."

Papa shifted again, but this time he couldn't find a comfortable position. "Well, you run an' tell Charles Earl to climb up on the stool an' set down, an' then you come back here an' keep the flies fanned away while I finish my nap." Alfie started away again and Papa added "And you tell Charles Earl not to make no racket while I'm sleepin'." Papa dozed off again but his sleep was disturbed by a fly buzzing near his head and he dreamed that the buzzing was Charles Earl's Mama's voice coming across the cotton patch, and he awakened to find the fly sitting on his forehead because Alfie had gone to tell Charles Earl and he had left Papa unguarded.

Papa got up from the hard floor, stretched his long limbs, and sat on the doorstep to put on his shoes. He walked back to the oak tree where he found Charles Earl sitting on the stool and holding Papa's clippers in his hands. Charles Earl was examining this instrument of torture fearfully and quizically.

"Give me them clippers, Charles Earl." Papa took the clippers and bent to examine Charles Earl's head. "Now if you'll jest set there an' don't move I'll finish this job in about two shakes of a sheep's tail."

The job was finished. Not in two shakes of a sheep's tail. And not without repeated hangings up, flexings and snatchings loose with consequent pain to Charles Earl. Not without vexation to Papa either. But finished. And Papa stepped back to look, and to give his final approval to the work he had done.

But when Papa stepped back, holding the clippers in his hand, a little screw that had worked loose while Papa was furiously flexing the clipper handles, or when Charles Earl was examining the clippers, this tiny screw fell out into the dust and fallen leaves and hair clippings and chicken droppings and the natural detritus which gathers under a giant oak tree when it has stood in one place for a hundred years. The clippers fell apart in Papa's hand. He looked, puzzled, at the pieces of the clippers in his hand, then he said "Well, that closes down the barber shop for today. Charles Earl, you pick up that stool an' set it yonder on the porch. Then you can run on home and show yourself to your Mama for inspection."

Alfie watched, wide eyed, as Charles Earl picked up the stool, and Papa dropped the pieces of the clippers into his overall pocket. Then a happy smile enveloped his face. He ran his right hand through the thick brown hair on his forehead and pushed it back from his eyes, and they shone now with an added luster of relief, of deliverance, of having got a new lease on life. Then he raced away on swift bare feet, calling out to Junior.

"Junior! Junior! Guess what! Papa ain't gonna cut my hair 'cause them ol' clippers broke! Junior!

Chapter Twenty: A Piglet for Alfie

A promise is a promise is a promise, and Alfie never let Papa forget that he had promised him a pig when the old sow had her next litter.

"When is the ol' sow gonna have pigs, Papa? Is it soon?"

"It takes the ol' sow nearly four months to make up a whole litter of pigs an' hatch 'em out ready to stand up an' run about an' take nourishment, not to speak of makin' a heap of racket squealin'."

"How long is nearly four months, Papa?"

"Well, to be exact, it takes her a hunderd and fourteen days. But she has already got a start on it, and I figure she has got about forty five more days to go. Now you bring me your pencil and tablet and I'll show you how to keep tabs on 'er."

Alfie came with pencil and tablet and Papa showed him how to count by fives. "You make a mark each day for four days like this ////, and on the fifth day you put a mark through it like this ////. And when you've done this nine times you'll have forty five days and the ol' sow will have about nine pigs." Alfie's eyes sparkled.

The old sow in question seemed to be in no hurry and the forty five days seemed like waiting for Christmas to Alfie. Each morning he went to see, and each morning he made a mark and on the forty fifth morning Papa came to breakfast and said "The ol' sow has got a litter of pigs."

"How many pigs has she got Papa? How many?"

"They are so piled up and the ol' sow ain't in a friendly mood, so I don't know exactly, but I'd say at least nine."

Alfie wanted to leave his breakfast and go to see them, but Mama said "Eat your breakfast. They will keep."

"And it will give them time to find where their breakfast is," Papa added.

When Papa and Alfie came to look the old sow was stretched out on her side with her belly exposed, and the pigs were lined up on her teats. They were pushing, shoving, squealing, and smacking their lips. One of them was smaller than all the others and he seemed to have got hold of a dry teat. Alfie said "That's the one I want, Papa. That little runt."

Then, "Can I have him, Papa? You promised."

"Well," Papa said, licking a cigarette paper in preparation for a smoke to celebrate the birth of the litter of pigs. "You can claim him.''

"Oh Boy!" Alfie clapped his hands in joy. "I'm gonna claim the runt because I like him better than any of the others."

Then Alfie's face became grave and thoughtful. "Papa. Does claim mean he's really mine? For keeps, I mean. Does it mean he's really mine?

Papa struck a match on his thumbnail and lit his roll-your-own-cigarette. "Claim means he's yours to raise," Papa said. "Hog-killin' time your claim runs out."

"Oh, Papa! I can't stand for my pet pig to be killed.!" Alfie's face reflected pain and anguish at the thought of his pig hanging by its hind legs from a tree limb and being prepared for making sausages and hams.

"Pigs are for pets. Hogs are to be et." Papa liked to make little word rhymes. "When your pet pig grows up to be a hog it won't be a pig no more. Maybe you won't even feel the same way towards him then."

"No Papa, I won't never feel different about him!"

Papa was eager to change the subject and he said "You sure that's the one you want to claim? Looks to me like he'll be the runt of the litter."

"I don t care if he is the runt," Alfie declared, feeling the pride of championing the littlest pig. "I'll feed 'im extra an' make him grow bigger than the others."

"Well now you do that," Papa said. "You feed that runt up real good an' make 'im grow... But how are you gonna' manage it so's he gets what you give 'im and he ain't shoved away from the trough by all the others?"

Alfie thought about what Papa had said, and he studied the litter of pigs crawling over one another to get at their mother's milk. Papa reached down and tugged gently at the hairs on Alfie's forearm. The hairs were long and light colored, like corn silks glistening in the early morning sunlight. They extended from the tops of his wrists to a point about an inch or two above the elbows. "Hairy arms is a sign of a good pig raiser," Papa said. "Always heard that. Even when I was a boy I heard that hairy arms was a sign of a good pig raiser, and if that's so you ought to be a Jim Dandy."

Alfie smiled his pleasure at Papa's touch and his words but he could not picture in his mind Papa as a boy. Papa had always been tall and straight, his reddish blond head going a bit bald in front - a high forehead, Papa called it - his blue eyes full of mischief when he was in a teasing mood, and blazing with anger when he was opposed. Papa's jaw had always jutted determinedly forward and he had always strode aggressively toward every task, long powerful legs carrying him forward like the legendary ten league boots. Papa had always been Papa, and Alfie would some day grow up to be big like Papa, or almost, but he could not really imagine that Papa had ever been little like himself. Alfie looked up at the curling red hairs on Papa's forearm, and he saw how the muscles rippled along the stretch of Papa's arm when he resumed his position leaning against the slab fence that stood between them and the old sow with her nine pigs, and Alfie said "I'll git 'im out and keep 'im in a little pen all by himself. I'll build a little pen specially for him, an' I'll feed 'im corn an' things to make 'im grow."

"Well, you wait 'till it's time to wean 'em all before you try to steal 'im away from his mammy. Right now he's too little to eat corn and he needs his mammy's milk. Later on you can feed 'im some clabber an' make 'im forget about wantin' to suck...Meantime I guess you could start buildin' your pen for 'im. I might help you when I get caught up with the plowin."

When the pigs were about three or four weeks old Alfie felt that he could not wait any longer, and he begged Papa to let him claim his pig and put him in the special pen constructed of chicken wire stretched about posts that Papa had set firmly in the ground. Papa and Alfie had nailed slabs to the posts to reinforce the wire, and Alfie had chosen a spot shaded by small persimmon trees. Alfie had nailed two boards together at right angles, then nailed shorter boards across the ends, forming a triangular trough the way Papa had shown him. Everything was ready and the separation of the runt from his mother and the other pigs in the litter was about to take place. "You better stay back here and let me get 'im for you, Son," Papa warned. "That ol' sow ain't gonna take too kindly to the idea of you kidnappin' one of her pigs."

"No, Papa, I want to pick 'im up myself. I know which one he is," Alfie said. In his eagerness he failed to take in the danger that Papa was warning him against, and Alfie darted into the pen and grabbed up the runt pig which began to squeal and kick with all four legs and to struggle mightily in Alfie's arms, and when the old sow saw and heard what was happening, she rose from the mud wallow where she was lying and cooling herself, and she threw off the other eight pigs which were in various positions of resting and feeding on her, and she went to the rescue of the little runt that was being stolen away. She was bristling with rage, her little pig eyes were filled with murderous hatred, and she emitted threatening sounds that were much closer to a growl than a grunt. As she made straight for Alfie, his own short legs were now moving like pistons as he ran toward the fence and Papa who was now inside the pig pen. Papa reached out for Alfie just as the old sow was closing the gap between herself and the pignapper; Papa snatched Alfie up into the air and swung him over the fence in one movement. He kicked the old sow soundly in the ribs, knocking her off balance momentarily and sprang over the fence himself in the next movement, and landed almost on top of Alfie and the struggling squealing runt pig which Alfie was still clutching in his arms. "God A'mighty!" Papa said, his face red with excitement and the exertion of leaping the fence. "A little bit more an' that ol' sow would'a et us alive!" Papa got to his feet and looked closely at Alfie whose face was white with fear, then at the runt pig which was still struggling and squealing. "You better go feed that pig some clabber an' get 'im to stop squealin''. Once you get him quiet the ol' sow may forget you stole one of her pigs, and maybe she won't come through that fence after us."

The old sow soon forgot that Alfie had stolen one of her pigs, for she had all she could take care of with the other eight. But Alfie did not forget so soon, and for many weeks, maybe months afterwards, he was awakened from the nightmare dream of the charging sow, bristling with rage, eyes glaring hatred, teeth bared and slashing at his unprotected legs, and in the darkness of the night, his sweat soaked body shaking uncontrollably, he would cry out "Papa! Papa" And when Mama and Papa awakened in the morning, Papa would look down at the small boy sleeping between him and Mama, and Papa would say to Mama "God A'mighty! How did this youngun manage to wind up in our bed thisaway?"

About the Author

Henry Buchanan's boyhood was an unfolding of the wonder and mystery of life on a one mule, red dirt farm near Macon, Georgia. His Mama and his Papa and Gran'ma, and his many brothers and one sister, and close neighbors and schoolteachers are the characters in his stories. And Sandy the dog and Kate the mule and Billy the goat. All God's creatures, big and little.

Colaparchee County is fictional in name only; the place itself is real. That's true of Ocumlgee too. From the beginning the author loved stories, hearing them and telling them. He grew up, with help from Miss Florrie, became a theologian, a mythologist, a linguist, a counselor and a teller of tales. ***Alfie's Story*** is his own tale. Not yet finished. More is coming. Watch for it!